FORWARD

C000153094

The novel opens in Geoffrey Foster waitii with Donald Rhodes, Hampshire,) and his new adviser flying in from Jersey. Foster, on his way to the airport has heard on the car radio some news which threatens to upset a period of relative stability of life back home and to open up old wounds.

The story then reverts in the most part to the turmoil of events in 1981 and 1982, and does not return to the opening scene at Gatwick until chapter 35.

The place names are factual with the exception of Gainsthorpe in Buckinghamshire and Fort Abbotshead in Gosport. The events and characters are mainly fictional, but some drawn from the author's experiences.

CHARACTERS AND WHERE THEY FIRST APPEAR

Characters & businesses	Chapter
Geoffrey Foster	1
Andy Harper	1
Donald Rhodes	1
Donald's cousin (un-named)	2
Saddler Hinds - accountants	2

Characters & businesses	Chapter
Rhodes Builders Merchants (Waterlooville) Limited	2
Rhodes Builders Merchants (Fareham) Limited	2
Bob Willetts	2
Gordon MacNeal	2
Arthur Lyons - accountants	2
Karen Foster	2
MaryAnn Foster	2
Philip Foster	2
Christina Foster	2
Jack Galliford - solicitor	2
Melanie Rhodes – Donald's wife	2
Bernadette Crotty (Bernie)	3
Joe Crotty – Bernadette's husband	3
Brendan Orford	3
Father Nugent	3
Angela – Donald's secretary at Fareham	4
Justine Formby – Rhodes' head bookkeeper and accountant	4
Susannah Jenkins née Threlkeld	5
Dave Jenkins – Susannah's husband	5
Hywel Petit Jenkins – Dave's father	5
Jack – senior auditor at Saddler Hinds, Southsea	9
Gillian – senior auditor at Saddler Hinds, Southsea	9
Evan Thomas - lorry driver at Rhodes	9

Characters & businesses	Chapter
Roy Burnside – buyer at Rhodes	9
George Godfrey – pastoral visitor from Methodists	11
Ingrid – secretary at Saddler Hinds, Buckingham	13
Jennifer – Jack's daughter	13
DC Dominic Baines	13
Martin Homer	15
'Ponytail'	15
'Boss'	15
Boris	15
Isaac	16
Vladimir (nickname 'Watch Man')	17
'Bully'	17
Oleg	18
Dr Nikolai Kuznestsov	18
Interrogator (later identified as Ivan)	20
Dominik	21
Tomasz	21
Marta – Tomaz's wife	22
Kowak – Tomaz's cousin	22
Bartek Felinski	22
Sebina – Bartek's wife	22

Characters & businesses	Chapter
Dr Lech Adamik	22
Fr Janusz Janowicz	22
Pastor Szymon	22
Piotr Gasiorowski	23
Krzysztof	23
Madelaine Macintosh	25
Laurence Bonham	25
Mr G. (man from MI6)	27
Mr S.	30
Mr B.	30
Mr W.	30
Andy – security unit	32
Denis Smalley	35

Chapter 1

Every few minutes I checked with my watch. Half past ten in the morning came and went, but Donald Rhodes was not to be seen among the relentless movement of humanity, going about its business with an apparent sense of purpose and determination.

"Next Wednesday, 10:30am in the Arrivals hall, at Gatwick North air terminal", we had agreed for our meeting; to give us half an hour in which to brief each other before Andy Harper, on a flight from Jersey, was due to join us. Neither Donald nor I had ever met him before. Consequently, I had printed out his name in large capitals on a sheet of A4 paper, knowing Donald would not have thought to do so. To be fair, it had only occurred to me at the last minute before leaving home to be a useful preparation, but I had failed to consider how I would hold it up with one hand without the edges curling inwards, and thus obscuring the lettering. The times when a third hand would be useful! The simple expedient of mounting the notice on a piece of card would have overcome the problem. More hurry, less speed! The handicap was my overloaded brief case which never left my grip in such places. Like many a lady's handbag, it contained much more than I really needed for the given moment, but old habits die hard.

By eleven o'clock, my patience with Donald was wearing a bit thin. There was still no sign of him. He was the one who urgently wanted this meeting. It had been necessary for me to plead with another client to postpone my appointment with her arranged for that Wednesday. She had been quite reasonable about it, but it was something I hated doing because it always felt as if I was treating one client with greater importance than another.

My state of mind was not helped by the item of news I had heard on the car radio on the way down to Gatwick. *'The remains of a man have been discovered in undergrowth near Buckingham by a dog being walked by a teenage girl. Police have cordoned off a large area of woodlands, but at this stage are not appealing for witnesses. It is believed that the badly decomposed body may be of a local man who disappeared eighteen years ago'.*

After the initial shock, my heart sank at the prospect of the lives of my family, our friends and our community being about to be turned upside down once again.

Chapter 2

I had first met Donald some nineteen years beforehand when he was in the process of taking over a couple of builders' merchant depots in Hampshire from a cousin, several decades his senior who was looking to retire, mainly on health grounds. The cousin was to retain some of his depots. Two years prior to this, he had taken on Donald to manage on his behalf the two based in Hampshire on an eighteen month trial period, and if all went well, he (a confirmed bachelor and philanderer) would give Donald a seventy five percent stake in them both, keeping twenty five percent for himself, with a vague promise it too would come Donald's way in time.

Donald, with a more than average endowment of the *arrogance of youth*, right from the commencement of his eighteen month probationary period, decided that his cousin's business modus operandi was flawed (*crap* was the word in the trade I think Donald used when I first met him). From what I can gather, there were constant rows between them, the cousin being somewhat paternalistic and Donald petulant in turn.

To begin with, Donald exhibited some flare at drumming up new business and getting to know the local builders, etc, by being flexible in his dealings with them. He achieved a measure of success in boosting trade, especially at Waterlooville, the newer of the two depots; a fledgling store when Donald came on the scene. This was not wholly reflected in the profit of the Waterlooville business as the margins were tighter, and the staff and overhead costs relatively higher than the older depot. However, to Donald, for ever the salesman, turnover was everything, whatever the cost.

I became involved at the point where Donald, more than two years after he had been appointed manager, was increasingly frustrated at the prevarication of his cousin in fulfilling his promise of the 75% share for Donald. I had been handed the case by a business partner of mine at our Portsmouth office of Saddler Hinds, Chartered Accountants, because Donald's initial enquiry was to do with structuring the proposed takeover, and the south coast partner felt I had more experience in such matters. An arrangement was made for an introduction at our Portsmouth office, 90 miles from my base in Gainsthorpe, Buckinghamshire. I was more than happy to make the journey, as I had been brought up, schooled and qualified as an accountant in Portsmouth, and it would provide me with an opportunity to take in a visit to my parents whilst there, time permitting. Such visits there were always tinged with a certain amount of trepidation because of an incident in my life in the late 1960s, but that is another story.

Our Portsmouth office, on the second floor of an Edwardian building, accompanied mainly by hotels and guest houses, was perhaps the most attractively located of all our nine offices. It overlooked Southsea Common and Spithead (the eastern end of the Solent), with the Isle of Wight as a backdrop. As I arrived at the office, the roar of a Hovercraft arriving on the pebble beach on the far side of the Common caught my attention, as it came to rest in a whirlwind of sea spray and shingle of its own making. It brought back memories of school lunch time walks in the late fifties, across the Common to the seafront with my college friend Bob Willetts.

A secretary knocked on Gordon MacNeal's partly open door, and informed him that a Mr Geoff Foster was here to see him, for which she received a gentle reprimand from Gordon for not knowing apart from my name, who I was. "Mr Foster is our partner from the wilds of Buckinghamshire". "Oh", she replied with little more than token interest. Her interest was slightly raised when I revealed that my origins were much closer than the wilderness of Buckinghamshire, and that I had served most of my Articles with Arthur Lyons, just along from them in Osborne Road. The old firm was still there I had noticed while looking for a space to park.

Gordon offered me a comfy chair facing a window, which afforded me an impressive view of a Brittany ferry, no doubt on its outward crossing to Caen in Normandy. It appeared enormous, almost out of scale, as it passed Billy Manning's Funfair and the War Memorial, a poignant feature of the Common. All along this part of the coast, hundreds of Naval and other craft left these shores on the great armada of Operation Overlord in June 1944.

We discussed Donald Rhodes situation for about twenty minutes, but ran out of things to say about it. Gordon's initial meeting with him had been brief, not much more than the twenty minutes we had just spent. We then moved on to pleasantries, our families, holidays, and before we realised it another half hour had elapsed, during which Gordon kept looking at his watch and becoming more and more agitated. "He did this last time – arrived long after the time of the appointment. No explanation or apology was offered. I didn't like to say anything – prospective new client and all that". "With all the travelling, I have written off the whole day for this", I replied, "but would like to have a bite to eat sometime, and squeeze in a visit to see Mum and Dad".

About an hour after my arrival, a loud and emphatic voice was heard coming from reception. "Rhodes to see Mr MacNeal". I raised my eyebrows, bringing a slight smile across Gordon's face, signifying acknowledgement of a somewhat arrogant visitor. "Ah! You must be the chap from up north", he said, turning to me the moment he walked into Gordon's room, and completely ignoring him. "Geoff Foster", I said offering a hand shake, which was accepted, along with an attempt to crush my fingers and palm. We agreed to address each other by first names, which was a good start towards establishing a working relationship. However, if we expected an explanation for why he was an hour late, we were to be disappointed. By way of consolation, he announced he would take us out to lunch at which we would get down to business. "The bastard we shall be talking about will be paying", he said, flashing a company credit card.

During the meal we were subjected to a highly emotional account of how Donald Rhodes' cousin had been a sly, scheming fraudster, who was trying to rob him of two years of his life of damned hard work for and loyalty to his cousin, 'who was now repaying him with vicious kick in the teeth'. "Since the eighteen months' trial period was up, I have been on and on at him to arrange the handover of the seventy five percent stake in the Waterlooville and Fareham businesses he promised to give me, and eventually I receive this from his solicitor".

Donald, with great passion, thrust down on the table a package of legal papers, narrowly missing a glass of Burgundy. I picked them up and scan read the first couple of pages of a share sale agreement for the company, Rhodes Builders Merchants (Fareham) Limited. "That one is mirrored by another one in the pack for the Waterlooville company."

I made the comment that these were sale agreements and not Deeds of Gift. "Exactly, that's my point", he responded. "It gets worse. There is a lease agreement in

11

there between himself and the Fareham company, whereby he personally receives rent of twenty five grand a year from the company for the premises. When he made the promise to me, the company owned the depot, so he is keeping it for himself, or the slimy reptile transferred it over sometime in the last couple of years without saying a word of it to me."

I asked, "Does the lease agreement provide you with any option to purchase now or at some future date".

"Nope. Not a dicky bird. The only thing it says about the future is that there will be five yearly 'upward only' rental reviews. It makes my blood boil".

"I can see that by the colour of your face", Gordon ventured to say.

"Can you wonder? Let's have some more wine. Waiter-another bottle of the same".

At the end of the meal at the Queens Hotel, just five minutes' walk from the office, we parted company with Donald, but not before I asked him for a copy of the original agreement he and his cousin had made. "It was between family! Of course there was nothing in writing", as if this was the obvious way such things operated.

Back at the office, Gordon and I wondered what our role in all this was to be. He had given us no opportunity to discuss it, which was just as well, given the state he was in, especially after drinking well over a bottle of wine himself. We agreed I would take Gordon's notes of the initial meeting, and telephone Donald the following day, hoping I would find him in a calmer mood, and see where we went from there. There was something about the man that enticed me into helping him, despite all the bluff and bluster. He had ambition, but it in my view needed channelling in the context of the real world, but perhaps that was just the accountant in my professional make-up. I had got into this at the age of sixteen, and had known little else, apart from the horrendous experience over eleven years previously.

I managed to spend a comfortable and homely couple of hours with Mum and Dad in the north of the city, catching up with their news and that of my five siblings and their offspring, before setting off back to the *northern* 'wilds of Buckinghamshire'. How parochial we southerners can be!

Home was a partially modernised farm house, long since detached from its farm, on the outskirts of the small town of Gainsthorpe, between Aylesbury and Buckingham. From the house there are long sweeping views of gently rolling hills, peppered with isolated farmsteads across the Vale of Aylesbury. The distant Chilterns to the south form an unspoilt edge to the Vale, carved out by an ancient glacier, marking the limit of the icecap of the last of the Ice Ages. Gainsthorpe still has some of the charm of a bygone era, including a town hall, its interior evocative of a time when town and parish councils had jurisdiction in much more self-sufficient communities than they are now, and their councillors were all known to their constituents.

Home for us was not simply the fabric of the building, but the life within its walls. In fact, to say that everything had its place, and was in its place, hardly described our domain. Housework was defined by the minimum you could get away with, and undeserving of the attention better focussed on more stimulating activity. The house was large, and we were unrepentant hoarders, especially of books. Certainly, we were better stocked than many a book shop we trawled around in towns we visited usually on holiday, although we were no competition for Hay on Wye.

My wife Karen (teacher) and I met on holiday in Italy in 1968. We had parted company immediately on return. After a period of mysterious incognito communications from Karen and her holiday companion, we rediscovered each other, and were married almost a year to the day after we had first met. Our children were born in the 1970s, MaryAnn, Philip and Christina in that order.

The journey back from Portsmouth was tortuous; the earlier part of it in the rush hour. I arrived home just after eight o'clock that evening, just in time for Christina's bedtime story. I dare say in most households this meant mum or dad, reading with exaggerated expression, Winnie the Pooh, Paddington Bear, James and the Giant Peach, or some such. Not in our house, the children read to us, which meant they could already read when they started school.

I very much treasured our home life, and made every effort not to let business impinge on it. My view was that having expended a great deal of energy and care on my clients' interests during the working week, I should ensure all my time and attention was devoted to my family, and to a measured extent the church, at the weekend, although very occasionally this was not possible.

The day after my trip to Portsmouth, I had a long telephone conversation with Donald. He was in a much more reasonable frame of mind, and he was able to give me a considerable amount of background information, and to say what he was expecting from us. Essentially, he was looking for professional support in challenging his cousin's meagre offer as Donald saw it, and to have some confidence that there was someone on his side. He explained that he had been to see a solicitor who had told him he hadn't a leg to stand on, and that his best bet was to walk away from the whole situation, or go back meekly to his cousin, work hard for him, and adopt a friendlier attitude towards him in the hopes that in time the cousin might promise him a new deal and if so, to ensure it was put in writing. "I imagine that was just what you wanted to hear", I remarked with irony. "Guess you won't be taking him to lunch", I added.

"Too right", he replied with a chuckle. "Well Geoff, do you think there is anything we can make of the situation, or do you think the solicitor was right? My inclination is still to go along to him and give him a good going over".

"The solicitor or your cousin?"

"Both perhaps, but I meant my cousin of course. I used to be a keen boxer and Rugby player – still am involved with the game – as a referee. Keeps me fit!"

"I have been through the draft agreements, etc. you gave me yesterday, which themselves provide a fair amount of the background. If they are correct, the Fareham premises have always been in your cousin's name, never in the company's, not at least in recent times. This arrangement is not unusual in small

16

businesses. Sometimes it's for family reasons, or ring-fencing assets against claims of creditors due to insolvency, or purely for tax reasons, for instance avoiding the virtual double taxation on capital gains, or even making the business more attractive to potential buyers where raising enough finance is an issue".

"The sod! He should bloody well have made that clear when he promised me a stake in the business".

"To be frank Donald, looking at it as an outsider, I'm tempted to say it appears to have been a very generous promise if inclusion of the premises were intended".

"But there was no rent being paid to him in the accounts, so I naturally assumed that was because the company owned them".

"If it had have done, they would have appeared in the Balance Sheets. Did you see them there?"

"Oh, I've never looked at them. I don't understand them; just seem to be an index to a load of irrelevant data, there for the benefit of political snoopers."

"They do contain vital information. What land, buildings, plant and machinery the company has, its bank balances, what its customers owe it, and how much it owes to the world at large, i.e. its creditors and bank and hire purchase loans and so forth. Basically, the difference between what it owns and what it owes is its capital".

"In other words, what the business is worth", offered Donald.

"Not exactly. The endless notes to the accounts set out the excuses as to why the real worth of the business doesn't appear anywhere. May be I'm being a bit cynical, but the worth of a business is very subjective, as indeed we shall find out if you do enter into any negotiations with your uncle, sorry, cousin".

"So it comes back to what I was saying, Balance Sheets are really a load of useless gibberish".

"Steady on Donald, we have to justify our fees somehow", I said with tongue in cheek.

This was the time I heard him really laugh.

"Does this mean Geoff, if we pull all this off, and I do get to own the companies, you can be the business accountant as well as my adviser?"

"That's up to you. I had envisaged that if we arrived at that happy situation, you would want Gordon as the accountant, as he is more local to you".

"No, I should want you to be both".

"OK, that's a decision for later. In the meantime there are a few formalities to be dealt with, a letter of engagement as your adviser – it's fancy speak for contract, but I shall write to you about that. Right now, let's just consider what might be possible".

"That's what I really want to hear".

"Our starting point is that realistically you can't force your cousin to do anything. There's no evidence of a contract made two years ago, only your word".

"Hang on. When a Rhodes makes a promise, he gives his word and it is his bond".

"Sorry Donald. That means nothing in a court of law, unless perhaps there are witnesses. I take it there are none".

"Well, no. This was meant to be strictly confidential. His girlfriend at the time, who worked for him, and who had expectations of marrying him, more fool her, would have gone ballistic. It doesn't matter now. She's dead".

"The fact that your cousin has instructed his solicitors to prepare these draft documents suggests something was understood between you, but no-one can prove what that was. Nevertheless, he has set out his stall in these papers, and I dare say these are in his mind only the starting point in a process of haggling, until an acceptable deal is reached. He probably thinks that 60 to 70% of the prices quoted are about the level we shall finish up at. I think that even this is way too high, given that the profit is not that remarkable in either business, especially when you deduct the value of the rent he is proposing, from the Fareham bottom line".

"How do you know what the profits have been? There are no accounts in the package I gave you".

"Gordon got copies from Companies House. Luckily they are bang up to date, and what's more, the fully detailed version of the Profit and Loss account has been filed. I have done a quick rough calculation of the share prices quoted in the agreement, and it is clear that they have valued them on the basis of profits without discounting for the proposed rent charge for Fareham, and a number of other factors, including the nuisance of having him continuing to be associated with the companies by virtue of his 25% stake".

"What about the ownership of Fareham premises? I was banking on that being an important feature of the promise?"

"Years ago, I used to work at Fareham, and I remember what was there before the depot became a builders' merchants. It was a car breakers yard. I couldn't afford new spares for the old bangers I had when I was an articled clerk, and so I was often there pulling off clutch plates, bits of transmission and even a carb. from the wrecks they had there. Customers were let loose on them, gleaning what they could. The chaps that ran the place were bone idle, and the yard, mainly bare earth, was swimming in oil, diesel and sometimes petrol. I shudder to think of how dangerous it was, especially with batteries lying around with still some charge in them, and customers with fags hanging out of their mouths. I mention this because we have recently had a case here in Buckinghamshire, of a car scrap yard where the ground was so heavily polluted as a result of similar activity, the cost of sorting it out was more than the value of the land once it was cleaned. Before the cleaning up operation, it had no value, and its ownership was a negative figure, in other words a liability. It bankrupted the owners. Before you even think of taking over the business at Fareham, let alone acquiring the freehold even it was on offer, I would strongly recommend you have the contamination question looked into".

"Oh! What joy! Geoff, you are making me even more depressed".

"Sorry, I'm like that. I should have been christened after one of Job's comforters. Anyway, the point is that this could be a bargaining tool, and certainly needs to be considered by the solicitor who will be acting for you in the transfer".

"Geoff, you are giving me lots to think about. Despite my remark, I do feel more hopeful now and in a stronger position to do battle with the old rogue. Should I arrange to confront him now?"

"No. Your next move is to get hold of a solicitor you can feel confident in. You and I see him together, and arrange for him to communicate with the cousin's solicitor. This is vital, as a wrong move now could prove far more costly than the fees you will be charged, which will not be cheap. No hard bargaining with the solicitor. You pay peanuts, you get monkeys. Say nothing to you cousin, except that you are thinking about it and taking advice".

My next journey south a week later was to the picturesque market town of Haslemere in Surrey, to meet Donald and his newly found solicitor. He came highly recommended by Gordon, and had had some dealings with a client of Gordon's in the late seventies, over the sale of a manor house and grounds in Liphook to a firm of developers, intent on demolishing the place and replacing it with an estate of luxury homes.

Donald, no doubt mindful of my reference to professional costs, was on time and wasted none of it on introductory pleasantries. The solicitor, Jack Galliford got straight down to business and readily supported my advice on no discussion with the cousin, and agreed that all contact would be strictly through the two parties' solicitors. This was not only to avoid Donald putting his foot in it, but to ensure they were informed and in control of the flow of information and developments. Jack would go through the papers with a fine toothcomb, look for pitfalls, etc., and report back to Donald, copying me in.

We both answered his queries, and made comments as necessary. This was followed by Jack writing to the cousin's solicitors with his observations and matters of due diligence, etc.

There followed a period when both solicitors hammered out the minutia, after which a meeting of both parties and their representatives including me, was arranged at the Petersfield office of the cousin's lawyers, with the object of coming to an agreement on share prices, property and rental values, and the trickiest of all, the terms of a loan agreement with the cousin enabling Donald to pay him a sizeable part the cost of the shares over period of time, with interest. The remaining part was to be covered by a bank loan I had managed to arrange for Donald.

The premises at Fareham were to be left in the cousin's ownership, after the report of a surveyor appointed by Donald did indeed highlight soil contamination and also subsidence and other issues, which were likely to lead to the need for a move to other premises in the short to medium term. This gave us the upper hand in negotiating a drastic reduction in the proposed rent for Fareham.

The whole process still took another two of such meetings, the second during which contacts were exchanged followed by immediate completion. Donald, Melanie his wife who was to be a joint shareholder with him in the 75% stake, Jack and I adjourned to a hotel afterwards for a decent (I would put it at no more than that) meal with champagne. All but Donald were relieved it had all come to fruition, but he fumed at his cousin's "skulduggery" or "sculbuggery" as he would keep referring to it, despite all the apparent matiness with his cousin during the meeting. This was to be a grudge we would never hear the end of.

It was several months before I heard again from Donald. I had duly submitted a bill to him at a fee we had agreed beforehand, for my advice and part in guiding him through the acquisition of the shares in the two companies. My subsequent letters and follow up telephone calls chasing him because of non-payment were met with stony silence. I was surprised and to some extent offended, after pulling out all the stops to help him. I was on the point of threatening legal action, when one Friday morning my secretary, during my meeting with a difficult client, knocked on my office door and apologetically whispered in my ear, "Geoff, there's that horrible man Donald Rhodes on the phone for you. I have told him you were with a client, but he insists he speaks to you now, and won't take 'no' for an answer". "Ingrid, would you tell him, please that I shall call him the moment I am free". "I'll try, but I don't think he will have it". Sure enough, Ingrid came knocking on the door again a moment later. She had a look of despair, said nothing but shrugged her shoulders. I turned to my client. "I am so sorry about this, but do you mind? I had better take this call in another room".

"You ought to train your clients better". That was a bit rich coming from him, as he also was prone to doing much the same thing.

"Donald, I have had to break off from a rather tricky meeting. I assume this urgency is nothing to do with your outstanding bill"

"Geoff, sorry about that. I swear to you a cheque will be off in the post to you tonight. I just rang to tell you the old rogue has become a saint. Literally! He died a couple of days ago from a heart attack, and guess what? He has left me the remainder of his shares in the two companies".

"The old rogue being your cousin?"

"Look Geoff, this is a big weight off my mind. It opens up a number of possibilities for me now, which I need to talk over with you as soon as possible. Any chance of you coming down tomorrow?"

"Not the slightest possibility".

The man is like a child with a new toy. The loss of a relative had brought him such shameless joy. How callous! Tomorrow was Saturday. No way was I going to give up my family's time to this.

"Tuesday is the earliest I can make it, on condition your cheque has arrived in the post on Monday".

"That's a bit mercenary of you. I wouldn't have expected that of you".

"Look Donald. If the boot were on the other foot, wouldn't you have done the same?"

"Yes, but I'm not nice".

"I shall give you a call on Monday once the postman has been, and we'll make the arrangements then. I must get back to my client now, before he walks out on me"

"Have a good weekend Geoff".

"I shall".

Chapter 3

Saturday was not a day to remember. We had invited my old school friend Bob Willetts for the afternoon and tea. He had moved up from Portchester to Milton Keynes, taking the post of assistant headmaster at one of its comprehensives. He had never married, and as far as I could tell, had never entered into a long term relationship with anyone. He was very devoted to his work, but not in a stuffy way. Last time the matter had entered into our conversation, he said that he was resigned to the 'fact' that nobody wanted him, and he would remain wedded to his teaching. He was a damned good teacher, and the kids loved him, but as it turned out on this occasion, not ours. He was always a shade uncomfortable with children under the age eight or nine, and quite intolerant of childishness in any age group, young or adult. Although our three children, ages ranging from four to ten, were by no means angels, they were usually reasonably well-behaved when we had company, but on this day, something seemed to get into them the moment Bob walked through the door.

It was probably my fault for asking them beforehand to be extra good, polite and no fighting. A feud developed just before he arrived, and reached a crescendo at the moment the doorbell chimed. Bob was greeted by the sound of Karen (unaware of his arrival) bawling them out, and ripostes of, "It was all her fault. It's just not fair". The children begrudgingly grumbled 'hello', and

27

acted for the remainder of the visit as if he were not there. At the tea table, their earlier animosity towards one another gave way to a belching competition, followed by silly descriptions of their teachers and delirious laughter. Bob was stony-faced for most of the tea, after which the kids were peremptorily packed off to bed, with a promise of a dressing down later. Karen and I agreed that discretion demanded I should take Bob down to the local, and reminisce over a pint or two, and hopefully work in an apology for our delinquents' behaviour.

Although our conversation was friendly enough, much in the vein of our weekly evenings before I met Karen, in various pubs around the countryside north of Portsmouth, the apology was not exactly accepted with magnanimity.

Bob's parents were blunt Yorkshire, and some of it had rubbed off on him, but the bluntness sounded natural in a Yorkshire accent, but somehow seemed much more hurtful when delivered in a southern accent. I often recall with some amusement an incident when were we were still at school. I had been invited to his home for tea one evening. The following day he told me his father had been quite angry that morning when he had gone into their downstairs toilet and discovered that the overhead heater was on, and the room was as hot as a henhouse on a blistering summer's day. As I apparently had been the only one to use the lavatory the evening before, it must have been me who had left it on, and they couldn't think why I had switched it on anyway. I then remembered. Yes, I had gone in there, yanked on the pull-switch next to the door. No light had come on, so I assumed the lamp had blown, but there was a kind of reddish glow coming from somewhere, which was just about sufficient for me to see what I was doing. I apologised to Bob for not letting them know about the lamp when I returned to the sitting room. "The switch for the loo is in the hallway, you dope. You pulled the heater switch." I was never invited back again, although I liked his parents. They were always interested in my family and what I was doing.

We returned from the pub in darkness. Bob popped his head inside the front door to say goodbye to Karen, and thanked her for the lovely tea. Perfect manners, our prim and proper Bob! As he climbed into his car, the angle of the light from the outside security lamp made his face look surprisingly old and care worn, yet he was the same age as me – thirty eight.

Once back inside, I asked Karen if she had said anything to the children about their behaviour. "I thought in the circumstances, that was better left to you".

"Fair enough", I said, "I shall do so, but after church tomorrow".

"Very wise! Did Bob say anything about it?"

"No, but I did apologise, although the look on his face said he was unimpressed".

"Talking about the look on his face, I thought he looked old, well, a lot older than you".

"I thought the same as he drove away this evening. It is a bit worrying. I must arrange to pop over to MK one evening soon and check if there is anything wrong....Half past ten! Is it bedtime?"

We sat in bed reading for a little while. Karen suddenly slammed her book shut. "I also am concerned about my friend, Bernadette".

"What's Bernadette been up to, then?"

"That's the point; she has been up to something".

"Oo, this sounds interesting. What's the gossip then?"

"It's not funny Geoff. It could make life very complicated over the coming weeks / months".

"It gets curiouser and curiouser!"

Bernadette was one of Karen's colleagues at the local Catholic school – a fellow teacher. She and Karen had become close over the last year, able to confide in each other, mostly about schoolwork and the ineffectual head, Jim Donnelly, so I thought.

"You know," Karen said, "or perhaps you don't, that Bernadette is very involved with the N.U.T., and regularly goes to meetings in the evening at Northampton. She is on some regional committee. En route, she usually picks up a chap called Brendan, a teacher at Roade. Now isn't that a co-incidence given what you were telling me about your day yesterday? Anyway, she was confiding in me yesterday lunchtime. Brendan is a bachelor; at least Bernadette thinks he is. At first Bernadette found him quite chatty and interesting when she stopped to drop him off at Roade on the way home. As time went on he would always get started on something deep and meaningful as they were approaching his home, and she found it was often up to about half an hour that they would be sitting outside his house in the car, deep in discussion. Then Brendan's conversation got more and more personal, and he took to leaning across and giving Bernie, as we call her at school, a kiss on the cheek as they parted. She thought little of it to begin with, but then on following occasions, he spoke increasingly about his Christianity, and how he had been absorbed by the works of modern theologians, particularly those who were advocating that marriages should be much more open, couples should not only look inward on their relationship, but be more inclusive in their friendship with others, and dare he say it, in sexual matters as well. The church, the Catholic Church in particular, was so out of step in all matters sexual, and so was society in general, despite the influence of the sixties. The love that Christ spoke of was all encompassing and not moralistically confined to the law or convention. Each time his conversation, although calm on the surface, became more intense and so did the parting kisses.

Bernie found his logic quite persuasive and was finding her conscience being more and more challenged. Yes, she thought, there was something rather selfish about the exclusive love demanded of marriage, which smacked of possession of one another. Surely this was at odds with the essence of Christ's teaching. As the weeks went by, the kisses were just the prelude to their deeper bodily contact. Petting became more and more adventurous until last Tuesday, when they almost reached coitus, and then all her instincts, her upbringing and love for Joe and the children conspired to interrupt. Brendan was soothing and understanding, and suggested perhaps it was too soon to be giving themselves to each other so completely in that way. Over the weeks, Joe had begun to notice how much later she was getting home and commented on it on Tuesday, being perplexed by what appeared to him to be her slightly excited and superficial mannerisms. She excused herself by saying there had been some contentious issues constantly on the boil at the N.U.T. meetings, mostly around the taking of industrial action. I thought that was quick thinking on her part, as the subject, as you know, is quite a live one at the moment".

"Well that's a bit of a bombshell", I said. "Bernadette of all people! She has always struck me as being the mumsy sort, devoted to Joe and the kids, and yet concerned for everyone. She clearly is caring about her job, the school and all the little darlings. She doesn't come across as prudish, but it is difficult to imagine her being manipulated in the way you have said. Of course, we never know what goes on behind closed doors, but I wouldn't have thought she and Joe have any deep seated problems in their relationship. Perhaps Bernie has latent passions, not entirely satisfied by Joe. It never ceases to amaze me what really throbs away in people's hearts. I mean, take you. Do I know all your secret yearnings?"

A pillow came at me fair and square, and continued in a path, taking my glasses with it, towards the tumbler of water on the bedside table on my side of the bed. "Now look what you made me do. My pillow's soaking", she moaned.

"Never mind. May be we can generate some heat to dry it out. Are my glasses intact?"

"Yeah. More than you deserve. Seriously, I don't know whether I should be doing anything and if so what? She's a friend, and I feel that her confiding in me is a cry for help. Or is it the comfort of justification from me, especially if she is nursing a submerged desire to take stock and let nature take its course? The way she was telling me all this did make me wonder".

"How long have they been married, do you think?"

"If the age of the children is anything to go by, I would say about ten or eleven years. Why do you ask?"

"Oh, just thinking about the seven year flitch?"

"What's a side of bacon to do with it? Do you mean 'itch', you chump?"

"Probably", I answered.

"She told me once that Joe wasn't the first. Actually, I should say she told us. Do you remember that staff Christmas party where we all got a bit squiffy?

"A bit squiffy! I had to go and collect you. It was reminiscent of a similar time in Venice when I was your prop on our way back to a certain boat. I pretty well had to carry you home from school. I don't think there was a sober one among you. A Catholic school and all! Good job the kids had all gone home and by that time safely tucked up in their beds. It was also a good job Father Nugent hadn't dropped by".

"Ah but he did, and when he saw the state of us, and we were only getting warmed up at that point, he said to us all, with that rueful smile, 'One to remember at your next confession. I shan't forget'. *You won't hear mine,* I thought. I'm not one of the fold. Methodists don't do absolution. Had he stayed he would have had a field day of confessions. The party rolled on and the alcohol took its affect, as it sometimes does like a truth drug. Out came the secrets, mostly about the loss of the flower of virginity. I can tell you Catholic or not, there were very few who stayed the course to the marital bed, and Bernie was not one of the few".

"Were you?" I asked mischievously.

Another pillow came my way; this time it was mine, but it stayed dry.

The air of mystery on that subject remained intact.

"All right, all right. Truce!" I pleaded. "We did reserve the ultimate intimacy between us until we were married. I gained sight of your bank statement".

Things often come in threes. On this occasion it was to be pillows, the third being the wet one.

We agreed it was way too late to do any more psychoanalysis of Bernadette's character, and it would be deferred until after the children's bedtime the following day. Bernie was bound to be at church. Tonight's revelation was obviously going to be a distraction during Mass, but where better to ponder what we might be called upon to do?

Indeed, Bernie was at Mass, but on her own. Her general demeanour revealed nothing of the subject of Karen's concerns. Nevertheless, it dominated my thoughts all through the service, aided by the fact that she was sitting directly in my line of sight when I was looking towards the altar, where most of the activity of the Mass took place. Afterwards, I caught up with her and said, part questioning, part in exclamation, "On your own today?!"

"Joe and the kids have gone to his parents for the weekend", she responded somewhat defensively, with no evidence of the smile she usually wore for Sunday Mass. *Mm*, I wondered. She probably would have guessed that Karen would have said something to me about her predicament.

I duly reported back to Karen before we as a family set off for my second bout of worship for the day; the service at Well Street Methodist Church in Buckingham.

The thought occurred to me that Bob was heavily involved with the N.U.T. and being at Milton Keynes, he could very possibly be part of the same Northampton committee that Bernie and Brendan were. This would make my proposed visit to see him at M.K. more pressing. I phoned him that afternoon. He was pleased, as he was thinking of calling me. There were things he wanted to tell me, but felt that yesterday afternoon had not been the time and place. We agreed on the Thursday coming, but at The Cock Inn in Wing rather than his home.

On Monday evening, after the children had gone to bed, Karen, who had been agitated ever since I had returned from the office, told me as calmly as she could that Bernie and Brendan had spent the weekend together,

36

and the inevitable had happened. They had taken advantage of the rest of the family being at Joe's parents', and having the house to themselves. He came over on Saturday evening and went back on Sunday evening before Joe and the kids returned. It was a close run thing, as Brendan pulled away just as Joe turned into their road.

Bernie said on Saturday they had gone out for a 'lovely' meal at Akeman. We must go there ourselves. She would babysit for us. They had polished off a bottle of wine with the meal, she having most of it as Brendan was driving. All through the meal they talked about their relationship, and how at one they felt in so many ways; teaching, the church and its refusal to accept the age in which it now found itself, and modern life in general. There couldn't be a better husband and father than Joe, and how lucky she was to have him. However, she felt everything had become so routine, so taken for granted. Brendan was offering a chance to risk something, even something quite earth shattering. By the time they arrived back at the house, she had made up her mind that she was determined to submit to his advances wherever they led. That deep pile rug they have in front of the fireplace was the setting for her moment of 'absolute submission and contentment'.

The following morning, she went to Mass with no feelings of guilt, save for the effect it would have on Joe and the children if ever they found out. She was resolved however, that although she wanted to continue seeing Brendan, the sexual side of it was to be a once and for all occasion, an expression of how deeply they felt for each other, but with no requirement to repeat it. "How naïve she is!" Karen proclaimed with exasperation, "How does she think she can ever be with him without all those sensual feelings bubbling up. If you cross that line, there is no turning back".

"That's a bit dogmatic, but I agree, she is naïve".

"What do you think we should do? She's right about one thing. The effect it would have on Joe and the kids would be devastating. We can't risk warning him, but it makes me feel how we would be betraying him to do otherwise. Why is she confiding in me, putting me in such an invidious position? Isn't that in itself being selfish. Has she even thought of that?"

"Perhaps she has chosen you because you are not a Catholic, you would be more understanding".

"You mean, having lower moral principles because I am only a Methodist?" replied Karen with some bitterness, and some anger towards me.

"I don't think that, but she might".

"Why do friends have to do this? Why mine?"

"You know love, you are very good at listening to people – lending a sympathetic ear, and I am the more fond of you for it."

"You are probably right. At college, my friends were always coming to me with their woes, usually boyfriend troubles or the lack of them, boyfriends I mean, but just occasionally it would be problems with their studies or tutors, or arguments with their parents. There was one poor girl whose dad was not paying the allowance he was supposed to, and she had no money, not a penny! I even had to pay for her phone call to her dad to beg".

"Couldn't she have used a reverse charge call?"

"She knew the mean old sod would not have accepted it".

"Yes, poor girl, indeed – literally", I said light heartedly.

"Listen. Do you think it a good idea to talk to Father Nugent about it? That is one of the things he is there for, isn't it?"

"I don't know. I suppose I could outline our dilemma without naming any names. He might have some advice for us. Yes, that's a good idea, love".

"I think you ought to hint that the unnamed are part of his flock, so that he can be vigilant, but for heaven's sake, get him to promise he will deal with it sensitively. You never know, Bernie might take the whole affair to Confession anyway".

"Blimey, that would bring on a sermon in the Confessional box, and cause a long queue outside, and what's more, precipitate a whole bunch of Our Fathers and Hail Marys, no doubt. We could of course pray about it".

"Believe you me, I am", retorted Karen.

"Let's sleep on it, and I shall give it some more thought on the drive down to Hampshire tomorrow..... God only knows what Donald Rhodes has in store for me".

Chapter 4

Tuesday did not start well. I spent an hour circumventing Oxford before getting on to the A34. The rest of the journey was reasonably stress-free, which meant I was able to turn my thoughts to the Bernadette/Brendan matter. Karen was right to be so concerned for her friend and the trouble she was getting herself into, but we had to be clear in our own minds where our sense of outrage was coming from. Was it the adultery or the deception and damage towards Joe and the children that most bothered us? If it were the former, were we in danger perhaps of moralising and being judgemental, sticking our noses in a place where they did not belong? On the other hand, if it were the latter, our friendship demanded something from us, but what?

I tried imagining myself in their place. I considered myself a hot blooded male, not incapable of having my head turned by an attractive woman, especially if she had the character and intellect to go with her looks. When I was courting Karen, in the initial full flush of love and infatuation, I would immediately stamp on such distractions by others of the opposite sex, and summarily suppress them as if they no longer should have the temerity to even claim my attention for a single moment. To keep that up after 12 years of marriage would be superhuman. If supposing some such lady were determined to step into my life with the prospect of an affair, could I in all honesty believe I would never succumb? In one off guard moment of temptation, perhaps in a situation where we had been thrown together, would I stand the test, could I always guarantee it, whatever happened? To be totally truthful, I had some slight doubts. Perhaps it was vanity to even contemplate that any woman would make such advances on me.

What about Karen? Would it be conceivable that she might find herself entangled in a relationship she had never contemplated or desired? May be we are (or I at least am) wrong or naïve to think that our marriage is inviolable in whatever circumstance that life might throw at us.

I tried to turn my thoughts to the purpose of the journey I was making, although it was difficult to focus on what felt less important than our friends' well-being. Donald's cousin had died, left him his 25% shareholding in the Waterlooville and Fareham companies, which would give him and his wife absolute control, but he was pretty close to that before. What about the loans outstanding to the cousin for the acquisition several months ago of 75% of the shares? Would the Will have said anything about them? There must be other important matters Donald wants to discuss.

My first priority was to obtain the overdue cheque for my fees he promised to hand me first thing today. As I had suspected, it was not uppermost in his mind after he had spoken to me on Friday, and therefore it did not arrive in Monday's post. I had phoned him on Monday afternoon about it. He said it must have been delayed in the post. When I threatened to cancel Tuesday's appointment, we agreed he would give me a 'replacement cheque' at our meeting, and he would phone the bank to cancel the original one. I thought to myself, if he had really sent the cheque to me as he claimed, and it was indeed late in the post, why could I have not simply destroyed it once received? I had to make it clear to him that if I was to continue acting for him, it would have to be on the basis of mutual trust in these matters. I would not tolerate being treated the way I imagine he treated his suppliers.

The Winchester Bypass was blocked by a broken down lorry. Nothing unusual in that! I swore it had been planted there. My irrational judgement of the local highway authorities was that they hated motorists, and loved to taunt us with deliberate obstructions, to remind us of who had the power. It gave me great satisfaction in defiance of those tin gods, to turn off the main road and cut across country by a route my uncle had shown me years ago. He had discovered it when he was stationed at RAF Barton Stacey in the late forties and early fifties. He would ride this route from Fareham with two handle bars, one set on his motor bike and the other the moustache he sported.

It was to Fareham I was heading. Parking was as diabolical as ever. (I had served a substantial part of my articles there in the offices of Arthur Lyons. Towards the end of that period I had bought my first car, a 1939 Standard 8, for £20, and very quickly discovered that there was a cost to the comfort of driving to work – docking it somewhere while I was there)

Donald had warned me off attempting to park at the depot. There were builders' lorries endlessly in and out of it, their drivers caring very little for anything such as a car in the yard. The Waterlooville depot was much better organised than this one. It was newly built for a start, but this one at Fareham was a complete shambles, with outbuildings in varying degrees of decay, one being kept upright by what resembled pit props. Stock taking here must have been a mightily optimistic exercise. The unauthorised taking of stock not so optimistic!

I eventually found a multi-storey car park, although it was a good fifteen minutes' walk to the depot. The weather had seemed quite settled when I started out that morning, but now it had become typical for April – squally showers blowing in from the north-west, with a bitterly cold edge to them. Attempts at hoisting an umbrella proved futile. Within moments a vicious gust of wind blew the thing inside out, the fabric breaking loose from one of the stays. Then it wouldn't close properly. I began to regret not hailing a taxi. It was highly unlikely that one would appear in the lane I was walking along. A Rhodes lorry scuttled past me, showering me with spray, as if I wasn't wet enough by now.

My mood brightened when I arrived at the terrapin hut which served as the office block for the depot, and was greeted by a very cheerful Angela, mid-forties at a guess, a little stocky but tastefully dressed in flecked grey sweater and deep red pleated skirt.

"I have only just found out you were coming today", she said. "Donald phoned five minutes ago from Waterlooville to say he was on his way, but he would have to call in at home first. Something about a new dishwasher being delivered, and Donald wants to supervise its installation."

I grimaced, thinking it hadn't been noticed, but Angela, being very attentive picked up on it immediately.

"I'm afraid Donald's always rushed off his feet, so busy-busy, he struggles to keep on schedule with all he has to fit in in the course of the day."

It was obvious her lines were well rehearsed, but they were delivered so pleasantly, with an assurance she was ever loyal to her boss, come what may. Although she did not say so, it was a reasonable assumption she was his secretary cum personal assistant, office manager, and most likely the only refuge of sanity in the place.

"You must be soaked to the skin from that hail storm just now. I can't think what I can do for you, but why don't you come and sit by the radiator", she offered, pulling a comfortable armchair from the other side of the office, revealing a part of the room the cleaner did not normally bother with.

"I shall now go and make you a nice hot coffee or would you prefer tea?"

"Coffee's fine, thank you"

"Biscuits – custard creams?"

"Just the ticket", I replied, wondering how long I would have to sit here waiting for Donald to condescend to gracing me with his presence.

Angela was very skilled at calming rising impatience in long suffering appointees to see Donald. She clearly had to be. Perhaps they were so enchanted by the time Donald arrived, he would be oblivious to the distress his lack of punctuality had caused.

Angela gave me a potted account of her life story, and after glimpses at the clock, realised she needed a change of tack to while away what she sensed was going to be at least another twenty minutes, I guessed. She asked me about my family, where I lived, our holidays, and so on, but when you move the small talk with an accountant to the subject of his career, you are really scraping the bottom of the barrel. At least that is the general public impression. In truth, for most of us, we pick up a good deal of potentially explosive gossip, but our profession demands we keep our mouths shut.

I became embarrassingly aware of the smell of warm damp clothing wafting around the office from my personage as I began to steam, at which point Donald burst in through the door. "What the hell is that smell?" he shouted, as he very markedly made for the windows and opened them. Nothing more calculated to put all present in a state of unease, especially as he must have known the origin of the offence to his olfactory senses.

"Right Geoff, I've just got two of three phone calls to make, and then we'll go and have some lunch".

Lunch time, I thought, and absolutely nothing achieved so far. I have not even got my hands on the cheque yet. All the running around I had done for him, and not a single penny received for it to date. Lunches, even if he did usually pay for them, were no compensation, and did not keep my family housed and fed.

Half an hour later we were on our way in his Bentley to a hotel in Wickham. The head waiter having taken our orders, and after some discussion about his favourite wines, Donald said, "Since the initial euphoria of hearing about the shares my cousin has left me, I had a chance to reflect over the weekend, and have come to

47

the conclusion, it is no big deal. Whom sensibly could he have left them to anyway? They are only of use to someone who is going to work in the business and help generate the profits, and there is no-one on his side of the family who would be prepared to do that".

"Donald before you go any further, there are two things to clear up", I chipped in.

"I know. I know. Your cheque. Here you are. You see I do keep my promises".

I opened the envelope, the address neatly typed out, no doubt by Angela. The bugger, I thought, he has only gone and rounded it down to the nearest thousand. Is this the professional relationship I can look forward to with this man?

"Well thanks Donald. You keep me waiting all this time, and then you dock four hundred and fifty quid from my bill. I shall expect the rest".

"Okay, okay! It was worth a try"

"It's not the way we do business in our firm. The fee was agreed long ago and that was our contract, not to be negotiated downwards at a later date".

After an embarrassing pause of a minute or two, I continued, "The other thing I wished to clear up was the loan from your cousin".

"What loan?"

"What you owe him for the 75% holding in the companies".

"Oh that! I was never going to pay that anyway. He could go sing for it".

"I just wondered if the Will says anything about it", I said.

"I've no idea. I've not seen it. What do you think it might say?"

"Well, as he has given you the rest of the shares, I thought he might have completed the job and forgiven the debt also. Who told you about the Will?"

"His sister, obviously another cousin of mine. They are all considerably older than me. She's not well herself – had a stroke five years ago. She is a heavy smoker and refuses to believe it has anything to do with her state of health, despite what all the medics have told her."

"Could you ask her for a copy of the Will? There may be other things in it. After all, they could affect your business plans. For instance, there is the question of the premises here in Fareham. Who inherits them? Not that the company will be affected in the short term, as the company's occupation is secured by the lease with your cousin, or rather now with the successor who has inherited it. You will also need to know how the Inheritance Tax is to be paid. Some Wills specify that certain non-cash bequests suffer their own share of Inheritance Tax."

"Geoff, you have really cheered me up; thanks".

"Now what were these plans you mentioned on the phone the other day?" I asked, trying to steer us on to something I anticipated would be a more cheerful subject.

"A couple of things, well three really. Two are plans, the other, something which worries me. First, my long-term aim as far as the companies are concerned. I should like to expand the operation. Originally I thought the one unique service we offer would take off, but it hasn't. You will remember it being discussed at one of the meetings when we and our solicitors were all together. My cousin wanted it patented in his name, so that he personally received royalties from it. We have two trucks with cement mixers mounted on the back of them. The idea is that for customers who only need a small amount of concrete or mortar, we mix it at the roadside for them, and barrow it to wherever they want it, and the customer does the rest. Despite efforts to promote it, the demand is very limited. Rather than pursue dead ends like that, I feel the way forward is to acquire existing depots which are floundering or someone wants out —say retirement, or start up new depots where there is a gap in a locality.

I also think I should introduce what we have at Waterlooville into Fareham, and any other future depots, and that is a shop, you know, selling tools and the small stuff.

Eventually, I hope I can develop a 'brand' and then reduce our trading risk by franchising out even more future expansion of the 'brand'. Once we have reached an appropriate size, we float the whole operation on the stock market, or seek a buyer for the whole lot".

"Sounds right for you", I said, "but you'll also have to build a dynamic team around you, not necessarily a large one. At the moment you seem to be rushed off your feet with just the two depots you have".

"May be, but I do like to be in full control of my domain".

"Hm", was my limited response.

"You sound doubtful. Don't you think I can do it? You did say it sounds right for me".

"I'm sure it can be. You certainly have the drive, the ideas and ambition. I'm just a little concerned that one person on their own could keep the whole thing together. I've seen promising starts before, only to stumble when their founder burns himself or herself out because they would not trust others, listen to or value their opinions".

"Okay. Thanks for the sermon. I shall keep it in mind", he said, sounding far from convinced.

"My other plan, which I am going ahead with anyway, is to have a third company – a holding company, which would not only have control of the depot companies, but engage in other activities, such as property investment and or dealing, and possibly the commodities market, and other interesting investments which might present themselves. I am already thinking of a restaurant, although that might be a separate partnership".

"What are your reasons for transferring the depot companies' shares to a holding company?"

It just seems the right vehicle for the expansion I envisage, and also my plan to give some equity to the depot managers in the company in which they are employed. I might even consider incentivising certain of the staff with an employees' share scheme".

"All good reasons", I commented.

"I should also like my children to have some of the shares in the holding company".

"Yes, that is a good idea. Quite popular!"

"I turn now to what's bothering me. Something I feel I must get right before I embark on expansionary ambitions. Justine Formby, my head bookkeeper/accountant prepares these rough summaries for me every month. They are not what you would call accounts, but they give me key information I can understand, and ought to know".

Donald handed me a couple of A4 sheets of neatly hand-written reports, one for each depot, showing sales, cost of goods bought for resale, wages and salaries, overheads and 'profit' for the last month, and accumulated over the last twelve months.

"Do you know , Donald, whether these are just cash and bank figures, or are they adjusted for bills owed to you and bills you owe?"

"You mean debtors and creditors? No, they are not adjusted for. It says so at the top", he said with slight irritation.

"My apologies. So it does! Well then, what is bothering you exactly, apart from the last month's figures looking a bit below average at Fareham, and generally not great compared with Waterlooville?"

"Well that is the point, and it seems to be a trend particularly for the last three months. The building trade, around here at least, is not in recession, and we have some good contracts with the Ministry of Defence".

"Would you like me to get some of my team to look into it for you?"

"Can't you tell from just looking at these reports?"

"They don't really reveal much *per se*. The bottom line is simply the movement of cash balances, not the profit. They provide a hint of something but are not really giving the full picture."

"How much is it going to cost for your blokes to do what is necessary?"

"I shall stick my neck out, and say we shall do a rough management report for a thousand up front, and we shall see what answers that gives us".

"Five hundred".

"No, one thousand pounds".

"You are a hard man, Geoffrey Foster".

"No I'm not. That's more than fair".

"Okay. Done".

"I shall set all of it out in writing, and get it off in tomorrow's post for signing".

Donald settled the bill for our meal, while I paid for the drinks and the tip. We then headed back on the ten minute drive to Fareham.

Chapter 5

"Sorry, I can't let you through", a policeman informed us, as we turned into Turnpike Road where the depot was. He stood between us and a panda car, forming a barrier. Further up the hill, I could see fire hoses across the road, the reflection of blue flashing lights in the puddles from a cloud burst about a quarter of an hour earlier.

"It's Rhodes' place up on the left", he elaborated, but Donald had left the Bentley and was sprinting up the road towards the depot.

"Must keep the road clear for emergency vehicles. Your car can't be left here". Luckily Donald had left the keys in the ignition.

"Leave it in the driveway just there. I'll explain to the householder if necessary".

Having cautiously manoeuvred the lumbering limousine into the drive, built for a typically Ford Anglia size car, I scuttled up towards the depot.

The scene which met my eyes was one of utter chaos. An explosion of glass from a large window intensified the drama consuming all one's senses.

Three fire engines with pumps screaming added a feeling of terror to the mayhem, a fourth was water cannoning the timber at the far side of the yard.

Two ambulances and half a dozen police cars with their lights flashing cast a blue hue across, each out of synchronisation with another, creating an impression that absolutely nothing was stationary. Even the rain drops sparkled like tiny Christmas lights.

A knot of people, a mixture of police and I assumed staff and customers was huddled around two or three medics (I could not tell exactly), crouching over what must have been a victim of the fire. Another victim, standing with the support of a medic and a police woman, had blood pouring from just above his left eye, as another person was trying to stem the flow with large wedges of cotton wool.

Everyone was drenched, either from the recent storm or the spray from the hoses playing over where the roof of the main storage shed had been.

Despite the volume of water flying in all directions, not helped by the incessant gusts of wind, the flames were unperturbed, leaping high above the buildings, defying any attempts at human intervention.

At first, all activity was concentrated on the emergency before me, as I tried to find Donald or Angela, but as I stepped towards the throng of people, all acting with great certainty of purpose, I was confronted by a senior fire officer. "What is your business here? Press?"

"No, I am visiting — came here with the company chairman, Mr Rhodes".

"Well I urge you to leave and make contact later. I shall have to be getting all except the ambulance and fire crew off site before this lot blows. There are gas cylinders present". He produced a loud hailer, instructing all except his own men to leave the site immediately, and that includes the police, who were busy taking instructions from a cacophony of car radios and walkie-talkies. Very few of the police were taking any notice at first, seemingly opting to only take instruction from their own discipline. The fire chief bellowed all the louder singling out the police, who then began to move, their body language suggesting they weren't happy about being told what to do, as if they were ordinary members of the public. I was probably judging them unfairly.

I joined the growing procession of bedraggled staff and customers walking down the hill towards the road block where I had left the car under the policeman's instructions.

Getting wetter and colder, I waited for some while as the trail of people passed by, which by now included residents being evacuated from the houses around the yard, some grumbling about the depot being allowed to be cheek by jowl with all the houses. Donald and Angela were not among them.

I decided , in spite of dripping water, I would risk spoiling the interior of the Bentley, and wait in a little more comfort inside it, watching all the while the comings and goings of ambulances and police cars, and some specialised gear for handling explosions. Suddenly, I was taken by surprise by a knocking on the driver's window. A lady without raincoat, peered inside from under an umbrella, as she doggedly competed with the wind for its possession.

I partially opened the window as she shivered and shouted, "I live here. Don't worry, I'm not going to ask you to move on, but if you would like to come indoors and in the warm for a cup of tea, you'd be very welcome".

"That's very kind. I'd love to, but as the car is not mine, I had better leave a note on top of the dashboard as to where I am",

The great British public, I thought. How they rise to an emergency! Perhaps they are reserved with strangers, all the more so down here in the south, but all that reticence goes on such occasions.

I explained that I had been visiting Mr Rhodes, and that the Bentley was his, but of course she knew that, as it was a familiar spectacle to those hereabouts.

"Such a nice man! Always the gentleman. He has been very good to us round here, often chipping in with building material when the community centre or local primary school have a project on".

Amazing! How there can be different sides to folk! How wrong we can be to judge simply by what we see.

While she was away in the kitchen making the tea, I felt my hair. It was almost dry. Being fine it dried out very quickly in the warm and dry. I took out my comb from an inside pocket, and found that my reflection in the glass of a photo frame was clear enough to use as a mirror to bring some decorum to my dishevelled state. The picture and several others about the sitting room built up an impression that this was the home of a family of a bald husband and three gorgeous looking children, a boy and two girls. The lady returning with the tea and some cake, caught me gazing at the photos.

"Our three monkeys", she chuckled. "Ages ranging from 3 to 8. Do you have any family?"

"Yes, the same as you. Two daughters and a son, he being the middle one, just as yours are. Mine are about a year or two ahead of yours I would guess".

She poured the tea and sat down, but I preferred to stand. Although my hair was dry, the rest of me was far from so. She had strikingly blue eyes, and long blonde hair down to her waist. Her cheek bones were quite high set, and gave her a slightly Scandinavian look, not unlike Agnetta of Abba, quite attractive!

As I drank my tea, she was looking at me intently, which became a little unnerving. "I feel I know you from somewhere", she said, with a quizzical look on her face. "Are you Geoffrey by any chance?"

I felt even more unnerved. "Well yes, my name is Geoffrey", I replied slowly, but in a wary tone.

"Geoffrey Foster", she seemed to draw up from the depths of her memory.

"Got it in one, but you have me at a disadvantage. You do remind me of someone. One of the Abba girls."

"That's what a number of people say. You will have known me of course by my maiden name, Susannah Threlkeld".

"Oh my goodness me! Of course! You were Hywel Pettit Jenkin's secretary at the office here in Fareham. Arthur Lyons and Co. as it was then, what seventeen years ago? Are you still there?"

"No, I trained as a nurse. The secretary job was just a fill in before I went off to college. I work part-time at the Q.A. It's all coming back to me. Weren't you attacked some time about ten years ago?"

"More like twelve or thirteen actually. It was the QA I was in then".

"It was all in the local papers. I was working at the QA at the time. I would have come along to see you but you were in high security, where they usually treat people from the prison. Were you attacked by people you knew?"

"Even now, I am not at liberty to say".

"Gosh! That sounds serious".

"It was; is".

"Well this is a co-incidence, Susie. I hope you don't mind my saying this to you, but I quite fancied you back in sixty four".

"I thought it was my sister you fancied".

"No it was you".

"Oh well, you missed your chance then!" she said with a mischievous smile.

"You were very shy and gave little away then".

"I really lacked self-confidence, but nursing had knocked all of that out of me, at least the shyness bit".

"Your husband…"

"Dave", she interrupted. "Dave Jenkins".

The cogs in my mind whirled, "Not son of Hywel?"

"That's my man".

"Well, well! So you married the boy next door, and the boss's son. Of course! You lived along the top road – Kiln Road. So you haven't moved far".

"Just downhill a bit!" she said with apparent deliberate *double entente.*

"I remember now, I used to give his sister Bronwen a lift home from the Gosport office when we both happened to be working there. She insisted that I dropped her off at the bottom of this road. It must have been just here. More or less outside your house right here! She would never let me take up to Kiln Road, and I could never think why. It's got to be a couple of miles walk from here to where she and you lived".

"Yes, she told me. She knew her mum would not approve. A lovely lady, my mother-in-law, but she has some old fashioned ideas about the boss's children fraternising with the staff".

"Probably more to do with the rough area where I came from. Anyway, didn't Bronwen take up with Kevin at the Gosport office, - the chap who lived in Stubbington?"

"Yes, that's Kev, my brother-in-law".

"My goodness me! It's such a small world…..What does Dave do?"

"Can't say. Not allowed to. It's secret work connected with the military."

"Ah! I suppose it's to do with the headquarters of Channel Command on the top of Portsdown Hill".

"I shall let you believe that".

"You mean that's not where he works".

"I'm not saying".

"Fair enough! I know what it is like keeping work related matters confidential, and indeed some of one's personal circumstances", I said, revealing more regret than I intended.

"You're a man of mystery! I suppose you can't tell me what connection you have with Donald Rhodes".

"Not really, ethically I mean".

"I see. He's a client. I remember how secretive you accountants have to be about even the names of whom you act for. I am assuming you are still a C.A.".

"Yes. Well, I must be getting home. It's a long drive. It's been lovely meeting you again after all these years, - perhaps not so many. It's not even twenty years. Thank you so much for your hospitality and the chat. I hope we shall meet again before long".

"Where's home, or is that a 'personal ' secret as well".

"North Buckinghamshire, where I live with Karen and my three kids".

"Not Karen from the Gosport office by any chance?"

"No, that is not one of these crazy bits of the Arthur Lyons jigsaw. I met Karen on holiday".

"What's she like?"

"The best of all that's happened to me. She's a teacher".

"Off you go then to the 'best that's happened to you'. It's also been lovely meeting you again. Mind how you go in all this awful weather. Feel free to call again if you happen to be passing by."

As I stepped outside, I called back, "It has just come to me. I was at school with your husband. He was a few years above me - a prefect in the sixth. A very popular guy and good sportsman, but I can't remember at what".

"Athletics", she called out as I was walking away.

As I inched down the side of the Bentley, the spectre of the disaster up the road, brought all emotions from the reminiscing to an abrupt end. I began going up to the yard to see if I could find Donald, but thought better of it. The fact that his car was still where it was suggested that he had his hands full, and I would be more a hindrance than any help. I left the Bentley keys with Susannah.

I retraced my route during a brief respite between showers to the multi-story car park where I had left my Audi, and set off home in the beginnings of the rush hour traffic.

The return journey seemed to take for ever. There were delays at Winchester, Newbury and Oxford, possibly avoidable, but the alternatives were probably just as congested. Bad weather invariably led to more and slower traffic.

Having listened to several bulletins of the news on the car radio, I felt information-saturated, and restored peace and quiet in my cocoon by switching it off. I began reflecting on the day, and how long it had felt. Uppermost in my mind, of course, was the fire. Who had been injured or possibly killed? Was Donald or Angela among them? Had the firemen managed to prevent the cylinders from exploding? Had they by now brought the blaze under control? Were people able now to get back to their homes? What would be the impact on the business and Donald's plans? Was the business fully insured?

These questions seemed to put into perspective the self- imposed pressures of resisting adulterous temptations. Perhaps the human race needs catastrophes to bring it to its senses sometimes, not that I would wish them on anyone. In a fleeting moment, I thought of how comfortable I had felt that afternoon in Susannah's company, much more so than when I had known her seventeen years ago. Could it have been simply that age and the experience of life in general made us less self-conscious, perhaps even more exposed to letting down our guard? If I had stayed longer and there hadn't have been the impending return of the rest of her family, I might have entertained notions outside my chosen boundaries. Who knows? Have they ever been seriously 'threatened'? Was all this just vanity? How fragile our lives and relationships can be! Be very careful before you pass judgement on others, I reminded myself.

Chapter 6

Once home, after providing explanations (but perhaps not quite all) for the late hour of my return, I peeled off everything as the effects of the earlier drenching, having dried out, had left an uncomfortable stickiness, besides which, they smelled of smoke. My suit was out of shape and would have had to go to the cleaners. I had a couple of spares which would do for the next few days.

Later that evening, Karen said that apropos the Bernadette saga, matters were getting very awkward. That day, one of her other colleagues who lives in the same street as Bernie, sidled up to Karen and expressed puzzlement over a male visitor Bernie had had over the weekend, seen going in and out of the house sometimes with her, sometimes on his own. The colleague knew Joe and the children had gone away. Karen suggested the visitor was probably her brother – she does come from quite a large family, and there would be a few to choose from. She hated having to lie, and was especially annoyed that Bernie had had it would seem little shame, and had taken no steps at concealment. In other words, if she was going to keep it from Joe, the rest of us would have to shield him from the truth.

"Have you spoken to Bernie today about it?"

"No, the colleague approached me after school".

"What about phoning Bernie to warn her that she is under suspicion?"

"Not out of school hours, as the children would be with her, and just now is out of the question. Joe will be at home, and it's far too late in the evening anyway".

"At this stage, the best you can do is to catch her as soon as you can in the morning... I'm knackered and ready for an early night".

"You haven't had anything to eat".

"Don't feel like it. The taste of that fire is in my mouth".

"Have you had a bath?"

"Yes, but that doesn't wash your mouth out, not unless you do as the kids did when they were small, - drink the bathwater."

"There's always toothpaste".

"I've scrubbed my teeth but the taste is still there. It's the burning rubber and plastic which lingers".

"Have a whisky".

"Now that's the best idea yet. How well you know me!"

How poignant my remark suddenly seemed!

Chapter 7

The following morning I phoned Donald. He readily took my call, but understandably couldn't speak for long as he had lots of calls to make many people to see – fire officers, police, insurers, staff, suppliers, builders and so on. Practically everything had been destroyed in the blaze, which was not out completely as yet. My observations of some months ago had been 'prophetic', he said, as the oil-saturated soil in parts of the yard had prolonged the burning. Thankfully, the gas cylinders had been saved by water being constantly played on them, and the intensive heat kept away from them.

I asked how many casualties there had been. I had seen at least two. Remarkably, there had only been those two and a fireman who had sustained minor injuries. Even more surprising was the discovery that the two, (who had been taken to hospital for treatment), had not come by their injuries from the fire, but from being embroiled in a fight with one another. One of them had been badly hurt. Obviously, the police were investigating, but there is a hint that one of them was responsible for the fire outbreak.

"Do you know either of them?" I enquired.

"Oh yes! They were both staff of mine, one a senior member who is a buyer and supervisor, the other a driver".

"What was the fight about?"

"Absolutely no idea! The driver won't say anything. The police think he was the one who caused the fire. He was taken into custody from the hospital, and interviewed at the police station, with his solicitor present, and clearly had been told by him to answer 'no comment' to all the police questions. This is often the advice to avoid incrimination where there is suspicion, to avoid self-incrimination, at least until more information and police evidence emerges."

"What about the other one – the buyer?"

"He's still in hospital – unconscious. Witnesses are saying that he took a hell of a beating from the driver, and eventually hit his head on a stack of concrete lintels. I have been asked not to name names at this juncture by the way".

"It must have been the driver whom I saw having his face swabbed. He had a cut just above his eye".

"The buyer at first was giving as good as he was getting apparently, and must have landed a punch which caused it. The staff have been saying he was aiming at the head, whereas the driver, much the stronger of the two, was lashing out in all directions".

"Is the driver under arrest?"

"No, he is out on bail. Look I must go now. The other phone is ringing…..Oh! Angela has just taken the call".

"Before you ring off, do you want our people to make a start on the investigatory work we discussed yesterday?"

"Yes please. As soon as possible as there are all sorts of reasons for it now. The records you will need are all kept and maintained at Waterlooville, thank God".

"I shall get it organised straight away. Do you want me to liaise with someone else as you are going to be so busy?"

"No. It's OK. I'd rather be in the picture at all times, given the circumstances, thanks. Thanks also by the way for looking after the Bentley yesterday".

"Sorry about the wet upholstery".

"No big deal! I'll send you the bill", he said chuckling to himself.

Some humour still there in the midst of all the trauma, I was relieved to hear.

I phoned Gordon at our Southsea office, and gave him a briefing on the latest events in the Rhodes saga. He said it had been on the Southern Television news, and was in the stop press of the Portsmouth Evening News, so that he was aware of the fire.

"The irony of it all was that Donald and I were out for lunch at Wickham when it started. Amongst other matters, we had been discussing his concerns about the

Fareham depot. He is convinced there is a leakage of profit, but can't put his finger on it. His fears may be unfounded, but in spite of the fire he wants us to investigate it. I have suggested to start with we prepare some detailed management accounts for each of the last twelve months for Fareham <u>and</u> Waterlooville, and see where there are anomalies, and where we should be taking a closer look. He wants this done urgently, especially now because of the fire, which is understandable".

"You are telling me this because you would like someone from this office to do the work?" Gordon asked. "I suppose it makes sense. You don't really want people coming down from Buckinghamshire if it can be helped".

"Quite so", I confirmed.

"We could manage a senior and a semi-senior for you on the job", he proffered.

"Actually, I think it calls for two seniors rather than the semi if you can possibly spare them".

"That'll be tough. I shall have to pull someone off an insurance company audit in Brighton".

"Anything you can do will be much appreciated. I have in mind one of them working on the accounts, and the other gathering as much information as possible about the running of each business, who the personnel are and their responsibilities, that sort of thing. Between you and me, I should like them both to keep a listen out for any gossip amongst the staff. I just have an uncomfortable feeling something's going on. The fire has heightened my suspicion."

"Will you be managing the assignment Geoff?"

"Oh yes. Donald insists on my personal supervision and input. I shall work out a full programme for your guys, and Fax it across I hope later today. When do you think they will be available to make a start?"

"I should like to say that's up to you Geoff, but practically speaking, I think it has to be Friday at the earliest. Would you want them to be working over the weekend?"

"I shall check with Donald, but if it can be avoided, I'd rather it were. The fee quoted does not allow for it. In any case, it is like pulling teeth getting him to pay."

"So I've heard".

Gordon, bless him, had the two seniors, Jack and Gillian working at the Waterlooville depot the following morning – Thursday. I decided to allow a day for them to get settled in, and would drive down on Friday for a preliminary meeting with them, and find out what they had already discovered, if anything at all. Jack and Gillian, I mused. Were they to have been based at Fareham, I imagined them going up the hill to the depot, not to fetch a pale of water, although there would have been plenty of it! An unkind thought perhaps!

Chapter 8

On Thursday evening I motored over to The Cock Inn in Wing to rendezvous with Bob, taking in the villages of Swanbourne and Stewkley on the way. Although the sky was heavy with cloud and dusk was fast approaching, it was as ever a pleasure driving through this quite unspoilt part of the county, almost unknown to those who lived more than twenty miles or so from it. Although I missed my favourite area of Hampshire, the Meon Valley, the pretty village of East Meon, and the surrounding chalk downs and the hamlets enfolded by them, my adopted Vale of Aylesbury, although very different, had much to console my pining.

Negotiating the very narrow way through to the car park behind The Cock Inn required all my car handling skills. My pride at accomplishing this was immediately shattered by the width of a large Mercedes and a Ford Pick-up truck, between which I parked. Bob was already there, and was settled at a table in a snug, pint of real ale in front of him, one hand in a packet of cheese and onion crisps.

The barman pulled me a pint of whatever Bob had, and discreetly informed me that Bob had opened a tab for us. Bob looked weary, and had none of the usual sparkle of enthusiasm for life, and nothing-daunted aspect about his person, I had been used to ever since we first met at twelve years of age, back in 1955.

He began by apologising for his mood the previous Saturday, and confessed he just couldn't help himself. He wasn't used to children of Philip and Christina's age and was simply unable to cope with them. It was not their fault, they were just acting their age. He went on to describe the dreadful fight he had been having with cancer. He had had half his stomach removed, and had undergone several bouts of chemo therapy. They would be followed by periods when the disease would go into remission, and then it would recur in some other part of his body. At the present time, it was again in remission, but only until the next time...... He broke off at that point, and tried to change the subject after he could sense the lingering shock in my appearance and demeanour.

I sipped my beer in an absent minded, perfunctory manner, trying to find something to say which would not sound trite, but all I could say was, "I am deeply sorry Bob. I had no idea. It's such a shock". I felt, but thought better of saying, how I had always regarded him as strong as an ox. It would have only rubbed in the premature deterioration of his health.

He changed the subject, and made a supreme effort to be cheerful and spoke of his fairly recently discovered passion of dinghy sailing. Milton Keynes offered plenty of opportunity for him to engage in this all absorbing hobby. It made him feel that controlling the boat in the vicissitudes of the wind and weather, was like overcoming what life and the disease were throwing at him. When times were bad, while packing up the boat after a couple of hours sailing on a blowy day, he would shake his fist at the wind and say, "This day has been mine".

As we had the previous Saturday in the pub in Gainsthorpe, we exchanged memories of our youth and early twenties together, and even the holiday to Italy and Austria we had gone on when I met Karen, and the fun we had had trying to track her down after our return from the holiday, but as the time drew on, I battled with the question of whether this was an appropriate moment to raise the subject of Brendan. There were some similarities between this and our quest over Karen, so I took the plunge and asked, "In your dealing with the N.U.T. committees, etc. have you come across a Brendan who teaches at Roade near Northampton?"

"Brendan Orford. Yes, I know him. Strange fellow! I can't quite make up my mind how genuine he is. He's very clever and a very good listener, but doesn't say a lot, but when he does, it is very deep and meaningful as the saying goes Trouble I have is that it's so deep, it's obscured from my reasoning".

"A Bernadette.."

"I thought that was coming", he interjected   "She of course teaches in your neck of the woods. She gives him a lift to and from our meetings. Are tongues beginning to wag in Gainsthorpe as they are around the N.U.T.?"

"I hope not to any extent. Bernadette is a colleague and friend of Karen's, and Karen is extremely bothered by it. It wouldn't be fair to say much more about it except that Bernadette and Brendan are not going out of their way to hide what they are up to".

"If they are up to anything at all, of course".

"I think it has got past the stage of speculation".

"Oh!" said Bob with a sigh of resignation.

After a little argument, we split the bill. As we parted, I felt a sudden chill. This may be the last time I see him.

Karen was very quiet after I had had given her an account of the evening.

Chapter 9

The offices were part of a small administration block and ground floor shop in an industrial estate down the hill from the main shopping street, which was in my childhood the A3 to London, but now partly a precinct. The Waterlooville depot was much smarter and tidier than Fareham. I parked in Donald's designated space, as he had invited me to do so. Since the events of Tuesday, he seemed to have taken on a more considerate persona, and had become much more rational. It had obviously shaken him severely.

I found Jack and Gillian in an upstairs room, which had been allocated to them. In one day they had made themselves at home, giving the room an air of an audit office found in nearly all accountancy practices - stacks of files everywhere, and little more than a square foot of space to work on each of the desks.

Jack was a _must have,_ commonly found in so many provincial accountants at that time, no formal professional qualification, but had worked in the same branch, man and boy, except during call up in World War II, which not only interrupted his career, but his studies under articles, for one reason or another, the latter not resumed after his being demobbed. His experience, common sense and nous knocked spots of many a qualified accountant with first class honours in

Economics, Ancient Greek and Roman Literature or Psychology. He was highly regarded by the clients he acted for, knew every inch of their businesses, and was bang up-to-date with all the regulatory requirements relevant to them. Farming was Jack's specialism, but he was equally proficient with builders' merchants such as Rhodes. He could also turn his hand to a bit of amateur building work around his own home as evidenced by his double garage, so Gordon told me, and Jack himself said to me he was often a customer of Rhodes.

He also said he winced at the sight of the customer being given a hand written invoice with a rubber receipt stamp applied to it, torn from a pad, with a sheet of carbon paper slipped behind each top copy page as it came to be used. This was invariably an indication that no stock recording system was in place. He had already observed during some testing the previous day, that towards the back of the sales invoice books as they were called, the retained carbon copied pages were so faint as to be hardly legible. Occasionally, the corner of the carbon sheet had been folded over, one assumes accidentally, and part of the information on the top copy had not come through on the carbon copy. Not only were the acknowledgements of receipt of payment rubber stamped, but also the letter heading of the company's name and address. Furthermore, although the pages were pre-numbered, the sequence went back to Number 1 with each new book. The opportunities for mistakes, muddles and worst of all, fraud, were manifest. Jack had found at least two breaks in the page numbering in one book alone, which was explained by the practice of tearing out pages where mistakes had been made, and the process started afresh on a new page.

"Are these sales invoice books used just for cash sales?" I asked Jack.

"Oh no, they are used for credit sales as well. In the case of cash sales, the carbon copy is, as I have said, rubber stamped as paid. The copies which are not so stamped are recorded once a week in the sales ledger".

"How often are the carbon copied invoices stamped as paid checked against money paid into the bank?"

"Daily. At the close of business for each day, they are totted up and the total checked against the banking made up for the cash and cheques in the tills for that day."

"Have the reconciliation workings been kept"

"That, I don't know. It's one of things I shall be looking into this morning. Before you ask, I plan to test check some of the unstamped invoices' postings to the sales (customers) ledger, and to see how money coming in for the credit sales is differentiated from the cash sales money".

"With the holes in the controls on the whole system, I would say you need to do quite an extensive test on that latter point in particular".

"Exactly!"

"Were you pulled off the Brighton insurance company audit?"

"Yes, but I am not sorry. It is a real drag. The records are all so perfect, we never find anything wrong, except once. They had recorded an agent as a 'Mr' when she was a 'Miss'. Great excitement that day! We went out at lunchtime on the last day of the audit and celebrated"..

"I thought you did that anyway".

"Well yes, but it added a certain soupcon to the occasion".

"You sad people!"

He shrugged.

"Anyway, I was quite pleased when Gordon asked me if I should like to do something I could get my teeth in to".

Gillian left the room.

"What is Gillian working on?"

"I have left her to get on with the management accounts."

"She's a qualified C.A. isn't she?"

"Don't rub it in, Geoff".

"As if...."

"That thing she has there that looks like a typewriter, is that a Personal Computer?"

"That's right. She is using SuperCalc on it".

"Is that so? "

"It uses spreadsheets. Bloody useful, so I am told", said Jack with a certain cynicism in his voice.

"No doubt it is their future, Jack".

"Come off it Geoff. You're still young enough to embrace it. Not yet forty, I bet".

"True! Perhaps Gillian can persuade me. What exactly is a spreadsheet?"

"How should I know? I am just the old man in the office. Old dogs, new tricks, etc."

"There are plenty of new tricks in you yet, you old dog".

"Bugger off, you puppy", retaliated Jack.

Gillian re-entered.

"Well Jack, I shall leave you to carry on. You obviously know what you are doing", I said with a touch of mock sarcasm and counter-retaliation.

I lurched across the room towards Gillian.

"Tell me something about SuperAdd and what this machine can do".

"SUPERCALC", barked Jack.

"Can it really help in preparing the management accounts?"

"Most certainly! I shall show you what I have done so far".

With great enthusiasm, she brought up on a little screen a template of the set of accounts I had envisaged.

"Did this come with the computer?"

"No, no. I compiled this myself. The figures you see in the little squares we call cells. I can change anything on here at will. No crossing out. What's more, those figures can be linked to other places in the spreadsheet. Take that one there in cell F6. If I go down here...". She scrolled down the screen to an area where there was a summary of data she had collated from somewhere, changed one of the figures, and instantaneously, the figure in cell F6 changed in accord.

"I'm impressed. I see the potential in this. I shall chew on that fact on the way home. Keep up the good work, and I shall look forward to seeing the end result. In the meantime, I shall pop along the corridor, and see Donald".

"He's got someone with him", Gillian informed me. "It sounded like some argy bargy going on".

Nevertheless, I walked in the direction of Donald's office. There was certainly something going on.

"Evan, why the hell won't you tell what the fighting was all about?" Donald shouted.

"Oh f*** off", came the response, at which point , whoever Evan was stormed out of Donald's room, roughly brushed past me, and stomped off down the stairs. I couldn't help noticing he had an X-shaped dressing just above his left eye.

"I can guess who Evan is", I remarked as Donald and I shook hands, greeting one another.

"He is one of our delivery drivers, the one you saw on Tuesday who was involved in the fracas. He's a sour character. Seems to have a permanent chip on his shoulder. Comes from South Wales – typical Socialist. Bolshie whenever asked to do anything. Takes an instant dislike to you if you have got a bob or two. I reckon he's driven by envy more than anything. Always has a Labour poster on his car whenever there's an election".

"Now you are showing your prejudices, Donald".

"I have every reason to considering what the Fire chief has told me. It seems the fire was started by a paraffin heater. Some of the staff saw it being kicked over by him when the fight broke out".

"Was it deliberate, or just an accident?"

"Who knows? It wouldn't surprise me if he lashed out at the stove first. He was in a foul mood, cursing and swearing at Roy".

"Is Roy the guy who was badly hurt?"

"That's right".

"What's the latest on his condition? Is he out of hospital now?"

"Far from it! He is still unconscious. They are keeping him in a coma because of suspected brain damage. He has also suffered extensive burns. He had to be dragged from the fire".

"I thought he had hit his head on the pile of concrete lintels".

"This is a bone of contention with the police. Witness statements are very confused over this. Certainly there is blood on the lintels and his head injuries are consistent with that".

"Perhaps he staggered towards the fire after hitting his head".

"Possibly. It's one theory the police have".

I said, slightly changing the subject, "I haven't yet had a look at the list of staff our Jack has given me". I delved in my briefcase and pulled out an envelope and opened it.

It showed Roy as one of two senior buyers, and indicated he was responsible for the contracts with the Ministry of Defence. I asked how much latitude and discretion he gave the buyers. "Virtually total. I rarely intervene. They are both very good at their job. They know the trade far better than I do, especially local. I trust them implicitly in that regard".

"Do you ever do any checks on prices independently from those they have negotiated?"

"Only if, for example, I bump into a wholesaler on the golf course, and we start talking shop. There was an occasion recently when one offered to quote for us, and give us a price we couldn't possibly refuse. I mentioned it to Roy, who followed it up, but found the prices we were already paying were just as competitive, except for one. Roy went back to our existing supplier, and managed to get them to undercut my golfing acquaintance's figures".

"Does anyone check anyone else's work?" I asked.

"What do you mean? Isn't that what an audit's all about? It's the auditors' job, surely, when they do the annual audit?"

"That's part of it, but auditors only do test checks on the system to verify that it is being followed, and to consider whether it is right and effective for the circumstances. Anyway, we shall be reporting briefly on any blatant weaknesses in the internal controls when we present you with the management accounts and our findings generally".

"When do you think the reports will be ready?"

"I'm hoping by this time next week, but don't hold us to that. There's plenty to do between now and then. I am going to need yours and someone else's help in establishing what stock you have in hand, and what went up in smoke at Fareham".

"The loss assessor from the insurance company was here yesterday, and we worked out between us roughly what it was at Fareham. He didn't seem especially concerned that there were no stock records apart from the annual stock take at the 31st March. I said the levels normally do not vary by very much. The big orders almost always go from our suppliers directly to our customers' sites", he said, subconsciously flipping back a strand of his blond hair, which had slipped down alongside his left temple. It probably was in imitation of my own action immediately beforehand. We both had trained hair from the side of heads to cover the thinning area on top.

"Can you let Gillian have a copy of your notes from yesterday's meeting with the loss assessor, please? Another thing — Is it possible to organise a stock take here at Waterlooville over this weekend?"

"At the loss assessor's suggestion, that's already been arranged. Do you want your people here as well?"

"It would be useful, but not essential. I'll see what they say. As it is not the annual audit, as I say it is not vital".

"Geoff, I have to go now. The fire people want a site meeting this morning".

On the way out, I looked in on Jack and Gillian again. They had heard that a weekend stocktake was in the offing, and had agreed between them to call in for a couple of hours on the Saturday afternoon. Clearly, neither could have been ardent Pompey fans, as there was an important near-end of season home game on. Had there not been things on at Gainsthorpe that weekend, I might have been tempted to stay over at mum and dad's, and watch the match at Fratton Park. It would also have been nice of course to have seen them as well.

Karen had warned Bernadette that her visitor the previous weekend had been spotted, but she appeared not to show any sense of alarm. Her only remark was to say that as matters stood, there were no arrangements in place for her and Brendan Orford to meet again until the next N.U.T. meeting, which was nearly three months away. Karen and I decided that being the case, we should do nothing to interfere in the hope that the affair would prove to be a one off, and would fizzle out. We did wonder whether Bernadette had confided in anyone else, but perhaps that was not our business, if indeed any of it was.

Chapter 10

I had not heard from Jack or Gillian by the following Thursday morning, and therefore phoned them from our South Midlands office in Buckingham, which was where I was based, for a progress report. Jack said that Gillian had produced a first draft of the management accounts for the two businesses, but they were not making a great deal of sense. She would spend the day going over her work, and where necessary see again certain individuals from whom she had obtained information, and review with them what they had given her. Although stock was an issue, there were also problems with tracing the banking of customers' cash and cheques, which had been recorded as received in the Sales Ledger at both depots.

The stock take over the previous weekend had lasted much longer than expected, but at least it had now been completed. Gillian and Jack were checking the pricing up of the inventories. Although approximate dates for the delivery to the depots of the vast majority of items of stock had been entered in the lists, Gillian had had great difficulty in persuading the staff to price them at the cost on those dates. Their inclination was to use current prices. The current rate of inflation was running high, and actual historic cost was likely to be materially lower than current cost value. Accepted accounting practice is that profit is not included in the accounts of a business until goods have been sold on to customers, hence stock is included at what it had cost the business. This causes difficulties if there is no proper stock recording system, as there often is no way of identifying when an individual item of stock was bought and for how much. This may seem a nicety, but when total stock on hand was substantial, the difference in the method of pricing could be quite significant, and so too the impact on the profit showing in the accounts.

Despite the crudeness of the monthly reports Donald had been getting from his staff, the trend they had revealed was being supported by the figures Gillian had so far produced, but in a much more marked way. There were still too many loose ends for Gillian and Jack to resolve before any reliable and useful reports could be released to Donald. More time than initially intimated was needed. They would aim to fax me everything on Monday for further discussion the same day, with a view of us all, including Donald, meeting on the Tuesday afternoon. That would allow time that morning to deal with any follow up from our discussion on Monday. Gillian stressed however, that there were likely to be many unanswered questions even then, especially relating to Fareham, in spite of the fact that very little in the way of vital records had been lost in the fire.

I spoke at length to Donald, explaining the necessary delay, to which at first he reacted in his usual bombastic tone. "Geoff, this is unacceptable. Your people have been here a week now, plagued us with all sorts of didactic questions, have probed into stuff the auditors have never troubled us with. They have stacks of files in the room they are working in. My staff are complaining that they have to keep going in there to look up ongoing information. Jack and the girl are constantly talking to each other about how they are going to tackle this and that. Do they not know what they are doing? They give the impression they don't, if they have to keep talking about it, instead of getting on and doing it, whatever it is. I'm afraid I got a bit shirty with whatever her name is – Gillian – last evening when they were still here while we were trying to lock up. I think you need to give them a kick up the backside. They are making a meal of this and it will be me paying for it".

I replied by saying I understood the strain and frustration he was under, and what it was like to be on the receiving end of questions, sometimes apparently trivial, from accountants, but there would be a serious purpose behind those queries.

I hinted at some of the areas of difficulty they were encountering, but as with a number of clients, he was more optimistic about the efficiency and effectiveness of their record keeping than reality justified. I had tried to convey this to him as discreetly as I could, but whatever way one expresses these delicate matters, they inevitably have an incendiary effect.

I let him rant for a minute or so, but gradually it became clear, as I should have recalled from previous occurrences, that it was part of his strategy in business, to establish control by wrong-footing his 'opponent'. How often one comes across this technique used by so-called captains (or lower ranks) of industry! This is all very well if the 'opponents', professional or otherwise, are resilient enough to avoid submission to inappropriate demands, but sadly many are not, with the result that some of these 'captains' surround themselves with sycophancy, which at best is nauseating to the observer, or at other times induces contempt for the unfortunate souls who have no choice but to kowtow.

Donald, now with his over-reaction (or play-acting) abating, and brought to his senses by the seed I had sown in his mind that we had made discoveries which could potentially involve calling in the police, began to listen intently, and became emphatic in his wish to have all problems exposed. "Speaking of police", he said, "they have told me that Evan, the lorry driver, wants to visit Roy, and apologise for the grief and injury he caused him. That of course, is not possible because of Roy's fragile state, but he is now conscious, although not well enough to be interviewed. Evan still will not say what the fight was all about".

Chapter 11

The following day, Friday, I worked, or rather tried to work from home. The school was closed to allow the teachers to attend a day long course at Missenden Abbey. MaryAnn and Philip attended the local school where Karen taught part-time. Christina, then at pre-school in the community centre, was due to join her brother and sister in the upcoming September. Karen was responsible for the seven to eight year olds, which included Philip. He would say that it was funny having mummy being mummy to all the class, which I suppose was his way of saying that she treated them all the same way she treated him. I felt that was a great tribute to Karen's teaching skills.

I had my day all worked out. Two jigsaws had been purchased in Buckingham the previous day. They had been gift wrapped and placed on the breakfast table, one next to MaryAnn's place and the other next to Philip's. It was a thrill to see their surprise turn to delight when they sat down for their cereals. "But it's not our birthday", they said almost in unison. With a great big grin on my face and full of self-satisfaction, I explained that the parcels contained their homework, in other words, something to keep them occupied while I got on with my work.

Karen stood looking on, somewhat unimpressed as if to say, 'You smart arse. You think you've got it all sussed. Just you wait and see'. Sure I didn't have to wait long. Christina arrived at the breakfast table. "Look what daddy has bought us", the other two chirped, again in unison.

"WHERE'S MY PRESENT?" she screamed.

Karen now spoke. "You just didn't see that coming, did you? Honestly, you bury yourself away in your work, not giving a thought to how it impacts on the rest of us. Now I'm off to Great Missenden with Bernadette. Over to you". Those last three words were spoken half an octave above her normal voice. The front door was closed with a little more clamour than usual.

Christina was not placated until we all set off in the car to the community centre to drop her off at pre-school. The day was squally and wet, so the excitement of dashing under an umbrella, desperate to turn itself inside out, to the centre's main door, provided the complete distraction from the overlooked breakfast parcel.

Back home, I was able to quietly get on with my work, while the other two became completely absorbed in joining the edge pieces of their puzzles, until Philip came into the study and wanted to know whom I was talking to. I then had to explain the purpose and workings of a Dictaphone. "Mummy writes her letters with a pen and puts them in the post box. How do the letters in that Dicta…thingy get to persons they are supposed to get to?" A few more minutes were lost in describing the office procedures involved in transcribing my recorded voice into a communication which would eventually find its way to its intended recipient. He didn't seem particularly enthralled, but just commented that what I had said to the machine sounded very, very boring. He was quite right. They were all letters to various Her Majesty's Inspectors of Taxes, enclosing business accounts, Schedule D Tax computations and completed Income Tax Returns for several clients.

My concentration having been broken, I reflected on Karen's words at breakfast time and the atmosphere they had generated. I then couldn't stop thinking about it. I hated our parting company when situations such as this had arisen. We very rarely shouted at each other as that solved nothing, but it meant we were both left brooding. Karen was an only child and I had guessed that not having siblings on hand, she had had to work out her problems unaided, hence her being prone to bottling things up. The coolness between us could sometimes last for a matter of days.

I had told Karen that I had taken the day off to devote to the children, and here I was trying to catch up on business correspondence, and almost resenting their calls on my time. My struggle to maintain due weight between the demands of work and family were more often than not the source of arguments, and I had to confess that there was a tendency on my part to overlook the importance of Karen's own career, and the sacrifices she had made in that direction.

What could I do to ease the strain? My train of thought was interrupted by MaryAnn and Philip getting restless as their interest in the jigsaws waned. They began arguing with one another and then squabbling which lasted for about twenty minutes until it was time to collect Christina from Pre-school. Although it was still raining steadily, I decided we would dress appropriately to brave the weather and walk, rather than more sensibly take the car. The kids loved the idea – Philip remarking it would be great to stamp in the puddles en route. On the way back, Christina also thought it was a fun idea. MaryAnn simply reminded me and them, there would be mum to be reckoned with later. 'What the heck?' I thought. There was plenty of time to dry out before she was due home.

Over lunch, my thoughts returned to lightening the mood for when Karen came home. Buy some flowers from the garage along the road. Too corny! Karen never fell for that one. Prepare a meal? No. I was expected to do that anyway, besides which I reckoned that she would have had a cooked meal at Missenden Abbey. Bake a cake, getting the children involved? That would keep us all entertained. They jumped with excitement at the suggestion. It was perhaps a bit devious on my part to use the children in easing my conscience, but they after all would benefit, having fun making the cake, and having a happy mum to follow.

I found a recipe for banana loaf which would have icing drizzled over the top. Perfect! It worked better by letting them do the work while I gave the instructions. MaryAnn and Philip's contretemps from the morning bubbled over into the culinary activity, while little Christina told them to stop fighting and grow up.

All went well, despite Philip insisting we included some apple and marmalade in the mix, although I drew the line at MaryAnn's suggestion of adding a dollop of Marmite. Further argument ensued over the licking out of the mixing bowl, but children the world over it seemed did that. The recipe's instruction to bake in a fan oven preheated to 160 degrees Celsius for half an hour proved to be an error so typically found in such publications. A whole hour was required, and even then it sagged a little in the middle. After cooling our creation, all three had a go at drizzling the icing and ensuring there was plenty over to lick.

At about quarter past three, the front door bell chimed its Big Ben theme. It was a fairly elderly gentleman I recognised from Buckingham Methodist Church, although I did not know his name. He often came round with the offertory plate along the aisle of the church where we normally sat on a Sunday. He appeared surprised, quite shocked in fact, to be confronted by me at the door. He introduced himself as George Godfrey from church. His name did sound familiar; I had simply not matched the face and name until that moment. It seemed the right thing to invite him in, especially as it was still raining. "Smells good!" he commented. My look of puzzlement prompted him to explain his remark: "Karen's been baking, no doubt".

"Oh no! The children and I have been discovering new talents, gifts from The Lord, you might say", I said, regretting my facile utterance instantly. It did not impress him very much either.

"I just wondered if Karen was about", he queried with diminishing expectation.

"I'm afraid she is away at a teachers' conference – all day actually; left me in charge of the kids."

He turned with a certain awkwardness towards the door. "Would you mind relaying to her that I called on the off chance", he said, again hoisting his umbrella.

"By all means. Can I say what it was about?"

"No..erm.. no. It's nothing that can't wait. Thank you anyway".

Strange, I thought. Odd chap!

"That was god, wasn't it daddy?" Christina said in a reverential tone." Mummy says that the money she puts on the plate in church is for god. Also, I heard him tell you he was church god".

"Not quite, darling. He said his name was George Godfrey, and mummy's money on the plate is taken to the altar, and is given to the preacher. He's the one who sort of gives it to God. I put money on the plate as well".

Philip, who was laughing at his sister's misapprehension, mischievously chipped in, "Suppose one day, instead of going up to front of the church, he turned round and ran out of the door with all the money. That would be really funny. It would make my day".

"I bet it would, you heathen", I said.

"What's that?" he asked.

"That's where you go when you die, isn't it daddy?" Christina said knowingly.

"No, that's heaven, silly", corrected MaryAnn.

Philip laughed all the louder, but probably would not have known the difference, without MaryAnn's intervention. At least he did not press for a proper answer to his question. I was relieved, as I was beginning to feel exhausted with the day's domestic duties. Poor me!

"That god who has just gone, comes to see mummy sometimes", revealed Christina casually.

Karen arrived home just after five o'clock in a much happier frame of mind than the morning, and in complete contrast to the weather. The wind had got up again, and the rain was lashing down, completely flattening the fine display of late tulips we had been enjoying so much over the last fortnight of mainly sunny days and unseasonal warmth. We had looked forward all winter to the bulbs we had bought in Spalding during a week's break in Boston, Lincolnshire over the previous October half – term holiday, spent with Karen's parents. There was an unusual glow about Karen's face, slightly flushed, and a smile showing an underlying attempt to repress it. There was also light in her expressive blue eyes which made them glisten.

"You've had a good day by the look of it!" I remarked.

"Yes. I have actually, I shall tell you about it later. What about yours?"

"We had quite a bit of fun, didn't we?" I replied, glancing at the children for affirmation.

"Yea", piped Christina. "Daddy let us splash in the puddles on the way home from playgroup. We really got really wet and it was lovely. Philip's trousers were ever so muddy and daddy had to wash them." Too much information, I thought.

However, Karen's glow was unchanged as she responded, "I should think so too".

She really is happy about something, I thought. Normally, I would not have got away with the sort of tales Christina was now regaling her with.

"Have you had dinner?" I asked Karen, changing the subject for fear the mood would not last.

"Yes, thanks. I shall not need anything to eat. They fed and watered us very well at Missenden".

"You must have some of the banana cake we baked for you", demanded Philip. It's specially for you and it's got icing on top as well".

"Sounds yummy scrumptious! I'll have some just before your bedtime. I expect daddy's looking forward to that. Daddy, have they had dinner yet?"

"No, not yet, but it's on its way. Can't you smell the beef mince pie in the oven?"

"You know I haven't much of a sense of smell. That's how I came to marry you", she chuckled.

"That was unkind, mummy", remarked MaryAnn with pathos.

"It's all right, MaryAnn, mummy was only joking".

"Yes, I was only joking", said Karen with a wry smile.

During dinner, Christina, in one of her audience-grabbing moments, informed Karen that "God had been again, and asked daddy to tell you."

"Sorry love, I forgot to tell you. It was actually a George Godfrey from.." Karen interrupted "Okay, okay. I know who God is". Her smile had gone. She quickly changed the subject.

"How far did you get with the jigsaws?" she asked, turning to MaryAnn and Philip.

"They were too hard, and we got bored", replied Philip with his usual frankness.

Karen's smile had returned. "I told you they were more for adults".

Okay. She was right. Whenever is she not?

After the children had gone to bed we watched an episode of 'I Claudius', which was being repeated over several weeks on television. We had both been gripped by it the first time, although some of it was extremely lurid, but the acting was superb, especially by Derek Jacobi who played the Emperor Claudius, a stammering buffoon with a limp, who was manipulated by his evil family and the ruthless characters who ruled the Roman Empire during the first century AD. Some scenes, I have to confess, I watched with relish, if not a little embarrassment, if Karen was watching as well, usually with her face in a book , but peering round the side of it, as much I guessed to observe my reactions to what I was seeing.

When the programme was over, she asked, "Did you enjoy that?"

"Yes. The acting was very good".

"And the rest", she said with some sarcasm. There was still a remnant of the glow about her when I asked, "So how was your day?"

"Excellent. For once it was really well worth going. The morning was taken up with the part computers are and will be playing in the future in education. I'm a bit unsure whether to look forward to that, but during the break-out sessions, some of the teachers were saying how the kids are really taking to them.. We also talked a lot about the Falklands War, Margaret Thatcher, the miners' strike and the Pope's visit".

"I'm surprised you had any time for educational matters".

"There was the usual smattering of 'true blues', who regard Thatcher as the new Messiah in female form, but the discussion was on the whole conducted in a generous spirit".

"That's unusual for you lot of Trots", I remarked.

"Well, we were all infants and juniors teachers, where you don't get too much of the party politics negativity...The lunch was good".

"Is it that which explains your happy disposition, compared with the 'out of the bed the wrong side' mood this morning?"

"Yes, I suppose that's part of it. In the afternoon we concentrated on child psychology, and guess who led the session".

"I've no idea. I know nothing of the various experts in the field of education. Perhaps I should pay more attention, Miss".

"I can now say I have met Brendan Orford".

"So he was there?"

"He actually led the whole afternoon's programme, and was absolutely brilliant. We all hung on his every word. He is such a good speaker – interesting, funny, and very much down to earth. During the break-out sessions he came round to each group, and was so kind and patient with everyone. A good listener and made us all feel we had so much to offer, whatever differing opinions we might hold. He and I had a long chat about the complications of being a Methodist teaching in a Catholic school, and although he claims to be a Catholic, he seemed to see everything from my point of view. Definitely what you might call a progressive. I can now appreciate what Bernadette sees in him. I could have listened to him all day with his Irish brogue and charm".

"Funny. I never thought of his being Irish, although his first name is obviously so".

"It was a surprise to me as well. Bernadette had said nothing about it, but then being Irish herself I suppose she is so used to it, and saw it as no big deal".

"So now do you regard him as a redeemed or acceptable character?"

"You could say I see him in a different light".

"What about Bernadette?"

"We shall see".

When I first knew Karen, I took it for granted that at the age of twenty one, having spent almost three years at teacher training college followed by a year employed as one, she had history as they say as far as the opposite sex was concerned. She occasionally mentioned relationships which were short lived, including one which was ongoing when I met her on a holiday. Between then and taking up with her again some months later, I had had for a very short time a girl friend who tragically died of a brain tumour. She, Catherine, was the first to show any great interest in possibly forging any sort of future with me. When I had eventually tracked down Karen and met her for the second time, our relationship blossomed rapidly, and we were married within a year.

All through our courtship and the first couple of years of marriage, I was terribly jealous when there was any threat, perceived or real to our relationship. Before Catherine and Karen, there had been no-one I could honestly regard as a girlfriend. Having lost Catherine, I was all the more fearful of losing Karen. As time went on, I grew more confident in the strength of our love for one another, and no matter what happened, our marriage would hold together, even if heaven forbid, one of us strayed.

Nevertheless, the old jealousy proved it had a little life left in it, when 'God', as Christina called him, appeared on the doorstep that afternoon. What was his business in doing so? "George Godfrey turning up that afternoon was a bit of a mystery", I said, trying not to make it sound of any great import.

"He is my pastoral visitor. He takes his job very seriously and delivers my membership card in person".

"Oh! Is that very often?"

"Once a year".

"Christina gave the impression it is more frequently than that".

"Is this an inquisition?"

"I'll drop the subject if it bothers you".

"Well, if you must know, he has called a few times on the off chance I'd be alone apart from Christina. His wife died quite suddenly of a heart attack while they were on holiday in the Canaries a couple of years ago. He gets very lonely and is desperate for someone to talk to. He tells me I'm a good listener and have a sympathetic ear, whereas he thinks that everyone else regards him as a bit odd. Why he singled me out in the first place, I'm not quite sure".

"Perhaps he fancies you. How old is he?"

"Not very old at all. He was fifty one last Thursday. I sent him a card. I expect that's why he called this afternoon – to thank me, and yes, I think he does fancy me. In actual fact I know he does. He told me so".

"So, how do you feel about that?"

"I think it is quite sweet, but I do feel quite sorry for him, as he obviously misses his wife and grieves for her".

"You do have this way of attracting loners of the opposite sex. You married one after all".

"You, a loner! You're just an odd ball".

"Granted. Why haven't you mentioned him before?"

"I don't tell you everything".

"Obviously!"

"A lady has to keep something back, some things to herself".

"If you say so".

I left it at that. This was part of Karen's mystique. I only had to recall the difficulty I and Bob Willetts had in tracing her after the holiday when I first met her. She and her friend knew where Bob lived, but to begin with I had no idea where she and her friend lived. It was for me to prove my interest in her through determination in finding her. That, at least, was my interpretation. If I were honest, I quite enjoyed that aura of retained mystery in our marriage.

Chapter 12

On Monday morning the fax machine at Buckingham was spewing out paper incessantly, with information from Gillian. While this was in progress, I spoke at length to Jack.

His conclusions were that there were essentially two if not three unresolved issues. The most important would need Roy's help, which of course, he was unable to give until he hopefully recovered. The second matter probably did not concern him, and the potential third would involve a frank personal discussion with Donald.

Jack was keen to deal with second first. "I'm convinced there has been good old-fashioned 'teeming and lading' with the cash bankings. It doesn't of course affect the gross profit percentage of sales that much, as it is a fraud that usually has its limitations. I think I know the identity of the culprit, but I feel we should approach Donald before we start naming names".

'Teeming and lading' often is the fraudulent retention of cash takings due for banking on a particular day (say day 1), by delaying the banking for say a day to day 2, and using some or part of the takings of day 2 to make up the misappropriations of day 1. Each subsequent day's takings have to be 'raided' to make up the shortfall of the rolled back takings of the previous day, and so on. The longer it goes on, the more complex it becomes, and usually involves cleverly altering the banker's date stamp on the banking's counterfoil. Auditors will invariably include in their programmes of work, checks comparing the dates on the counterfoils with the dates appearing on the bank statements. If the counterfoils show earlier dates, it can be an indication that something untoward is going on. In serious cases banks are requested to produce the original bank paying in slips which they would otherwise retain. (This at least was the practice in the 1980s).

Jack checked a month's worth, and was convinced the date stamps on the counterfoils had been altered. In fact, in one instance the alteration was made using a pencil. The simple application of a rubber clearly revealed the original date. From this he was able to estimate that the defalcation was around £3,000.

The third matter related to round amounts of cash removed from takings of the Waterlooville shop, and recorded as paid to Donald for expenses 'unsubstantiated'.

The prime matter however, was much more subtle, and had the potential to make an impact on profits to a much greater extent. Jack explained that he and Gillian had paid close attention to the whole process of purchase and supply of the businesses, especially at Fareham, where the gross profit margin was noticeably weaker than that at Waterlooville. Gross profit in Rhodes' case was the amount by which sales income exceeded the cost of the goods supplied. The margin is expressed as a percentage of sales income. For example, in the simplest terms, suppose goods were bought for £60 and sold for £100, the gross profit would be £40. The gross margin would be 40% of the value of the sales. Merchants and retailers would generally carry stocks of goods for resale. Where there were sophisticated stock recording systems in place, the cost of each item sold could be identified. However, particularly in relatively small concerns, full stock records were rare, and for many were rudimentary, if they existed at all.

In those circumstances, many businesses relied on an annual stock take to provide an inventory of stock items held at the end of the financial year, and price them as accurately as possible at the cost the business paid when buying them. The gross profit the business will have made in say a year would be sales income, less the cost of the goods sold. That cost will consist of the cost value of the stock in hand at the beginning of the financial year, plus the cost of goods bought during the year, less the cost value of goods still in hand and unsold at the end of the year.

The gross profit margin percentage on Sales therefore, will be an important guide as to the performance of a business, and a check on many aspects of how it is being operated. As most businesses sell a variety of products, the gross profit margins on them can differ, often significantly, depending on the mark-up on them.

If the sales mix of products is fairly consistent from one period to the next, the overall gross profit margin should not vary very much from year to year, but there are many factors to consider where there is a marked variation, such as competition for sales, the availability of supplies to the business, and the deals made with the suppliers, discounts and so on.

Some merchants will apply the same mark-up on virtually all the products they sell. Such was meant to be the case with Rhodes. If we take the example above, the £60 paid for the goods had a mark-up of £40, being 66.67% (2/3rds), to produce the 40% (2/5ths) gross margin on sales value.

Jack had established with Donald that their target mark-up was on the whole being achieved at Waterlooville, but at Fareham it was a very different picture, it having deteriorated noticeably according to the audited accounts of the last two years, and in particular during the period covered by the draft management accounts produced by Gillian.

Hers and Jack's investigations had thrown up some anomalies. They had worked out that around three quarters of the sales for each depot were related to goods which were delivered direct to the contractors' (customers') sites. In other words, the goods did not go physically via the yard, thus at no stage becoming stock in hand as far as Rhodes were concerned. This enabled Jack and Gillian to match exactly those goods purchased by the depot with those supplied by it, by comparing the invoices and delivery notes received from Rhodes' suppliers with the detail on the invoices issued by Rhodes to its customers. This showed that that aspect of the business was operating consistently, and supported Donald's assertions.

However, Jack had observed that at Fareham, over a period of two and a half years, the sales for Ministry of Defence projects had risen from about 10% to roughly 15% of total sales. These were not sales of goods direct from suppliers to customers' sites as one would have expected, but were delivered first to the yard.

Nevertheless, it has proved relatively easy to follow the trail as the bulk of the goods had come from the same supplier of plaster board and plaster products, and the quantities and dates of purchase and supply matched the descriptions in the supplier's invoices and the Rhodes' invoices rendered to the Ministry of Defence. The surprise was that the profit margins were less than half those expected, and were it not for the exceptional delivery charges made to the Ministry, would have been almost zero.

At this stage, the discovery had not been discussed with Donald. We agreed we would leave it until our meeting scheduled for the following day. Jack however, confirmed that Roy was the buyer who handled all the Ministry supplies. He, apparently according to the staff, regarded the account as his "baby", and personally looked after the sales contracts as well. It was not an Ideal arrangement from the internal check and control operation of the business.

"I couldn't help noticing how thin the partition walls are at Waterlooville. You can easily hear conversations in adjacent rooms", I said to Jack.

"You can say that again. Donald's loud voice can be heard throughout the building. It can be embarrassing for everyone at times, especially when he makes personal comments about people who are there, or ribs them about their sex life".

"I am convinced because of that, we should have tomorrow afternoon's meeting with him in the Southsea office. I shall call Donald now, and make certain he understands that. He can be so vague about his appointments. Incidentally, did you or Gillian pick up any useful gossip from the staff?"

"Not much. They are not a particularly friendly office. I heard someone comment that Roy was a law unto himself. The other buyer is quite a jolly chap, and seems to lighten the atmosphere when he is in the office. I get the impression he is out and about a great deal, travelling the length and breadth of the country, chasing down the last penny on prices, and ensuring continuity of supplies and delivery commitments. He is the one who is well-respected around the premises. You never see anything of the sales team. There are only three of them - Donald's sister Jenny and two chaps. It's all in the report I have just faxed you. Donald as you might imagine, is the real 'go-getter' for new sources of business. He barks a lot at the staff, which is why they don't chatter much".

"I shall be with you around ten o'clock tomorrow at the Southsea office. We should aim at two thirty don't you think for seeing Donald. I shall drum into him the importance of being punctual as we have a lot to get through. He might suggest lunch, but I'd rather steer him away from that idea. We shall have plenty to do before he arrives".

"You miserable git, Geoff!"

"Can't have the staff enjoying themselves!"

"Won't do any more overtime for you then".

I persuaded Donald to accept our Southsea office as the better venue, despite his moan about parking. He told me that Roy was now out of hospital and desperate to return to work the following week. When Donald asked about the fight with Evan the lorry driver, he said that Evan had taken exception to insinuations he Roy had made about Evan's wife being not particular about the men in her life. Evan had since confirmed this with Donald that this was what the fight was over, and that he and Roy had since apologised to one another and shaken hands. Donald had said to him that this was all very well, but he had still been left with a burnt out depot and all the associated hassle, all because of their stupidity.

As Roy and Evan were not pressing charges against each other, the police were no longer interested in the case. The fire people had yet to make their final report, on which the insurance claim would depend.

Chapter 13

When I arrived at the Southsea office the following morning, there was much consternation. Neither Jack nor Gillian had put in an appearance. The secretaries were doing their best to find out why, but no-one in their respective families could be contacted, although it was known that both lived on their own.

I phoned my secretary Ingrid at Buckingham, but there had been no calls from Jack and Gillian, although Gillian had sent a fax the previous evening after we had all left for home. I asked Ingrid if she would read it out. The fax said, *"Geoff, my enquiries about Midland Counties Plaster and Lining Supplies Ltd with Companies House say that it was struck off eight years ago, after continued non-compliance in filing accounts and other documents. The Inland Revenue on the other hand refused to divulge any information, but may write to us after making further enquiries"*.

I phoned Donald to check that Jack and Gillian were not at Waterlooville, but he said they had left at about six o'clock the night before after monopolising the depot's fax machine, and were not expected to be there that day (Tuesday). He made his apologies that he would not be able to make that afternoon's appointment after all, as he had double booked. He suggested we dealt with all outstanding matters over the phone, and the reports be posted to him, after I complained that I had had a wasted journey down to Portsmouth. With Jack and Gillian absence, it was promising to be a fruitless day anyway.

News began to filter through that Jack was seen being mugged in a Waterlooville car park the previous evening by someone looking out from a window in a block of flats, but by the time they had got to the scene, no one was to be found, not even Jack. Although they didn't know Jack, they had spotted him several times before, returning to his car on other evenings, usually with a bulging briefcase. The person said his car was still there that morning, and so she decided to inform the police. Why, I thought had she not thought to do so the previous evening?

The police had put two and two together after receiving a call from Jack's daughter Jennifer. She had been alerted by a call from our office earlier in the morning, asking if she knew where he was. His daughter was well-known to us, as she used to be one of our receptionists. She went round to his house and let herself in as there was no response to the doorbell. Everything looked normal. She checked the answerphone. The most recent message was from 'Gillian someone', who seemed agitated and confused. What she was saying was very indistinct, and after a few moments she hung up. Jennifer then phoned the police.

She later telephoned our office to confirm that the car in the car park was definitely her father's and was unlocked. There was no briefcase inside, or keys. The car had been cordoned off as a crime scene.

By this time we were pretty shaken. Something very serious had happened to two of our colleagues. The police had asked me to stay put, as they would be sending someone along from C.I.D. to interview me at the office.

This was beginning to feel all too familiar after a series of bad experiences I had undergone some fourteen years earlier, which culminated in my being abducted.

DC Dominic Baines from Havant C.I.D. was at least six foot ten. I rapidly introduced him to a chair as my neck was straining during the brief preliminaries to the interview, uttered in a mild country Hampshire accent, quite distinct from that of Portsmouth.

He began by asking if we (I presumed we at the office) had considered the possibility that Jack and Gillian (the 'potential absconders' as he preferred to dub them) had run off together, especially as they had been working closely in each other's company for nearly a fortnight. It certainly had not occurred to me, but I supposed it was not beyond the bounds of possibility, but highly unlikely. There was a considerable gap between their ages. One of the Southsea secretaries had told me Gillian was only 24, and commented how clever she was to have obtained a university degree and achieved qualification as a Chartered Accountant by such a young age. Gillian had struck me as a quiet and studious lass, who would not engage in office tittle tattle, and that my suggestion that she and Jack should listen out for gossip at Rhodes would have been an anathema to her. 'The strong silent types are often attractive to the older man', I thought, but without attributing much credence to the notion. Even so, perhaps DC Baines was on to something.

I had naturally assumed that their disappearances were connected and related to the discoveries made during the course of their work at Rhodes. My dilemma was how much I should reveal to the policeman in fairness to Donald. I had yet to discuss any of it properly with him. There was also the question of client confidentiality. Nevertheless, as a citizen, one was duty bound to inform the police of anything of a criminal nature. At this stage, the only reasonably certain matter involving fraud was the teeming and lading issue, and it was conceivable that Donald was aware of it, and had come to an arrangement with the member of staff concerned to recover the missing monies. In the end, I decided it was wiser to say that Jack and Gillian had been conducting at the offices of Rhodes, an examination of the accounting systems, and were on the verge of making their report on the observations. A meeting with Donald Rhodes had been planned for that afternoon, but for obvious reasons had to be postponed. Perhaps they had unwittingly disturbed a hornets' nest, serious enough in someone's mind to provoke the compounding of their criminal activities. DC Baines asked me for an example of what I had in mind. "This is purely hypothetical, and for illustrative purposes of course, but suppose a member of staff in a fairly senior position had been discovered creaming off profits in a big way by making personal deals with either suppliers or customers. I am not saying that has happened here, you understand".

"It happens", he said with a knowing expression and a nod.

He acknowledged there were some worrying factors, namely the apparent mugging and Gillian's message on Jack's answerphone, but he still had doubts that the whole affair would prove to be a police matter. However, he asked that I let him know without delay if anything pertinent sprang to mind or emerged from my eventual meeting with Mr Rhodes.

His 'parting shot' was to inform me that someone at Rhodes had told one of his colleagues that Jack and Gillian had been seen on one occasion, clutched fervently in an embrace, and were very sheepish when they realised they had been spotted.

Before setting off for Buckingham, I tried contacting Donald again, but was told by a disinterested male voice that he was unavailable. "Can I leave a message, please?"

"If you must".

Somewhat taken aback by his rudeness, I said slowly and deliberately, "If it is not too much trouble, would you ask Mr Rhodes to call Geoff Foster at his Buckingham office. He knows the number".

On the quiet country road between Corhampton and Winchester, during the drive back to my office, I could not help worrying about the safety of Jack and Gillian, despite DC Baines' inclinations in thinking it was an elaborate tryst. I was becoming more convinced it was something sinister, a feeling heightened by my experience years before. I briefly prayed for their wellbeing, whatever had befallen them.

I wondered what had happened to the highly sensitive papers in Jack's briefcase, and those no doubt which were, or had been in Gillian's possession. The more I mulled it over, the more frenzied my thinking became, to the point that I started to shiver violently. I had to stop the car and allow myself to calm down. I turned the radio on, which worked momentarily, and set off again, but the shaking resumed.

I tried to think of something to take my mind off the day's events, as in that instant, my priority was to complete the journey. I thought of the game we as a family often played on long car trips. It was fairly mindless, but it kept the children occupied, and I considered had the benefit of increasing their powers of observation. The number element in UK vehicle registrations at that time ranged from 1 to 999, with a few exceptions, such as military and diplomatic transport. The idea, as we drove along, was to spot in numerical order registrations starting at number 1. Over a period of several weeks we had reached 327, which meant we were now looking for a 328.

It was perhaps not the wisest mental exercise to be occupied whilst driving, but it did shift my train of thought. After a certain amount of traffic coming towards me passed by and their registrations duly observed, I glimpsed in my mirror. There was a car some way back. Every so often I checked the mirror to see whether it was close enough to read its registration, but it remained too far behind to do so.

In due course, after descending a steep hill with a magnificent view over the city, I reached the Winchester bypass. As always at that time of day, it was extremely busy. I had to wait for a gap in the traffic. In the meantime the car which had been behind me for some miles, a greyish BMW, caught up and was close enough for me to see its registration number which was 38, my age.

The next part of the journey entailed at first heading north on the Winchester bypass for a few minutes, then joining the A34 towards Newbury and Oxford. Both were fast roads with heavy traffic, requiring the driver's full attention, so the little numbers game was out of the question.

It was not until more than an hour later I had to stop at temporary traffic lights at roadworks between Bicester and Tingewick, when I noticed the greyish BMW was again behind me. Apart from observing that the driver and companion were male, there was no time to take in anything further except the first two letters of the registration, before the lights changed to green. This was most disconcerting, as I had covered roughly 50 miles from the last sighting, and in my general state of agitation, I concluded that it was more than a coincidence, and for the next twenty minutes until arriving at the office, the shivering and shaking resumed more forcibly.

I threw my brief case on to my office chair and made a dash for the loo, but not before spotting the BMW passing the office window. I was unable to take in the third letter of the registration.

My sojourn in the boys' room was an opportunity to compose myself and decide what to do next. DC Baines had invited me to call him with anything pertinent. Was this such a case, or just me being paranoid? After all, was it so unlikely that a car had made the same journey as me from just south of Winchester to Buckingham? It may well have gone on to Milton Keynes afterwards. Would that be so remarkable, even if made simultaneously with me? After all, Buckingham was en route from central Hampshire to Milton Keynes, and Milton Keynes was a burgeoning metropolis, both of people, industry and commerce? Rightly or wrongly, I decided to let it rest.

Despite having previously left a message at Rhodes to call me, I decide to try Donald again, but still no luck. For the next hour or so, I read again through all the faxes I had received from Jack and Gillian over the past fortnight, in preparation for my conversation with Donald once I next succeeded in making contact.

I was still on tenterhooks when I returned home that evening. The news on the television had for several weeks had been virtually non-stop focussed on the Falklands' War, and the build up to British troops gaining a toe-hold on the Islands. It brought some distraction from the immediate thoughts running through my mind. The children had been fed about an hour earlier, but as Karen and I had separate meetings to go to, we independently snatched a bite to eat, while waiting for the baby sitter, Bernadette. Various friends and acquaintances have formed a group referred to as the 'circle', whereby tokens were earned from babysitting, and later used to 'pay' for sitting by other members of the group. Bernadette and Joe, and indeed we, were founder members of our group.

I had debated when or even whether to let Karen know of the day's events, but decided to put off doing so until after we had returned that evening. Karen however, asked just before going off to practice with a local choir, "Are you coming down with something? You look as white as a sheet".

"Perhaps. We'll discuss it later".

Once Bernadette had arrived and we had exchanged a few pleasantries, Karen set off in her car. I had planned walking to my meeting which was at the church, but the sky looked ominous, and so I chose to drive instead. As this provided me with a few spare minutes, I tried Donald's home phone number, but again I had no success. I took the opportunity in the remaining minutes to ask Bernadette a few somewhat loaded questions.

"Did you enjoy the conference at Missenden last week?"

"Yes thanks", she replied curtly.

"Karen said it was excellent, especially the afternoon session".

"Yes, it does seem to have made an impression on her", she said with some diffidence.

"Oh! It sounds as though it didn't quite cut the mustard with you".

"Well, it was okay".

"You must know my friend Bob Willetts".

"What makes you say that?"

"It is just that when I saw him recently, we were talking about the proposed teachers' strike, and he said it was a contentious matter at the N.U.T. meetings. I happened to mention that Karen had told me you also attended those meetings in Northampton, and Bob said he knew you, and the guy who spoke at Missenden last Friday afternoon".

"Come off it, Geoff. You know damn well what's been happening, and that guy as you put it, is Brendan Orford. Why pretend you don't? You're just fishing".

I felt belittled and quite deservedly so and mumbled, "Yes, well, erm... I had better get going. Is there anything you would wish me to raise at the meeting tonight?"

"Such as?"

"Nothing really, Just asking".

"Well there isn't".

"Hope the kids behave themselves. I shall leave you to it. See you in a wee while".

This is simply was not my day, I concluded, feeling more than a little sorry for myself.

The rain justified my decision to take the car. As I drove it out of the driveway into the lane, I was shaken to the core by a frantic young woman yanking on the passenger door handle, and banging on the window at the same time. The door was locked, deliberately so, in view of the fears spilling over from my journey that afternoon. She was soaking wet and in sheer panic, with water and make-up streaming down her face, contorted by a wild and fearful expression. Without thinking straight, I leaned across to unlock the door, but she was gone. I parked the car along the little bit of kerbing we had outside our house, and went looking for her, but she was nowhere to be seen. Perhaps my mind was playing tricks. I returned to the car, and waited for a while in case she reappeared, but after six or seven minutes there had been no sign of a anyone, so I drove off to the church.

I was home well before Karen, and described to Bernadette what had happened earlier outside, and then wondered if I should have mentioned it. It might have frightened her unnecessarily. She did not seem that perturbed, and probably thought I was exaggerating and being melodramatic, as a distraction from our earlier conversation. At least she let me see her safely away in her car.

Later, I mentioned Bernie's strange mood to Karen. "She's been like that in the last couple of days. I've obviously said or done something to upset her, but I cannot think what. I can only imagine it's to do with last Friday afternoon. Possibly my singing Brendan's praises has somehow wrong-footed her. Perhaps they have fallen out".

"Or, she's jealous of your enthusiasm for his words of wisdom, or admiration for him at an intellectual level", I tentatively suggested.

We changed the subject at Karen's instigation to my peaky appearance. In view of where this might lead, I had firmly decided not to mention the incident in the road outside earlier that evening. However, Karen said she had noticed something odd. When she drove away to choir practice, she observed that there was a grey car parked just up the lane, with two fellows sitting in the front, simply staring into space, as if totally bored out of their minds. When she returned, they were still there, but once she stopped in our drive to close the gate behind her, the car came by at some speed, and disappeared on up the lane into the wet gloom.

"Did you see what sort of car it was?"

"As I said, it was grey".

"I mean, what make, for instance?"

"You know me. I haven't a clue about makes of cars except my own, especially when it's wet. They all look the same to me, other than their colour".

"What about the registration?"

131

"Ah! Now that I did notice. Ever since we started that silly game with the kids, it's got me looking at car numbers. I particularly remember thinking its number was the same as your age. Anyway, why are we getting all excited by it?"

Karen, in many respects, had a strong character, very capable and down to earth, and marvellous with children in the school environment. She was popular with her charges and parents alike, although she would not stand for bad behaviour in or out of the classroom.

She was fun-loving, and she and I shared a similar sense of humour, important in any relationship, but there was a breaking point. My childish practical jokes would occasionally and unpredictably traverse the boundaries. Our own children knew how far they could push her. They, after all, had been brought up from the beginning to recognise the signs. I, as yet, despite thirteen years of marriage, was still an amateur. When the line was crossed, I wished I had the facility of Captain Kirk to say, "Beam me up, Scotty". How I loved her all the same!

However, her sense of security was very acute, and especially as far as the children were concerned, was paramount. Any hint of jeopardy in the family set up had to be resolved IMMEDIATELY, and threats avoided at all costs. The suspect car business was not to be mentioned unless it became absolutely necessary, otherwise it would fester and make her sick with anxiety.

I waited until Karen had gone up to bed, and telephoned Havant C.I.D. from the study, in spite of the late hour. As it happened, DC Baines was still on duty, which surprised me, given that he had interviewed me twelve hours previously. I described the whole saga, and he readily took the matter very seriously. He asked if I had any inkling of the year letter in the registration of the BMW, but I had not, although I said the car was fairly new, which would narrow down the tracing of the car. He would contact Thames Valley Police straight away to at least alert them to the situation, even if they were unable to do much about it until 'business hours'. They might for example call on our neighbours, etc, for further information on any sightings, and perhaps the full registration of the BMW, or even discover who the frantic young lady was at my car window. He assured me I had done exactly the right thing in phoning him even at the late hour. He also confirmed that there was no further news of Jack and Gillian.

I purposely kept myself awake through that night, not that I would have slept anyway.

Chapter 14

The following morning I resolved to stay as close to my family as possible until further news from the police, but somehow finding a way of doing so without alerting Karen of my fears.

As a rule, we all left the house at the same time. On fine days Karen would walk to play group and school with the children. She taught mornings only until lunch time, collected Christina from play group, and went home for lunch. At the end of the school day, she and Christina would usually return to school to collect Philip and MaryAnn, although increasingly Karen would allow the two of them to walk home together without being collected.

As a precautionary measure that morning, I surreptitiously followed them on foot to ensure they arrived safely at play group and school. I then returned to the house, collected the car and drove to the office, watching my rear view mirror constantly.

Donald was in his office that morning, but it was hopeless trying to have a serious telephone conversation with him regarding our work over the last two weeks. I managed to bring to his attention the teeming and lading of cash issue, but he said he really did not follow the detail of what I was saying, but understood that the cashier had "buggered off with £3,000 of his cash". Apart from saying "he'd have her guts for garters", he had little more to add. He dismissed my attempts to deal with the major problem of unexplained poor profit mark-ups on plaster products, etc. He had had a skin full the night before, and was having difficulty concentrating. "Come down one day next week and we can go into it face to face".

To his credit, he asked after Jack and Gillian, but I had no extra information to give, so he repeated what his staff had said about the canoodling, and concluded, "Says it all really".

I gathered up a pile of papers, Dictaphone, etc, and set off home. I worked until midday, collecting Karen from school and Christina from play group.

I explained to Karen that I had reported to the police what she had observed about the car, and I confessed to her about not mentioning the frantic woman incident, of which I had also made the police aware. It occurred to me that if the police were conducting house to house enquiries in the neighbourhood, Karen would need to know about her, besides which, Bernadette might have told her.

"Why had you kept the woman bit from me?"

"To be honest, I didn't want to frighten you unnecessarily".

"Don't you dare keep that sort of thing from me again".

I gulped at the thought that what she knew now was only the tip of the iceberg. Thankfully, at this stage she did not appear to wonder why the police (and I) were taking the matter so seriously.

The telephone rang while we were having lunch, but Karen got to it before I could.

"It's Havant C.I.D. for you, Geoffrey. Why Havant?"

"Perhaps they've traced the car to their area", I said disingenuously".

It was DC Baines colleague, to say that the car had indeed been traced. It had been hired initially in London, but returned that morning to the Oxford branch of the hire company. Efforts were being made to trace who had hired it, but it was looking increasingly as if false names and addresses had been given. They had foreign accents, according to the London based staff, who had no clue of the nationality. The Oxford branch staff thought they might be foreign because of their looks rather speech, because they had hardly said anything at all. They seemed to be in very much of a hurry to catch a train, as it was towards the railway station that they partly ran, partly walked, after dropping off the car. I asked, "When did they first hire the car?"

"Monday morning".

"That would have given them plenty of time to be involved in the abduction of my colleagues who were working at Waterlooville".

"Always assuming there were any abductions".

"Any other news?"

"Thames Valley Police called on a number of addresses in your lane this morning, but very few people were at home. Three of your neighbours noticed the car, and one thought they heard a scream around seven thirty, but couldn't see anything when they peered through their net curtains, but noticed you sitting in your car, and therefore assumed there was nothing to get excited about".

After I had hung up, Karen stood before me with her arms tightly folded, and a grim look on her face.

"What was that about abductions for heaven's sake? It's getting to the point where I can hardly believe a word you say. Is that why you looked so pale faced last night? Even Bernie remarked on it this morning".

"Jack and Gillian, the pair I have had working at Rhodes this past couple of weeks, didn't turn up for work on Tuesday".

"I thought you went down to Portsmouth yesterday morning to meet them. If not, what did you do?"

There was no longer much to be gained from shielding Karen from knowledge of the events of the past two days. I explained everything of what we knew, what we suspected, apart from one or two theories I had about the revelations at Rhodes, as they were only wild speculation, which at that stage I had not mentioned to anyone.

"Where does all this leave us, the kids, me?" she asked angrily. "Are we in any sort of danger? I can tell you I am really scared". Her eyes were electric with fear.

"Now that the hire car has been returned, I imagine they have done what they set out to do, so there's a good chance the danger has passed".

"Come off it Geoffrey. Can't you see that means nothing of the sort. It tells me they now know where we live; their work, whatever it is, has only just begun. I am not the least reassured by your delusional optimism. In fact I am bloody frightened. What are you going to do about it?"

"We shall have to be vigilant", I offered rather tamely.

"WAKE UP, for goodness' sake. If you don't get on that phone right now to your policeman friend and demand some protection, I shall".

At that moment, Father Nugent called round. He wanted to discuss one or two matters emerging from the meeting the previous evening. Karen, without saying anything, pointedly took herself off into another room.

"Oh dear, Geoff! Have I called at an inconvenient moment?"

I told him something of the difficulty we found ourselves in.

"I shall speak to some of our ladies – see if we can't organise a watch on you and your safety – be all eyes and ears for you, Karen and the children", he said in an Irish comforting way. "And there's always the power of prayer, especially in situations like this. Let's forget what I came round for. It will keep".

After he had left, I found Karen sitting in the dining room, slumped over the table, her face buried in her folded arms. From behind, I put my arms around her and pressed my cheeks against the back of her head. Slowly, she unwrapped herself, turned and stood up limply. We held each other tightly as she began to sob quietly, shaking gently. Neither of us said anything for several minutes. Karen then released herself from my grip, and turned to face me, the area around her eyes red from weeping. "Geoff", she said in almost a whisper, "What are we going to do?"

I was silent for a minute or two and then, as calmly as I could, replied, "First, right now, I shall do as you suggested, and phone DC Baines, or speak to his superior if he is not available, about what protection they can offer. I suspect it will be very little if any. I shall also ask them for any advice on hiring professional surveillance. Clearly, it won't come cheap, but to hell with the cost, ours and our children's safety is priceless. Second, I shall speak to my partners about our concerns. They know nothing of them at the moment. My inclination is to avoid the office and stay here as much as possible, although somehow, I must arrange to see Donald Rhodes as soon as I can. I am convinced the whole thing is linked to the Rhodes businesses".

"Do you think Donald would come here?"

"I could try to persuade him I suppose, but it's difficult enough to get him to come into the Southsea office, let alone drag him all the way up here".

"Well, he seems to have no qualms about expecting you to go down to Hampshire, and often with no commitment on his part to turn up".

"True!"

I pondered on my experience fourteen years ago, and how I had not heeded advice to engage personal security surveillance. (*Note for reader: These experiences are referred to in several places in this book. More can be discovered in 'The Ledge', an account of earlier difficulties for Geoff Foster, set in 1968.*)

As I expected, the police were not able to offer much support 'at this time', but agreed it would be sensible to seek personal protection professionally. They provided me with three names of firms which operated on a national basis, who catered exactly for what we needed.

I also spoke to my co-partner at Buckingham, who assured me that they would support any arrangements I made for working safely during this crisis.

It was time to collect MaryAnn and Philip in the car from school, in spite of the prior arrangement made for them to walk home. I asked our neighbour if she would mind keeping Karen and Christina company, while I fetched the children. She invited them round for a cup of tea and a chat instead.

'Just my luck when I'm in a hurry', I thought as I reached the bottom of the drive. A learner driver had just pulled away in my direction from the kerb on my right. I had to wait while he made hesitant progress as he passed in front of me. Then much to my annoyance, the learner, (or rather his instructor more likely) decided it was that part of lesson when a three-point turn was called for.

This was in the narrowest part of the lane, and the only undeveloped section between our house and the town. There were no pavements or verges, but high banks on either side of the road, with tall field-hedges atop. The learner unsurprisingly completely blocked the lane, as he struggled to make any impression on getting the car point in the opposite direction.

I cursed the fact they had chosen such a ridiculous and dangerous spot to practise the manoeuvre, but there was nothing to be done but wait patiently. But patience was in short supply as the minutes ticked away. I was desperate to arrive at the school before my children would set off across the fields to our home, using a short cut where any would-be child snatcher might be lurking behind trees or bushes, and would have no difficulty in abducting them.

A car came up behind me, and hooted no doubt to register the driver's anger at the impediment before us. The sound of the horn prompted me to again look in my mirrors. The driver had got out and was walking towards the obstruction in front of us, but as he was passing my car, he suddenly veered towards my offside rear door and climbed inside. As I turned to address him, another man who appeared from nowhere, yanked opened my driver's door, and ordered, then pushed me over to the passenger's side, while the fellow in the back revealed the long shining blade of a knife. *'Why had I not locked the car from the inside before driving off from home?'* I scolded myself internally.

The learner promptly completed his three-point turn and set off towards the town, while the intruder at the wheel of my car drove closely behind. I managed to catch a glimpse of the car from which the hooting had emanated. It was now being driven by yet another person. It was clear the whole saga had been an ambush, a trap I had fallen into so easily.

As we neared the road leading down to the school, there were already children, mums and dads walking home from it, many of them familiar to me. I moved my left hand towards the window button to open it and shout for help, but a voice from behind me warned, "Don't even think about it", as I noticed the silencer of a gun in the gap between the two front seats.

I thought of calling his bluff, but then considered the possibility that not only might he shoot me, but a mum and the children surrounding her , who were at that moment showing her with great enthusiasm, the work they had done and were bringing home.

Someone was bound to recognise the car, but no one seemed to, but then why should they? It was Karen who usually collected the children in her car; consequently, mine was not such a familiar sight.

In a matter of seconds, we were in open country heading towards Steeple Claydon, a neighbouring village to the west of Gainsthorpe. The man driving my car appeared to be only a lad in his late teens or possibly early twenties, but nevertheless a confident driver. "Suppose the gate to the quarry has been found with the padlock broken and replaced with a new one," he said to the man in the back.

"The place is not visited much, and the gate is not likely to have been checked out since we were there this morning. Anyway, keep your bloody mouth shut", uttered the voice from behind, in a heavy Russian sounding accent.

After we had travelled through Steeple Claydon, and were heading on a near deserted lane towards Marsh Gibbon, we drew to a halt in front of what must have been the gate in question. The learner car had parked just ahead of us. The driver of the car behind us which had also stopped, opened the gate, and his car and mine were driven through the gate along a short track which led into a small gravel quarry, with a tumble down shed, backing up to a shallow cliff. My car was driven into the narrow space between the cliff and the shed, where I was forced out of the car at gun point, and ordered into the back seat of the car, a Vauxhall Cavalier, which had been behind us since Gainsthorpe. I observed that where my car was now parked, was well hidden from the road and anyone who happened to be passing. Indeed, I had used this road many times in the past, and had never noticed the existence of the quarry.

Now we were a convoy of merely two vehicles, as the journey to goodness-knows where was resumed. The learner car, a Peugeot 504, again took the lead, its L plates and driving school signs having been removed. I made a point of memorising its registration, in case it came in useful if ever I regained my freedom. The young lad had moved to the Peugeot car, and seemed to be disappointed he was not driving.

The driver of the Cavalier I was in, was a middle aged man with dishevelled thinning grey hair, tied back in a ponytail, his face unvisited by a razor for at least three days. From the few words he spoke, I assumed he was from the Birmingham area. The Russian gunman sat beside me with the gun in his lap. His face was almost without expression or movement as if chiselled from stone, and heavily pockmarked.

Conversation was sparse. I gained the impression that the two of them were not well acquainted, and did not even know each other's names, the driver being a hireling for simply the job in hand. The back of his left hand was tattooed with the head of an eagle clutching in its talons what might have been a banner carrying a name, but this was mainly covered by the cuff of his donkey jacket.

"Is someone going to tell me what the hell this is all about?" I railed. Where are you taking me?"

"Shut your mouth, or I shut it for you", the Russian growled, laying his hand upon the gun.

It was no more than, or should I say as little as, I expected.

Silence then reigned supreme as we circumvented the centre of Bicester, took the country route via Bladon to

Witney, where we joined the A40 as far as just beyond Burford. At that point our route veered south west and on towards Cirencester. A few miles the other side of Cirencester our convoy pulled into a layby for a pee break, using cover provided by mother nature in the form of brambles, hawthorn and privet. In my case it was an opportunity to throw up. The thought of Karen and the children, who by now would have realised something had happened to me, had churned my stomach to the point where everything inside me was bursting and busting to escape. I imagined Karen being so frantic, she would have needed sedation. The police would be looking for me and the car.

It occurred to me that it, having been abandoned only a few miles from our home, would soon be discovered, notwithstanding its invisibility from the road. However, I was acutely aware that nothing was likely to be known of our present convoy.

I had not properly seen the driver of the Peugeot until this moment in the layby. He had quite a bit to say, mainly giving orders. He also spoke in a Russian sounding accent, and appeared to be the ring-leader of the gang. For a moment, I had been left alone behind the bushes, when I heard him shouting at the others, "Is anyone keeping a watch out for Mr Foster?"

No-one answered.

"You imbeciles! He could be making a run for it".

'Just what I had in mind', I thought.

He scrambled through the undergrowth as I was about to take off at all the speed I could muster, down an overgrown track I had spotted. He stood before me brandishing a gun. "Oh no you don't. Turn around and go through to the cars, NOW". He pushed me violently through the bushes. I felt a sharp thorn catch the top of my leg. At least, that is what I thought.

After the natural break, I began to feel increasingly drowsy in spite of all which was going on in my head. 'Ponytail' spoke as if from a distant shore, for the first time in quite a while, "Has he passed out yet?"

I had not, but almost. The gunman put his hand on my face and forced open my left eye and declared that I was 'out for the counting'. I had managed to fool him, but my mind was beginning to drift. Through the haze of semi-consciousness, I could just about take in their self-congratulation in pulling off the ambush in Gainsthorpe, after several failed attempts, including grabbing the wrong woman in the lane the night before. Today's had worked, but only just. The three point turn should have been much quicker after the hooting signal had been given.

The last I remember, we were speeding towards Bristol on the M4.

Chapter 15

Sometime later, much later, I came to, with a gradual awareness that we were being bumped around as the car was moving across a very rough surface, its tyres scrunching on scalpings, and then coming to a skidding halt. It was pitch black. The place at the top of my leg where I had been pricked was extremely sore, and as I became more awake and began to focus my thoughts, I guessed that the sensation of being jabbed by a hawthorn must have been a stab from a hypodermic needle, injecting some kind of drug to knock me out.

As my mind grew clearer, I could hear the lapping of waves, and the rushing of their retreat, in normal circumstances, such a comforting and familiar sound to someone brought up on the coast. It was just possible in the darkness to make out the silhouette of cliffs and a headland against a moonless but starry night sky.

My gun toting companion, and Ponytail seemed unaware of my regained consciousness. I decided it was better to keep it that way.

Suddenly, a dazzling spotlight shone in front of us. The two men jumped out of the car, leaving the doors on the offside open. They walked around the back of the car to its (left) nearside. I half opened my eyes to take in the scene. The bright light was mounted on a fishing boat, moored alongside a small stone jetty, about fifty feet away. As the lamp bobbed up and down, and from side to side, it illuminated the feverish activity of seven or eight men, including those who had travelled from Gainsthorpe. They were off-loading crates from a pick-up truck, standing on the right hand side of the Cavalier, facing away from the sea. The pick-up had been left with the throb of its diesel engine running, and its driver's door wide open. The crates were being stacked up on the jetty, next to the boat.

The men finished unloading the pick-up, raised and fastened its tailboard. All activity then switch to the left hand side of the Cavalier, where the Peugeot had been parked. I very slowly moved my head to half-face that side, in order to observe what was going on. The Peugeot's tailgate was open. The men were unloading boxes from the car.

The Russian who had been driving it on the way from Gainsthorpe, came across to the door of the Cavalier against which I was leaning on the inside, and pulled it open. I had in the split second beforehand anticipated this, and feigned unconsciousness as the door swung partly open, but caught a bump on my head as it hit the arm-rest on the door. It took all my powers of self-control not to show any physical reaction, but to remain limp, as the man they were now calling Boss, poked me with his gun. "The stuff I gave him still seems to be working", he said to Ponytail. He closed the door, again banging my head in the process, and forcing me back into the position I was in before. The window of the door was slightly open, allowing me to hear him say something in Russian to the gunman who had sat beside me on the way down, whom I decided to nickname 'Boris'.

Boris moved to and stood on a nearby seaweed covered rock, where he could see me, and still supervise the unloading of the Peugeot. He then must have noticed the right hand rear door of the Cavalier was open. He walked round the car and much to my disappointment, closed it. He returned to his rock on the left hand side of the car, vaguely pointing his gun towards the opening in the car window and me.

'Curses', I thought, 'the open door on the right could have been a means of escape'.

Boris gradually gave more of his attention to the unloading operation and looking at his watch as if he were growing impatient at the time it was taking. As he looked away from me, it gave me the opportunity to gaze upon the scene through squinted eyes.

I wondered again what all this was about, and how it could be connected with anything Jack and Gillian had discovered at Rhodes, and why Russian speaking kidnapping gentlemen would be involved, and strangest of all, what was the meaning and purpose of this mysterious shipping of crates and boxes into a fishing vessel at dead of night, with a drugged accountant in tow? It would have been comical if it had not been so terrifyingly real.

I also wondered if the lad had been drinking, as he was staggering and slipping on rocks as he went backwards and forwards to the jetty assisting in the unloading of the Peugeot. Carrying a box, he came over to Boris and began shouting something he thought was amusing. As he laughed at his own humour, he knocked into Boris, unbalancing him from his lofty perch on the rock. The gun went off and the shot hit the search light on the boat, plunging the whole scene into darkness. Boris started shouting and swearing at the lad, and demanding a torch, as he had dropped the gun among the rocks. All attention swung towards him, as the few torches the gang had between them were concentrated on the search for it.

Amongst the hue and cry, I saw my moment, and without any thought of the consequences, I seized my God-given chance, pushed open the off side rear door of the Cavalier with all my might, and dashed across to the pick-up. I sprang into the driver's seat, slammed the door shut, shoved the stick into what I guessed was first gear, let out the clutch, with the engine screaming at high revs, and drove like a maniac into the lane which led away from the jetty.

Within seconds, someone was firing shots at the truck as I drove it as fast as it would go, up what became a steep hill away from the inlet. The pick-up was difficult to control at the speed we were going around the many sharp bends, but all I could think was to put as much distance between myself and my captors, before they organised themselves   sufficiently to make pursuit. Eventually, I reached the top of the rise, where the road opened up onto moorland.

The headlights were not very effective. It was all I could do to keep on the road, and to avoid the sheep, which did not expect their peace to be disturbed at that time of night. The clock on the dashboard displayed a time of ten past two, much later than I had imagined.

In a short while I reached a T junction. The sign post indicated that Port Isaac and Delabole were to the left, and Polzeath were to the right. Polzeath was the shortest distance, so I swung right, but in doing so, the truck slewed violently at the back end. As I regained control and accelerated towards Polzeath, it became obvious that the near side rear tyre was flat, probably punctured by gun shot in the getaway.

Before long, the clattering and screeching from the back indicated that the flat tyre had parted company with the vehicle, and the truck was running on the rim of the wheel. I knew it was only a matter of time before the wheel would become so hot it would seize up, and no further progress would be made. My only hope was that my pursuers, as by then they must have become, would take the Delabole direction at the T junction. However, they had two cars at their disposal, so if they had any sense, one of them was bound to head in my direction.

I managed to reach the first signs of habitation of Polzeath, before the inevitable happened. With the accelerator on the floor, and the resistance from the back wheel, the engine could do no more and stalled, with the truck coming to a halt, straddled across the road, blocking it entirely.

I ran further along the road for 200 yards or so to the nearest cottage, and knocked sharply on the front door, in the faint expectation that someone would answer. The house remained in darkness. Once more I rapped on the door, this time much more vehemently. At last a light appeared in an upstairs window. To my great relief, I could hear sounds of movement in the hallway. A shaky voice called, "Who's there?"

"I urgently need some help. My truck has broken down and it's blocking the road".

There was a pause of about a minute, when I saw the figure of an elderly lady at the lit upstairs window, looking down at me, and then towards the road. A few moments later, she was again just behind the front door. "I can't see any truck. Go away or I shall call the police".

"Oh please do. Tell them the truck is roughly 200 yards from your cottage, on the Delabole side."

I could hear her speaking on the telephone and giving her address, then shouting, "Please hurry".

I asked if she would let me in, but quite sensibly she refused to do so.

By now, I could see headlights, their beam dancing across the moor and approaching from the Delabole direction. I had to assume it was the gang on their way. I made my way along the Polzeath side of the cottage to avoid being seen by my pursuers, and into the back garden. Although it was apparently quite large with plenty of trees and shrubbery, it was the obvious place for them to come looking for me. It was too dark to see what was beyond the garden, but I had to take my chances in running that way.

After a few frantic moments negotiating a six foot post and rail fence with wire netting, covered in dog roses and ivy, I ran hell for leather across a paddock, inadvertently disturbing some ponies, which puffed and spluttered in disgust at my approach. Vainly, I bade them to keep quiet. Reaching the far side of the paddock, I climbed a much easier fence than the last, and entered a copse, providing me with some dense and welcome cover.

My instinct was to keep moving away from the cottage and road until there was enough daylight to see the lay of the land, and work out what to aim for. At that point, I was only about 300 yards from the road, and light from the pursuant car could be seen through gaps in the intervening foliage. What was more, voices could be heard clearly enough to make out something of what was being said. "You, try the cottage; you, round the back of it, and you, carry on down the road as fast as you can. He can't have got very far yet".

By my reckoning, that made at least four of them. The orders seem to come from the boss, who struck me from the little I had seen of him, as being quite young and fit.

I made my way through the thicket as fast as I could, but trying to make as little noise as possible. A footpath cut across the course I had been taking. At first I thought the path would be helpful in getting me away from the vicinity much more quickly, but then, it would be of equal benefit for the others if they happened to come across it.

I used the path for about five minutes, running as fast as the darkness would allow, and then turned off, diving sharply to the right into even denser undergrowth. Progress was slow as it became increasingly boggier underfoot. However, the sound of the voices had been replaced by complete silence, hopefully I thought, because I was now out of range of immediate discovery. It was eerily quiet, the peace only unsettled by my own footsteps crunching twigs, brushing against foliage, and the occasional sucking sound of my shoes being withdrawn from the bog. Then I disturbed a pheasant, which let out a piercing cry as it scuttled into the blackness of the night. To my bitter despair, the lad, at close hand, shouted, "Did anyone hear that? Might have been a bird or a fox".

'Ignorant townie', I thought uncharitably.

"Someone must have disturbed it", continued the lad.

A response, a little more distant, came from Ponytail, "Probably you, you stupid arse".

The lad was so close by then, that I concluded making any further progress would give away my position. I could now see torchlight getting nearer and nearer. 'Should I spring him? He was quite puny and drunk', I thought. If so, it would need to be before he found me, which was now imminent. The alternative was to crash through the undergrowth not seeing where the hell I was going, making a heck of a din, and probably literally getting bogged down. The former had to be my choice, and acted upon NOW, as I could now see him, luckily at that moment looking away from me, and making so much noise, it was covering my own sounds of movement.

I leapt on him from behind, putting my hand across his mouth, and pushed him face down into the mud. He tried to bite me, but I forced my thumb upwards into the gap behind his chin, which took the pressure of his bite. I contemplated my next move. There was no intension of causing him any more harm than was necessary, but I had to weigh this against potential harm these fellows had in mind for me, and heaven knows what for Karen and my children.

Ponytail's constant calling out to the lad, (whose name was evidently Martin), was now more and more distant until it became inaudible. I had Martin in an arm lock, still with his face and my hand in the bog. I withdrew my thumb and hand, and forced his head sideways. He let out a yelp, but with so much soil in his mouth, he spat and spluttered, and any attempt at shouting was ineffectual. With a threatening clenched fist, I demanded he gave me chapter and verse on whom he was working for and what they were up to. He complained my knee in his back was excruciating. I pushed it in even harder, until he cried, "Okay, okay, I'll tell you what I know, which isn't much. They are a couple of Russian guys who have hired me and two of my mates from the pub we drink at in Oxford. They are paying us four hundred quid each to drive them around, do as we are told, take some stuff to down here in Cornwall, and ask no questions. We didn't know there was going to be any kidnapping until yesterday. We said we would back out unless they paid us another four hundred each. It's not to be sneezed at where I come from."

"Do the cars belong to you and your mates?"

"No, they are hired. I know that because we had to pick them up from a hire place in Oxford, yesterday morning."

"Is this the first job you have done for them?"

"Yep".

"You didn't go down to the Portsmouth area this week?"

"Nope".

"Have the Russian guys said anything about Portsmouth, Waterlooville, or anything at all about what this is in aid of?"

"Nothing. You've seen how talkative they are".

"Sounds as if your work for them is over".

Picking up the torch, I said, "Now do I knock you out with this and leave you here, or drag you along with me until I can find some help?"

I did not really want his company, but could not bring myself to clobber him. In the end my dilemma was resolved by what followed. When I released Martin, he was as sick as a dog which left him very dazed and unsteady. He had either drunk an enormous amount of alcohol, or more likely, the Russian Boss had given him one his special prescriptions.

I took his torch and left him to his own devices in a semi collapsed state, propped in a sitting position against a tree. He should have been able to sort himself out once he had recovered from his immediate problem.

My next problem was recovering my sense of direction. With no moon visible, I had no means of regaining my bearings. I had not studied the stars, so they were of no help except to give a rough idea of travelling in a straight line. My only hope was to find the unreliable signs of disturbed foliage, and head the opposite way, otherwise I might have found myself back on the road.

In the dark, even with the aid of a torch, this was easier said than done. In the end, I simply relied on instinct. As I did not come across the footpath again after trudging some distance, I concluded I was moving in the direction of safety, and the prospect of renewed captivity was receding.

It then dawned on me that Martin had not opened up to me with much at all which could be relied on. He or Ponytail, I could not remember who, had referred at some stage to attempted abductions before mine, in particular, the woman in the lane on Tuesday evening. The car used then was the BMW, which had travelled up from Hampshire, and returned to the hire company at the Oxford depot on Wednesday morning. That suggested Martin had been in the Portsmouth vicinity.

I began to retrace my steps to where I had left Martin, but I had completely lost the trail. For my present safety, it would be wiser to keeping heading away from the area.

After about ten minutes or so, I reached the edge of the woods, climbed a similar fence as before, and began walking across a meadow, at least that is what I thought. It was not until the ponies I had encountered earlier came ambling towards me, I realised I must have gone round virtually in a circle, finishing up at another part of the paddock. Before me loomed in silhouette the cottage and its garden.

At that moment, the dimming light offered by the torch, died. The batteries had given up the ghost. In frustration, I tossed the torch into the undergrowth.

Before I had a chance to take stock, I was grabbed from behind by the Russian Boss, who pushing and shoving me, brought me to the roadside between the cottage and the pick-up truck I had abandoned. I was frog-marched to the awaiting Peugeot beyond the pick-up, and unceremoniously shoe-horned into the third row of seats at the back, which by then had been put back in position after the offloading of the boxes at the quayside.

"Where's Martin?" the Boss asked his accomplices.

"Don't know", answered Ponytail. "We lost him in a wood at the back of the cottage. He's probably sleeping off the skin full he must have had on the way down. God knows where he was hiding the booze. I s'pose he had a flask in his jacket, although I've never seen him with one before".

"No matter", said the Boss, "We have to go quickly now before anyone comes. I think that woman in the cottage has called the police. I heard her shouting at someone in the house to watch out at the window for them".

The Boss, who was in the driver's seat, now performed a three point turn which outscored the earlier feigned attempt in the lane back home. We soon reached the T junction, and turned left into the road leading down to the inlet. As we did so, blue flashing lights of a police car passed at seventy or eighty miles per hour, heading towards Polzeath, regrettably no doubt oblivious to our presence.

By now I was terrified of the reception I would receive once we were back at the jetty. Once again, Boris was sitting beside me, nursing the gun on his lap. I thought about the old lady in the cottage and how frightened she and her companion would be. It was possible she had seen nothing of the men or the car, as the slight bend in the road may have hidden them from her view. In any event, the police would soon be on hand to allay her fears. How I wished they would have cause to turn round and follow us to where we were going.

Chapter 16

To my surprise, there were no recriminations for the trouble I had put them through, although the pushing and shoving whenever they wanted me to move, was markedly more ungentlemanly than before.

The boat had been turned around during my little excursion into the Cornish countryside, as it was now facing out to sea, and its engine was ticking over gently, in anticipation of its next trip ocean-wise. The tide had risen, and there was much more of a swell. The Cavalier had gone, but was probably still out looking for me and the pick-up.

No time was lost in getting me on board the rusty vessel, stinking unsurprisingly of fish and diesel, although there was some delay when I stumbled on the door sill of the Peugeot while in the process of extricating myself from the back seat, and badly grazing my knee on the rough ground. I was led limping down into a compartment, behind and below the wheelhouse, and shackled in a standing position to part of the superstructure of the cabin. Boris had at least the grace to leave me with my left arm free, which enabled me to nurse my injured right knee. In the act of falling I had ripped my trouser leg, and blood was running down my shin. The temptation was to rub the source of the bleeding, but I resisted, as to do so would increase the risk of infection. It was already stinging like billy-o, and beginning to throb.

Boris, the Boss and his land-side cohort departed, and left me in the hands of the crew of my new metal prison, three Cornishmen. They were so adept at moving about the rocking craft, one could be forgiven for believing they had evolved from a race of sea born humanity, capable of staying upright, whatever the angle of the deck. Two of them wore Guernseys, at least I think that was what they were, while the other sported a red sweater with 'Port Isaac' emblazoned across its back.

The mooring ropes were released and thrown on board, as one of the two Guernsey clad crew, the only bearded member, scrambled aboard. The boat immediately leapt forward at full throttle, its engine being much more powerful than I had expected.

My new companions were refreshingly more cheerful than the other lot had been, and, I had to admit, kept me entertained by their constant banter. They referred to me as 'Jim Boy'.

Despite the initial acceleration away from the jetty, the boat proceeded with caution, as 'Port Isaac' called instructions from somewhere ahead of the wheelhouse. The bearded one explained to me in friendly fashion, that they were having to navigate the treacherous inlet approach by torchlight, until they had rounded the headland, because that Russian 'dickhead' had put their spotlight out of action.

There was absolutely no doubting when we reached the headland. The boat lurched violently from side to side, and bucked as if it were an unbroken colt with weight on its back for the first time. Had the circumstances been less frightening, and my knee less painful, I would have found the experience exhilarating. Previous trips out to sea had led me to believe I was not prone to seasickness, but this was surely to be the acid test.

Once we were on the open sea, the engine increased to maximum revs, and it felt we were travelling at a hundred miles per hour or more, but of course, we were probably doing less than 30 knots.

'Port Isaac' moved inside and climbed down to sit beside me, after repositioning my shackles, so that I had the choice of standing or now sitting on a metal bench bolted to the deck.

"Don't know, and don't want to know what you've been up to, but orders is to keep you fastened like that", he said pointing to the clasp around my right wrist and attached chain wrapped around a leg of the bench.. "Sorry, an' all that, but orders is orders. Keepin' 'em is what we're paid for. Fancy a tea or coffee? Don't suppose that miserable lot gave you anything all the time they 'ad you".

"Only a shot from a hypodermic".

165

"Yea! That's their style".

"Coffee, please… Who are they and where are you taking me?" I asked displaying little humour.

"Can't tell you. No can do".

"Orders is orders?" I discerned.

He nodded, and went up to the wheelhouse. I could just about hear above the roar of the engine, the lashing sea and the wind, the comforting sound of a kettle boiling tailing off to a whistle, followed a few moments later by 'Ta mate' and then repeated.

Once again, 'Port Isaac' appeared before me, bearing a steaming tin mug. "Sorry, we haven't washed up the china tea cups and saucers yet", he said, chuckling as he handed what was a most welcome treat, although being right-handed, I struggled at first to hold the mug. The strong dark brown liquid tasted sublime. He then offered me biscuits. "Take two", he said. "Cooked by the wife. Better keep your strength up. We'll be in this boat for a long while yet. Sorry! I didn't offer you sugar, did I?"

"No thanks", I responded. "Is there anything orders will allow you to tell me?"

"What like?"

"Well, we are not crossing the Atlantic are we?"

"No", he laughed at the thought of it. "No Disney World for you, Jim Boy, I'm afraid".

A huge wave shook the boat violently, and hot coffee splashed over my face and down my front. 'No hope of a change of clothes', I thought. The way things were going, I would be stuck with my present ripped and coffee stained apparel for the indefinite future.

"Are we going fishing?" I asked facetiously.

"We are, but not you, and not until after we have completed what we have been paid to do".

"That sounds ominous! Are you dropping me into the deep blue ocean, only I can't swim?"

"Neither can we", he said with a grin. "Most fishermen are discouraged. It means we don't easily desert the ship. Besides, once you're out here, swimming ain't going to help you".

"So, what are you going to do with me in completing your mission?"

"Don't blame you for asking, but I'm not telling you…Do you play chess?"

"I used to, but haven't done so for years. Strange question! One can hardly play in these conditions, with the pitching and tossing".

He produced a pocket set where the pieces slot into peg holes. I agreed to play, more to humour him than the other way round as I think he intended, although I wondered if I really had a choice.

I was never that good at chess, and the only person I regularly beat was the person who had taught me the game, my grandfather. However, on this occasion I could not concentrate for obvious reasons including an overwhelming urge to sleep. After a couple of very brief games, we both concluded it was all a bit meaningless.

I asked, "Why are you involved in this these shenanigans? It is clearly illegal... You seem a fairly decent sort".

"Most of us struggle to make a living just from fishing, so we have to turn our hand to whatever is going. Some of it is a bit close to that fine line between what's allowed and what isn't".

"Yes, but kidnapping is hardly close to that line. It's way the wrong side of it. Put yourself in my shoes and think of what this is doing to my family and loved ones, let alone the illegality".

"Don't try that guilty conscience stuff on me. I lay my life on the line every time I put to sea, so that I can feed my wife and kids. That's what important to me. How I do it and the risks I take are all the same to me. Stuff what the ruling classes say. So what's a bit of smuggling if it pays well?"

"But holding me prisoner in this rusty old bucket is hardly just a bit of harmless smuggling"

"What's the difference; delivering goods, delivering people I know nothing about?"

"When you might and probably are delivering me to my death, I should say there's a hell of a difference"

"Who said anything about you being killed?"

"No-one in so many words, but body language, waving guns around, sticking hypodermic needles in me, somehow give me the odd hint that I am not being invited to a picnic. You and your mates up there in the wheelhouse, your banter and laughter, all very entertaining, but how do you live with yourselves?"

"Well, who said crooks shouldn't enjoy their work?" 'Port Isaac said facetiously.

I had obviously rattled him. He threw a pile of grubby rugs at me. "Make yourself as comfortable as you can with these", he said, and then joined his mates in the wheelhouse.

It was now broad daylight, and a sky filled with billowing white and dark grey clouds, racing between patches of blue. The wind, if anything, was getting stronger, and the waves responding with ever greater attempts to swamp the boat.

The men up front appeared totally unperturbed, discussing football, the prices obtained for recent catches, and the ever rising costs of maintaining their boats and fishing tackle, and 'Port Isaac', the unrealistic demands of his wife and kids. "The eldest", he bemoaned, "wants to go to university. I told him to get off his arse and get a job, and forget all that stuffing his head with bloody law and politics, which he wants to do. Now take the bloke back there, I'm told he's an accountant. Don't mind if my boy does a bit of that. If the fees they charge me are anything to go by, he should make a handsome living out of it. You know that guy was having a go at me not having a guilty conscience. I think that's a bit rich coming from one of them. Tell me, what's the difference between us smuggling a few fags, and them fiddling the taxes of the rich? They get all hoity-toity when the likes of us tell a few porkies, but I bet they're licking the boots of the big company bosses and that".

One of the others intervened, "Ah Isaac, you astound me. You really tell porkies to the accountant and tax man? I'm quite shocked". All three found it hilarious. I had heard this sort of conversation many times before. My only surprise was that the man actually was called Isaac.

The scream of a jet fighter lasting for no more than a second, pierced through all the noise of the engine, wind and waves. This was followed by four more in quick succession. It was a salutary reminder that there was a war on. Amid all that had been going on in mine and my family's life in the past few days, Britain had been engaged in an all-out campaign against Argentina to retake the Falkland Islands, South Georgia and the South Sandwich Islands. It had been almost the sole topic of the BBC news bulletins since the beginning of April, with the exception of the impending controversial visit to Britain of Pope John Paul the Second. I suddenly remembered that I had volunteered as a parent assistant on our school visit to Ninian Park in Cardiff on the second of June, when the Pope was due to address about thirty thousand young people. Several buses had been booked to take the entire school to various locations in the Welsh capital. This would be in just a few days' time.

Isaac continued the conversation in the wheelhouse. "The trouble is the ruling classes don't care tuppence about us seamen. Thatcher, Galtieri, they're all the same. All those poor buggers lost when the General Belgrano went down! Our nuclear sub had orders to attack when it was known the cruiser was already in retreat. Disgusting!"

"Come off it, Isaac. It's war. The Argies are the aggressors. That old boat shouldn't have been there in the first place", responded the bearded one. *(Although at the time it was widely believed that the attack on the General Belgrano, while in retreat, was callously personally ordered by Margaret Thatcher, many years later there was confirmation from the Argentinian side that the cruiser was not in fact in retreat.)*

An argument then ensued about the wisdom and appropriateness of the Papal visit, especially while we were in conflict with a nominally Catholic country, and how religious leaders should keep their noses out of politics. At times I was sorely tempted to join in, but thought better of it. There was plenty I could say about the integrity of the majority of accountants, politics and religion, imperialism and war. These were controversial enough at home, let alone doing battle with these guys in these circumstances.

Isaac returned to the cabin I was in.

"Want another drink?"

"I could most do with a loo at the moment", I replied.

He obligingly unlocked the handcuff on my right hand and indicated the appropriate door. When I emerged, he stood in front of me twirling the cuffs around one of his fingers. I asked, "Is there really any necessity to clamp those on me? After all, where is there for me to go?"

"Orders is orders".

"You can always put them back on when we arrive at where we are going, or just beforehand".

"We are being paid for delivering you alive, so I'm not taking the risk of you topping yourself by jumping overboard".

"There's no risk of that. I'm too much of a coward. How much longer before we get where we are going?"

"Couple of hours", shouted a voice from the wheelhouse.

Isaac dutifully replaced my handcuff, this time around my left wrist, which improved my dexterity in handling the replenished tin mug. He continued to stand in the cabin, leaning his back firmly against the wall opposite me.

"Is this your boat?" I asked in order to prompt conversation, which he appeared to want.

"Yea, that's right".

"It's a good sized vessel", I remarked. "How far out to sea is it safe to go with it?"

"Depends what you mean by safe. She is built to cope with anywhere in British waters within reason, but we have to be sensible about weather conditions. The shipping forecasts are vital to us".

"So you could fish fifty or sixty miles offshore, all being well?"

"Oh yea, easily. Most of the time in actual fact".

"I'm surprised you can't make a living from a boat this size".

"It's the competition we're up against. I don't just mean prices. The seas have only got so much fish. Those huge trawlers the Spanish and the Russians have got, just scoop up most of what there is in traditional Cornish waters, leaving us to go out further and further, sometimes for days on end, and even then what we catch doesn't always cover the costs of the trip."

"Russians!" I exclaimed.

"Oh yes! They're the worst".

"Hence, your earnings on the side!"

"You've got it. If you can't lick 'em, join them, that's what I say".

'Now I wonder what he meant by that?', I thought.

He did not seem in any hurry to re-join his mates, and for a while gave the impression he wanted to say something, but could not quite bring himself to come out with it. I wondered if orders forbade him to fraternise with the prisoner, but his instincts were to chat or even feel sorry for me. As I felt under no such prohibition, I asked if he had anything I could eat as it was nearly twenty four hours since my last meal. The crew were treating me with some civility and as my anxiety diminished, my appetite increased.

"We have not got much on board; just enough to keep us going for today and tomorrow, as we plan to put in at…." He suddenly stopped himself, obviously for fear of giving away too much information. "I'll see what we can share. Be back in a minute".

He returned with a plate of three sandwiches and half a pasty, which I considered very generous of them, and was indeed moderately grateful.

"Look, you're an accountant…".

It was me who interrupted this time. "How do you know that? "

"I don't know how. Somebody must have mentioned when we were loading up."

To my mind, they all must have known, and that confirmed my abduction was linked to our investigation at Rhodes, not that I really had any doubts.

I managed a smile in response. "You were going to ask if I would act as your accountant?"

"No, no. Not that".

"I was only joking. Anyway, there is no way I would, even if I were not in my present predicament". If I were your accountant and I heard what you were talking about in the wheelhouse and knew what you've already told me, I should have to inform the authorities. I would be duty bound to do so, otherwise I could be accused of

175

aiding and abetting, and most certainly would finish up in prison. Ironic really, considering the liberty I am enjoying at this moment."

"Hm..So I should watch it with my present accountant. You see, he knows I have more income than I put down in my books, 'cos he says that after expenses, it doesn't leave enough for me and the wife and kids to live on. So when I see him once a year, he insists we work out what our living expenses are, roughly of course, and then he calculates a figure and adds it to my turnover. He reckons it is the cash sales I haven't put down. I don't argue with him, although I truly do not have any cash sales, as all my fishing is strictly under contract, but I daren't tell him where the extra money actually comes from. Does that make sense to you, or is my accountant pulling a fast one I haven't caught on to?"

"I can't really advise you, but I would say what your chap is doing makes sense. He should be insisting you record all your sales, contract, cash or otherwise, but I follow your reasoning about letting him believe there are missing cash sales. Incidentally, you do realise that if anyone, whether they are your accountant or not, knows you are committing fraud, which includes smuggling, and they fail to report you, they are technically guilty of aiding and abetting".

"Well, that might be so in theory, but it's not living in the real world, is it?"

"You would be surprised. There are plenty of people who take their civic duties seriously. What's more, those in business can easily make enemies, enemies who find they can do a lot of damage with what they know, including disgruntled wives".

"So, are you saying that when you are let loose, you are duty bound to inform on me?"

"Surely you don't need to ask that question, with all that's gone and going on?"

"S'pose I can't demand my sandwiches and pasty back. I see you've eaten them".

We both managed a grin. He then returned to the wheelhouse, leaving me to my own thoughts.

The semi-congenial interlude had been a distraction from the uncertainty and potential dangers I was facing. Where were we heading? The south coast of Ireland? Brittany? Bay of Biscay? It was clear to me it was south or west or something in between. There were moments of sunshine in between clouds of many shades of colour, racing towards what I assumed to be the north west and Britain, but how sure could I be?

I remembered from orienteering exercises that it was possible to use one's watch as a compass, if one could see the sun. I had a limited view through a porthole opposite from where I was sitting, but I realised that the sun would be too high in the sky for me to glimpse it through my window on the world. I tried laying on the floor, but my manacled left wrist would not allow sufficient leeway, and merely induced comments from the wheelhouse. "What on earth is Jim Boy up to?"

"Venting his frustration, I expect", speculated another.

During the brief periods of sunlight streaming into the cabin, I closely observed the angles and lengths of shadows, and reflections on shiny metal of which there was precious little, and endeavoured to work out where in the vast heavens above the sun was sitting. It was reminiscent of those 'Spot the Ball' competitions one found on the sports pages of newspapers. It was not easy. For one thing, the boat was being tossed about by the tempestuous sea, and was continuously having to correct its bearings.

Having made an educated guess, I pointed the hour hand of my watch towards the imagined position of the brilliant golden globe, and calculated that we were heading due west. If our direction had remained the same since setting sail, we were not heading for any landfall. However, I should need to repeat the exercise a number of times to establish whether I could achieve a consistent result, before I could have a modicum of confidence in my speculations. Each time my answers were in a range between west south west or west north west, which meant that the only possible landfall was the coast of Ireland.

I then tried to calculate the distance we had travelled, but I had nothing realistic to go on. My best bet would be to engage Isaac in a conversation about the boat's power, speed and how it fared against headwinds. I began to wonder if he would ever return to the cabin, but eventually he did to retrieve a lifejacket from an overhead rack.

"It amazes me how boats like this don't get swallowed up by these mountainous waves out here in mid ocean".

"Oh, you ain't seen anything yet".

"I can understand why you need such a powerful engine. I imagine in calm waters you can achieve quite a turn of speed, but with this headwind it must take all your power to virtually stand still".

"That's why fuel is such a large part of our costs".

"Still, I suppose you have the wind behind you as often as you have it against you, so it would be swings and roundabouts with fuel consumption".

"Yea! Our return journeys down here can be half the time of our outwards".

"So double the speed then?"

"More or less, but it can depend on the weight of our catch".

"So a trip might be one day getting to your fishing area, one and a half days fishing and half a day to get back?"

"Could be. 'Course it varies a lot. Depends how long it takes to find a catch".

"How far out would you go on say a three day trip".

"I personally don't like going more than 150 miles or so".

"Still, that's quite some distance".

He did not answer, but put his lifejacket on.

He rummaged around and found another. "You'd better put this on", he said.

When I did not move, he recognised that my donning it with one hand attached to the leg of the bench was not without its difficulties. He warily unlocked the cuffs, and helped me on with the jacket which was a tight fit over the jacket I was already wearing. I understood by this that we were nearing a point of disembarkation, rather than the sea becoming more hazardous.

Now that I was able to stand fully upright, the weight on my right leg reminded me of the injury I had sustained. I asked if they had any painkillers on board. While he went to find some, I had foolish ideas of escape, but instantly calculated the futility of such notions.

"Ah! I see her – starboard", came a shout from the wheelhouse, which drew my attention to the bearded one who was looking through binoculars.

Isaac produced a couple of Aspros and tumbler of water, for which I thanked him. There was always a place for good manners, even in adversity.

After about quarter of an hour, the un-bearded Guernsey wearer asked the bearded one, who had remained with binoculars glued to his face, "Can you see if they are sending a lighter?"

"Can't see one".

"How the bloody hell are we supposed to get him up that great wall of metal, especially in this sea?"

Although I could not see much from the cabin, I was able to make out at eye level the hull of a large ship as our boat turned to starboard and came alongside it. The rise and dip of the waves at one moment brought us almost level with the main deck of the ship, and in the next moment seemingly staring at virtually the underside of the vessel.

The ship moved around until it was broadside on to the prevailing wind and waves, with us on the leeward side of it. I was allowed into the wheelhouse to watch the operation, while the crew described to me what was happening. From there I was able to see that the ship was in fact a large trawler, much bigger than the fishing

181

boat we were in, and certainly more sophisticated with derricks and huge gantries fore and aft, and two parallel funnels, but just as rusty.

A rocket with a lead rope attached was fired from our boat across to the trawler, enabling all sorts of rope and tackle to be passed to us. A breeches buoy arrangement was rigged up between the two vessels which seemed to take for ever. Once all was in place, I was led along the deck to the buoy, feeling like a lamb being led to the slaughter, and unceremoniously manhandled into the contraption. The conditions were absolutely atrocious, and it was quite obvious how precarious this whole operation was going to be, but I was beyond caring by this stage.

Instructions were being exchanged between the respective crews, but it was clear neither could understand the other. One of the ship's crew began swearing and violently gesticulating at the Cornishmen. Isaac shouted back, "And I love you too sunshine", and then under his breath, "Bloody Ruskies!"

They had hauled me about half way across the divide when the heavens opened; and the wind, the rain and the sea combined to make the whole experience seem terminal as far as any chance of survival for me was concerned. The men on the trawler appeared to dive for cover although goodness knows why. They were soaking wet anyway. I was left hanging in the lurch, suspended like a sack, with water pouring from the bottom of it. A more senior member of the crew arrived on the scene and got them back to completing the task of inviting me into my new home.

In the meantime, a life boat had been lowered from the trawler and positioned between it and the fishing boat. The fishermen began offloading the boxes and crates which had been transferred previously from the pick-up and the Peugeot. The lifeboat would then have been hauled back on board the trawler. This was I presumed considered a more expedient way of transferring the cargo than using the contraption to which I was subjected. The whole operation had taken nearly two hours, but had struck me as being extremely un-seamanlike and foolhardy, especially the wedging of a lifeboat between the two vessels. It was a wonder it had not been crushed given the conditions, but then why should I have cared about that?

What did I care about? Strangely, I did not overly care about my own safety, perhaps because of an inherent trust in the future, in spite of the dangers which were all too clear to see before me. I cared desperately about Karen, MaryAnn, Philip and Christina. I cared about our parents and siblings, our friends, especially Bernadette and Joe, their marriage and their children, of Bob Willets and his battle with cancer, our respective churches, Jack and Gillian, and yes, just at that moment, Isaac and the crew of the fishing boat. I had been with them for only a few hours, but they had treated me with respect; they had challenged my pattern of thought, they had got under my skin, and made me think about the journeys we take in life, some chosen, but in truth for many, mostly imposed by circumstance.

What did Isaac care about? Were his priorities very different from mine? His own safety? He put on his lifejacket only when we were approaching the trawler, yet the dangers in the rough sea were with us from the moment we left the coast. It seemed inevitable that his and his mates' nefarious activities were bound to be exposed sooner or later. What impact would that have on his life and family? One might reasonably say that it was his choice to follow a life, dominated by great risk on the high seas, made all the more so by his criminality, and, as it now appeared to me, treachery, treason. In his mind, what was choice or what was blinding necessity?

People sometimes say that in moments of great danger, your life flashes before you. These thoughts were uppermost in my mind whilst I was suspended in mid-air, being assaulted and battered by the elements. In the midst of all this, I was feeling a tinge of regret that I was parting company with my Cornish jailers, for whom I prayerfully wished redemption. For a fleeting moment, I was warmed by the thought of St. Paul's treatment of his jailer in the Acts of the Apostles, chapter 16.

Chapter 17

A small team of seamen, clad in heavy yellow waterproof gear and southwesters, carefully helped me out of the breeches buoy trouser-like hoist, while an impatient officer of sorts shouted at them in, I presumed, Russian. Once freed from the gear, I remained unrestrained by chains or handcuffs of any description. However, the officer wasted no time in making me feel I was a prisoner, a *persona non grata,* someone over whom he had power and authority, and in whose face he would dearly loved to have spat.

There were no guns in evidence, for which I felt mightily relieved, but the officer was extremely aggressive, pushing and shoving me through a doorway, and then down steep steps in to a lower interior deck, and then along a passageway leading to a mess area. He indicated to me to sit on a long bench with an equally long table in front of it, and beckoned to a crew member, a burly fellow with a weather-beaten ruddy complexion, to stand watch over me, while he disappeared through a door at the far end of the mess.

It struck me that there was a surprising absence of the smell of fish, which had been all pervasive in the previous boat. Perhaps the strength of the wind was causing it to be dissipated from the hold before reaching this part of the ship.

I asked the crewman standing guard if he spoke English, using exaggerated intonation to ensure it sounded like a question. He merely shrugged his shoulders, which I took to mean that he had no clue as to what I was saying. There was then a moment of mistaken enlightenment in his facial expression, as he showed me his watch. To acknowledge at least an attempt on his part to understand, I read out the time, and he nodded with a half-smile, which was possibly a hint of gratitude for lesson one in learning English. I almost showed him my watch, but thought better of it. It would perhaps be unwise to draw attention to the possessions I had about my soggy person. So far, on neither land nor at sea, had anyone thought to search me. I earnestly hoped that would remain the status quo. My trusty Swiss Army penknife had been a life saver in a previous incarceration, the biro might possibly proof useful, but the house keys and Dictaphone had dubious potential, the latter probably ruined by the dousing I had endured during the ship to ship crossing.

The officer bully returned. If I thought I would remain unfettered, my hopes were dashed when he handcuffed me behind my back, then beckoned me with his right hand index finger to follow him, the proud watch-owning crew member taking up the rear.

I was led and shown into an extensive shower room and toilets block, which suggested the ship was manned by a sizeable number of crew. Everything looked clean and well maintained in complete contrast to the outside appearance of the boat, and I began to wonder if fishing for fish was the main purpose of this particular vessel.

The officer pointed to a towel and some clothing on a peg inside one of the shower cubicles. He removed the handcuffs, and steered me in to the cubicle. I was more than a touch relieved that he permitted me to close its door, not out of any sense of modesty, but because it allowed me the opportunity of transferring unseen my possessions to the clean clothing.

Although the water was only lukewarm, I was in no hurry to complete my ablutions, as it was the one chance of having some privacy in the past twenty four hours or so, with the exception of the brief interlude of freedom in the Cornish countryside at dead of the previous night.

I considered singing as an act of defiance, but abandoned the idea, as I would find the sound an assault on my own ears, let alone those of the officer and watch man. My attempts whilst on my own in the car always convinced and shamed me into declining any invitations to join local choirs.

No matter how relaxing and pleasant having a shower or bath can be, there comes a point where one's skin begins to resemble the texture of a prune, and, paradoxically, feel quite dry. I supposed a skin care specialist would explain that the body's protective oils were being washed away.

I dried myself off and while so doing observed that other than socks, there was no replacement footwear. My shoes were still covered in the mud from the Polzeath bog. I judged that they could not be any wetter than they were, and so washed them in the shower. I noticed at first with dismay that the soaking had partially loosened the insole in one of the shoes, but it then occurred to me that this might be a blessing. If I was to be searched, my emergence from the shower cubicle would be the most likely opportunity for my guard to do so. The flap, facilitated by the loose insole at the toe end of my shoe, provided a place to secrete at least one of my belongings. The obvious choice was the penknife, as it had the potential to be the most useful, and consequently, the one most likely to be confiscated. I was to be proved wrong in this, but more of that later!

I put on the clean underwear provided, and what was a type of boiler suit which served as my only over garment. It clearly was not new; a little tattered and ill-fitting in fact, but clean. The lining of one of its several inside pockets had a small tear, into which I inserted the Dictaphone. It immediately made its way down into the general lining of the boiler suit and settled near the bottom hem. The battery had earlier been removed to make the Dictaphone lighter, but it did pose the problem of where to store the battery. The other pockets of the boiler suit offered no secrecy. There was only one other place I could think of – down the front of my borrowed underpants. The boiler suit, being very loose fitting, deprived me of the chance to exaggerate my manhood, not that I ever had any intention of displaying such vanity.

Reasonably confident that there was no hidden camera in the cubicle, I walked bare-footed out of it, carrying my shoes, still dripping wet, and the clean socks to put on once I was on a dry floor. My own clothes were left on the peg. Whether or not I would ever see them again was open to speculation. The odd coinage left in the jacket pocket, would serve as a bonus for its new custodians.

True to expectation, the officer made his search, first looking into the shoes, but his disgust thankfully put him off a close examination. He began to frisk me, picking on the biro clipped to the breast pocket. After unscrewing it, taking out the refill and scribbling on the palm of his hand, he satisfied himself it was genuine, and reassembled the pen, and popped it back in the breast pocket. 'Two up, three to go', I thought. He started to run his hands down my sides, when fate or God stepped in. A deafening alarm went off. The officer rushed to the door, and ran along the passageway, leaving me with watch man, who had no interest in completing the search or responding to the alarm.

"Forserti", he remarked.

I wondered if it were Russian for 'alarm'.

For a moment we stood gaping at each other, he apparently looking to me for his next instruction. He vaguely reminded me of Tommy Cooper, the comedian, but without his fez.

I moved to a dry patch on the floor, and dried my feet as best I could, with a very damp towel, and one-leggedly put on the socks, while the guard ('Watch Man'- my temporary nick-name for him) held the shoes – he insisted by more or less snatching them from me. I prayed he would not look inside them. Again, fate was in my favour. The officer returned, and I guessed explained to Watch Man why the alarm was sounding. As he dashed off again, he shouted at Watch Man, clearly with fresh instructions as to what to do with me.

Watch Man led me through to another part of the ship, which allowed me the opportunity to glimpse through port holes as we went. The sun was now shining and the sea much calmer. I paused for a second at a porthole and pointed the hour hand of my watch at the sun, and made a quick calculation that we were still heading west, and probably south west of Ireland.

Two decks lower, we found ourselves in what must have been where the sleeping quarters were. I was directed into a cabin approximately seven by eight feet, with bunk beds, both with mattresses, but only one with a sheet and a rug.

Watch man tried to tell me something, but when I looked completely blank, he switched to using signs, quite comically, but effectively, first eating with a knife and fork, and holding his index finger up to signify 'one'. I pointed to the one o'clock on my watch, and he nodded, and then confirmed what I thought by running his finger clockwise around the watch face from the one round to the one again. I interpreted the message to be that I could expect something to eat in an hour's time. He left me to myself, locking the door of the cabin from the outside.

Although I was desperate for some sleep, I certainly did not want to miss out on any food offered. It was not so difficult for I also had other bodily functions demanding much needed relief, which left me with no choice but to stay awake.

It was Watch Man who came an hour later with a plate of salad and salami. No embellishments, limp lettuce - symptomatic of the surroundings in which I found myself. Next problem – how to sign language my urgent requirement for a toilet? All I could think of was to bounce up and down whilst holding my crotch. That worked anyway, and without further ado, I was led to the door next to mine belonging to the communal lavatories, which doubled up as a washroom, with an array of hand basins each overlooked by an illuminated mirror. Again, it suggested this ship had a sizeable occupancy.

Although the meal was very basic with minimal variety, it was more than welcome after such a long fast. Watch Man returned to take my plate and empty cup. I wondered if he had been assigned as my keeper for the duration, whatever that was to be. If so, I could be grateful for small mercies, as he appeared to be reasonably inoffensive. I would try to discover his name, as it was not in my nature to remain stand offish for long. I believed he thought mine was 'Forserti'. I hoped it was not something insulting.

I slept soundly for several hours, being lulled by the gentle rhythm of engines, and the swaying of the boat from side to side and rocking from front to back. I awoke when it was still dark, except for a chink of light from under the door. The partitions between the cabins were not particularly sound proof. I could hear faint chatter from distant cabins, and snoring from those closer to hand. However, having woken up, I was unable to get to sleep again, as thoughts of what was happening at home and my present predicament kept crowding in.

Apart from being fed and watered, and visits to the wash room, I was confined to the cabin for most of the next two days, and developed some sympathy for those incarcerated in prison for years, serving long sentences. During this time, by using my watch and the rare glimpses of the sun, I was able to work out our approximate direction of travel, that is to say, due north, then north east on the first day, followed by east for a short while and then south east on the second, by which time I guessed we were somewhere between the Scottish and Norwegian coast. In all that time, the only person I saw was Vladimir, Watch Man's real name, so I suppose I could say I achieved one thing, how to address him.

I was still 'Forserti' for some unaccountable reason I had yet to fathom.

Chapter 18

By the third night I was well rested, which probably in part explained why I had great difficulty in sleeping. Anxiety over kith and kin and of course, my own safety, gripped my consciousness, and became mentally all-consuming. The almost total lack of human contact left an increasingly intolerable vacuum and feeling of uncertainty. The greatest cause of frustration was having no real knowledge of why anyone, especially Russian or having connections with fishing, should think I was important enough to be abducted. There had been no interrogation, I had not been thoroughly searched, not that I wished to be, but some kind of explanation as to the purpose and intention, good or evil, on the part of my captors, might, just might, fill a void in my present state of being.

Another concern was my grazed knee which was becoming more painful, bruised and a mixture of red, yellow and dark grey around the affected area. I resolved to bring this to Vladimir's attention at the next opportunity, rather than to continue suffering in silence.

In the early hours of the morning, in the midst of my restlessness, the much quieter than day-time yet unrelenting drone of the engines, the general creaking and noises of the ship, I thought I could hear the sound, not far away, of someone sobbing; a quiet restrained, but deeply impassioned sobbing. It was difficult to tell whether its source was male or female.

At first, I thought it was my imagination. I climbed down from the bunk, and cupped my ear in my hand against the partition wall of my 'cell'. It was clear from the sniffles and the intensity of the sobbing that someone was in great distress. I called out, "Is there anything I can do to help?" which seemed a ridiculous question given my situation. The crying ceased instantly, but was immediately followed the snap of the key in the lock to my cabin, and the door being flung open. Vladimir stood in the doorway, for the first time without his usual mildly friendly demeanour, but eyes wild with fury. He shouted something in his own language, and pushed me back towards the bunk. "Sh,sh", he uttered, moving a finger horizontally across his throat, the international threat of something serious if I did not comply.

He retreated from the cabin, relocked the door, and went next door to remonstrate with the unhappy resident.

After that, all was quiet, but I suspected that sad soul in the adjacent cabin continued to weep quietly. The whole incident made me very angry to the point of wishing to retaliate in some way. It was a distraction from my previous anxious state, which burnt up sufficient energy to enable me to sleep until daylight, and the sounds of activity in the washroom as a hoard of crewmen descended upon it before beginning their day shift.

I had previously dismissed the urge to sing, but my anger from a few hours earlier returned, and revived a desire for modest retaliation and relief from frustration, by breaking forth into song. It was a ripe moment while all those chaps showering and shaving were within earshot. What to sing? I knew very little by heart. All I could think of was the Credo we sang at High Mass in Latin. It was Sunday after all! I cleared my throat, took a deep breath and sang with gusto, 'Credo in unum Deum, Patrem omnipotentem, factorem caeli at terrae..'

To my utter amazement, one by one a contingent from the wash room joined in with equal enthusiasm. By the time we reached, "Et unam, sanctam, catholicam et apostolicam Ecclesiam...", I had stopped to listen to them, a veritable glorious male voice choir. However, it caused great consternation among the higher ranks of the ship, as a group of what I imagined were officers, including the bully of the welcoming party who had seen me on board four days earlier, charged in upon the scene, screaming orders no doubt to stop the singing. I felt quite triumphant when the men answered back, while two or three continued in fine fettle, determined to finish the last few words of the Credo.

It sounded as if there were a few minor scuffles, and then it all died down, as the crew must have returned to their quarters to dress and report for breakfast and duty.

I felt more than satisfied by my attempts at defiance, as it seemed to me that I was not alone in venting pent up emotions. It was unlikely that there would be any sanctions imposed on the men especially whilst at sea, as the officers would be dependent on the cooperation of the crew, especially when the conditions were particularly rough. Furthermore, the officers most likely were unaware that I had initiated the little bit of religious expression of faith.

My assumptions about the nationality and make up the occupants of the ship had been shattered. The language used by the men who had answered back did not sound the same as the officers, even though I guessed that some of it was swearing. My impression was that they may have been Polish. Poland had been in the News a great deal over the last two years, with unrest aimed against the Communist leaders and Soviet domination, and growing self confidence among the people now the leader of the Catholic Church was a fellow compatriot.

However, I had not got away entirely with my own little rebellion. I was deprived of my breakfast, and my visit to the washroom postponed. I became so desperate that I banged like a madman on the door, until Vladimir could stand it no longer, and led me to the toilets.

On the way back, I noticed that the cabin next door was open, with a small pile of laundry in the doorway. Just inside I could see Vladimir's jacket hanging on a peg. I knew it was his as it had a small tear by one of its outside pockets I had observed before. There was also a holdall that had been tossed on a bunk, and which he hurriedly grabbed before letting me into my cabin. I surmised that whoever had occupied the adjacent cabin had now been moved elsewhere, and Vladimir installed in their place, perhaps to better keep an eye on me. I wondered whether the sobbing in the early hours of the morning was an indication of my not being the only prisoner on this trawler.

By mid-afternoon it was beginning to look as if this was to be another pointless day, when suddenly the sound of the engines stopped, and the rocking of the boat became more pronounced as it slowed gradually to a halt. Another noise replaced that of the engines, only growing to something much louder. A helicopter passed by the porthole so close, hovering tentatively as if it were about to land. Perhaps the vessel had a helipad. The helicopter's engine continued for some minutes and then the sound faded. This was followed by silence, complete silence. After the unending noise from the engines of the last three days, it was eerily quiet, not a sound from anywhere. I realised that the constant noise had numbed my sensitivities during all that time, for I was immediately overwhelmed by the stark reality of my situation. I would never have thought until that moment that a bit of peace and quiet could be so disarming, so frightening. There were no voices or footsteps, no whirring of machinery, nothing except the slight creaking of the ship. It felt as if I were the only human being on board.

I heard the meow of a cat in the passageway outside my cabin. At least there was some life aboard.

After ten minutes the silence was broken again, this time by the approach of at least two people striding with purpose along the corridor. A key turned in the cabin's door, which was flung open. The bully officer stood in the doorway, while Vladimir squeezed past him and fastened handcuffs around my wrists, behind my back, although I made some effort in making it difficult for him.

They led me, rather prodded and pushed me, up two flights of stairs and into what I believed were the captain's quarters, a comfortable, but modestly furnished room, except for a long deep leather sofa. On the wall hung framed photographs of Soviet leaders, but not including Stalin or Krushchev.

The handcuffs were removed. Another door opened. A grey haired gentleman possibly in his sixties, entered wearing a smart suit, immaculately pressed, followed but another much younger suited man, but not so smart, making no attempt to conceal the gun just inside his jacket, which explained why his suit did not hang well on his stocky form.

Bully officer and Vladimir were dismissed, while I was invited in English by the smart one to sit on the leather sofa.

"Geoffrey Foster", he began. "May I call you Geoffrey?"

"I would say that was your prerogative", I replied, staring pointedly at his henchman's gun. It was tempting to say, 'You call the shots', but I did not feel it wise to encourage anyone.

He offered me a cigarette, which I declined. I had not smoked for six years after a pact I had made with Karen, when she was expecting Christina. "Don't let that stop you", I said, trying to display a little bravado. I do not know why, but it made me feel a whole lot better.

"When did you arrive here?" he asked.

"On Thursday, three days ago", I replied.

"Have you been treated civilly?"

"How am I expected to answer that? I would not be here if there had been a modicum of civility in what has happened to me since last Wednesday. No-one has explained to me what the hell all this about. I am a British citizen, leading what one may regard as a normal life, with no international intrigues; some might say a boring humdrum existence. What possible interest you can have in me, I cannot begin to understand. I have had to console myself with the conclusion that the whole thing is a case of mistaken identity. Who are you, by the way? Are you English? You have no trace of a foreign accent that I can detect".

"Trinity College, Cambridge. Mid nineteen thirties", he said, rather full of himself. Thank you for the compliment. I pride myself in keeping up my grandmother's tongue."

"I suppose you are going to tell me you had something to do with the Cambridge Five, the British traitors, the spies, Philby, Burgess, Maclean, etc?"

"On the fringes, old boy. On the fringes".

'Pompous ass', I thought.

"They are not traitors, but brave men acting according to their consciences and high calling".

"You don't expect me to accept that?"

There followed a diatribe about my Western arrogance, which eventually gave way to his life history. The third man in the room, who had been standing by the door all this time, yawned. Perhaps he was bored; perhaps he had heard it all many times before. On the other hand, perhaps he had not understood a word of it. His eyes began to glaze over, until he became aware that I was watching him. He transferred his weight from one leg to the other, wriggled a little, fiddled with his gun for reassurance. My staring had obviously unnerved him a touch. 'Perhaps I should try it more often', I thought with a modest internal chuckle.

I transported my staring technique to the interrogator to see what effect it would have on him. All it achieved was for him to play the same game with me.

"When I asked if you had received civil treatment during your stay here, I meant that no-one had physically hurt you in any way", he elucidated.

"A bit of pushing and shoving from that objectionable officer who conducted me in here, but nothing much else. However, the actual abduction was a very different kettle of fish. One of your compatriots shoved a needle in me, and I was out for the count. He also hurried me out of a car; I stumbled, the consequence of which I received a badly grazed and infected knee, for which I have had no treatment. It is now becoming very painful. Would you like me to write a report?" I asked heatedly.

The henchman moved towards me, but the interrogator signalled to him to back off. "He does understand a bit of English, you know", he said as a warning to me.

"I shall ask the ship's doctor to have a look at it when we have finished", he continued. "My name is Oleg, by the way Geoffrey. Now let's be clear, I am the one who asks the questions, not you".

"Fine by me! May be I shall get to know eventually why I am here. Incidentally, I need the loo".

"You can wait", he said severely. I thought, 'Perhaps he is concerned his helicopter will leave without him if this interrogation is delayed any further'.

"You have been investigating a British company by the name of Midland Counties Plaster and Lining Supplies Ltd, I understand."

"I cannot discuss with you any of my clients, or the work I undertake for them."

"But, this company is not your client".

"Then why do you have the idea that I am investigating them?"

"I shall assume you have been investigating them as you are not denying it", he conjectured.

"You can infer what you like, but I am not going to divulge anything".

He brushed my comment aside, and then continued, "The company is a major supplier to your client, Rhodes, of plaster products. We know you have made certain enquiries about them". He reacted to my dismissive expression by declaring triumphantly, "We have documentation which confirms this".

We sat in silence for a while, he staring intensely at me, and I looking towards the window, wondering if this was all just a bad dream. It just seemed so surreal.

"Well, what do you have to say to that?" he asked.

"To what?"

With mock exasperation, "To the fact that we have documentation which proves you have been investigating Midland Counties Plaster and Lining Supplies Ltd".

"Even if what you say were true, I haven't the foggiest idea why anything I may or may not have been investigating could be of the slightest interest to you, let alone understand what there can be which would justify the elaborate lengths you have gone to in bringing me here".

Already I had intimated more than I intended. I excused myself with the consolation that this was down to the skill of my interrogator. I must avoid falling into any trap he was setting. Not only was I defending matters of principle, but I had to consider my own safety. It was time to clam up completely. No more quips!

He continued for another twenty minutes, asking the same questions from different angles.

I gained the impression he was under some time constraints, as he kept looking at his watch and became more and more agitated by that, than my non-cooperation. Finally, he said, "Just consider this. You are totally in our hands. You cannot escape to anywhere. Your entire future is at our discretion. We know where you live and your family circumstances and routines. I shall leave you *to stew in your own juice,* I think the saying goes. We shall have another chat in one or two days' time. In the meantime, I shall send you to the ship's doctor and to a toilet".

That reference to my family certainly rattled me.

Oleg pressed a button on the desk he had been sitting at, spoke a few words in Russian, and left with his henchman, as Bully Officer reappeared on his own. He signalled for me to get up and proceeded to push me through another door into a private washroom and toilet, and left me alone in there.

It had a porthole, surprisingly with clear rather than the usual frosted glass, which lent me the opportunity of having a good look outside, as opposed to surreptitious glimpses I had managed since I had been on board.

The ship remained more or less stationary, I presumed to facilitate the coming and going of Oleg's helicopter. I could see a large aircraft high in the mainly blue sky, with its attendant vapour trail, occasionally popping in and out of the clouds, and imagined its crew and passengers looking down at us, without any notion of our being anything other than a vessel going about its legitimate business in a vast expanse of ocean. What possible means of attracting their attention had I? Absolutely none at all! Oleg's words of my chances of escape rang in my ears. However, what if the aircraft were an RAF Nimrod on reconnaissance, regarding the ship as a spying Russian trawler, which it obviously was? Its altitude was far too high for me to identify what sort of aeroplane it was. Even if it was a reconnaissance aircraft, what possible help could it be to me in my present predicament?

Bully Officer banged on the door and shouted something, the gist of which no doubt was, "You have had long enough. Come out at once", or words to that effect. I obliged, hoping I had left an atmosphere sufficiently unpleasant to his olfactory senses.

He attached the manacles once more, and shunted me along a corridor to the medical room. How I wished I had had the guts to turn around and kick him where I could damage his prospects of a future happy sex life. His propensity to shove and poke was an intense irritation, and was totally unnecessary, but possibly simply a rare enjoyment of expressing his control over someone. Perhaps his wife nagged him. Good for her!

The medical room was light and airy, overlooking the whole area from the superstructure to the bow. It was a shock to see the devastation spread out before me. The gantry and derricks which should have stood astride the forecastle, had collapsed into a tangled mess sprawling across much of the bow area, some it leaning against the superstructure and communication equipment of the ship. There were men with metal cutting equipment and acetylene torches making slow progress in disentangling the sorry scene.

I guessed that this was responsible for the alarm which sounded on the day of my arrival on board. The conditions were extremely rough that day, severe enough perhaps to have brought down the machinery meant to be used during trawling. Much of it looked so rusty, it probably needed little encouragement to topple over. I could not see any helipad. Perhaps it was astern somewhere.

The doctor arrived and introduced himself as Nikolai Kuznetsov. I was pleased there appeared to be no aggression in his manner.

He spoke English fluently, but unlike Oleg, with a strong Russian accent. "You observe the damage outside. Quite terrible you think?"

"How did it happen?" I asked.

"The storm on Thursday caused electrical wires to lash against a crane and short, making an explosion. The crane crashed on to the gantry and the whole lot fell like dominos in the high wind, I am afraid to say. It is making the ship difficult to handle, the captain tells me".

The doctor looked to be in his late fifties or early sixties. He had a kindly, but very pale face, which accentuated his dark, bushy and somewhat unkempt eyebrows that curled downwards on to his eyelids, and must have interfered with his ability to see properly. However, one's attention was drawn more to a shock of silver hair which, despite a want of grooming, had a brush-like quality, staying in shape and place whatever movement he made with his head.

"I see your clothes are bloodstained at the knee, which I am told is painful. Would you remove your clothes while I make a call?"

It was a struggle with the handicap of being manacled. He picked up a telephone receiver and judging by the inflection in his voice, made a request.

"Another set of clothes is being found for you. Now let me look at that injury. How did it happen?"

I explained, and complained at the lack of attention it had received up to that point. Although he shrugged his shoulders, I detected a look of disapproval of the absence of care, and I dared to hope, of the process I had been subjected to.

"I am afraid it is quite badly infected", he said as he dabbed the affected area with a swab of cotton wool soaked in anti-septic, which stung with eye-watering ferocity.

"I shall give you some antibiotic tablets, and leave instructions for you to have plenty of drinking water". He then dressed the wound, which having been cleansed, looked pretty awful.

"I shall make arrangements to see you each day to change the dressing until I am satisfied the infection is clear. You have a temperature a little on the high side. I shall make sure you have enough bedding".

"You have been most kind, doctor", I said and really meant it. "May I be permitted a question or two?"

"About your health, yes".

"Is there not a sick bay I could stay in?"

"Normally there would be, but all the beds are taken up with men who were injured when the storm damage you have seen, occurred".

"My other question is where this ship is going to, and where am I being taken?"

"I should very much like to tell you, but I am not permitted, but please be assured, I shall do the best I can for you".

"Thank you. Do you know anything of my circumstances?"

"A little, but it is considered not my business to know. It is very unusual to have what _you_ might regard as prisoners on this ship. It is normally just crew and..erm...shall we say *professionals*".

"Professional what?"

He thrashed around for a description which I guessed would not betray state secrets, and replied, "Scientists".

"Scientists, my foot!"

"You have a problem with your foot as well?"

"No, no. It's just a saying when one doesn't believe what one has just been told".

He shrugged his shoulders again.

"You said prisoners. Have there been others?"

"I am not permitted to say".

"I shall draw my own conclusion which is that there have been. I do have one other question. It's personal. Do you like your job?"

"That's a strange question", he remarked. "Your occupation is just something you have to do, not like".

"Do you have a conscience about the set-up, the circumstances in which you are working? Perhaps you don't have a choice".

"I do not think about it much. I suppose ultimately we feel we are working for the good of the State, society you might say. It is different for you in the West. You are either part of the bourgeoisie, working to make as much money as possible for yourselves and the capitalist bosses, all for your inflated life-styles; or you are part of the much larger proletariat who are repressed by the bourgeoisie and the political classes who are in the pockets of the capitalists. Look how your governments have crushed the working man in the last ten years, and how Thatcher is now breaking the trade unions, the power of the people".

"That is a very cynical view. Certainly you will find people in Britain who would agree with you, but they are in the minority, or if that is not the case, a large number of them are not using their entitlement to vote. We pride ourselves on being a democracy, where people are free to express their opinions, to vote or not to vote, and if the majority do not like the government, they kick them out at the next election. Well that's how it should work. Accepted, our political parties are past masters at deception, but by and large our fundamental freedoms remain intact. I readily acknowledge our attitudes towards other countries, and ethnic minorities in our own, have a very long way to go. Nevertheless, as for the working man or woman in the street, whether bourgeois or proletariat, they, as you do, endeavour to feed and house themselves and their families, and have something left over for luxuries, which I accept are not generally available to the majority of people in your country. Leaving aside the criminal classes, we work in the knowledge that what we are doing is legitimate, does not involve harbouring suspicion and spying on others, and imposing heavy restrictions on them and their activities. Most of us are conscientious in what we do, as we take some pride in it, and it consider it is for the benefit of the society of which we are a part. Many of us are fortunate enough to work with colleagues with the same work ethic, and enjoy a collegiate and sometimes social working environment, which has the benefit or by-product of greater productivity, and importantly, job satisfaction".

"How bourgeois that sounds", he retorted.

"Perhaps you are right in part. However, this is all very interesting, but it is not what I was trying to imply when I raised the original question. To put it bluntly, how do you live with your conscience when you are colluding with those who are in the business of abduction of innocent people, for goodness knows what illicit purposes?"

"As I have said or implied, it is justified by the greater good of the State, just as you might think that the work of your own Intelligence services is for Great Britain. We are of the same world my man, except that I think our country's motives are much less tarnished than yours".

"Oleg likes his job; so does that objectionable officer who brought me in here", I said.

The doctor looked up and beyond me. I turned to see what had caught his attention, and realised with a sense of foreboding that I had insulted Bully Officer in his presence. He stood there with a fresh set of clothes for me.

"Don't worry", the doctor reassured me, "He doesn't understand English".

I hoped he was right. The cuffs were removed while I dressed myself, and then promptly reapplied.

On the way back to my 'cell', Vladimir, the watch man, took over from Bully Officer, so I was spared the annoying shoving and prodding for most of the return trip.

Once back in my quarters, the handcuffs were removed, and I was once again locked in. I was pleased about three things; I had had the foresight to hide my personal belongings, such that they were, inside my mattress, courtesy of a small tear in it; someone had placed two large bottles of water on the floor beside the bunks; and I had been in the company of someone who had shown some humanity and civility, in spite of our political discourse. I hoped that the inevitable ubiquitous and abounding bugging would not land him in any trouble. Where life went from here, goodness only knew!

About half an hour later, I heard the helicopter again. I clambered on to the top bunk to get a better view from the porthole in my room. It was pointing in the same direction as before, although I concluded that it was taking off with Oleg on board. However, within a few minutes, I heard it again, but this time I could see it taking off, and heading off into the distance. Perhaps I had missed this on the first occasion as my mind was not so well focussed then. It was now clear that it had not stayed on the ship while Oleg was on board, but had gone most likely back to its base. Roughly two hours had elapsed between the helicopter visits, which suggested its base was a maximum of an hour's flight away, possibly a round trip of between three hundred and three hundred and fifty miles.

I reckoned that the base was not on land. It would have needed to be somewhere behind the Iron Curtain, either close to the Baltic Sea, or the north Russian coast. There had been insufficient time to have reached either since leaving the Atlantic south of Ireland. Northern Russia could be eliminated anyway, as my watch navigational skills had indicated consistently that our course had been due east and then south east for quite a while, which would not have taken us north of Norway in order to reach Russia. The helicopter's base must have been another ship, possibly an aircraft carrier. This then begged some questions, such as the helicopter's maximum speed and range; all beyond my knowledge. How relevant were my conclusions to my ultimate destiny? I had no idea of course, but it gave me a modicum of satisfaction to have worked out something of our present location, and of the situation beyond the confines and isolation of imprisonment.

How mariners of old, having spent weeks and months on end at sea, must have yearned for knowledge of what was happening the other side of their apparently unchanging horizon! How they must have cursed the endless impenetrable silence of the world, disconnected from their barque and the limited vista it offered them! The occasional sightings of foreign shores would raise little hope of news of home. All would have a consciousness of being day by day on the edge of life. Those of faith would have felt particularly close to God, their maker, very much in his hands and mercy, and the vicissitudes of the forces of nature, all part of his creation. *O hear us when we cry to thee, for those in peril on the sea.*

As the sound of the helicopter receded, the ship's engines once again came to life, and the boat's course was set once more. It was time for another navigational check, using the watch. I worked out that were continuing to head south east.

I began to reflect on the conversation with the Dr Nikolai Kuznetsov. In my mind I repeated the name several times over. It had a fascinating rhythm and almost noble ring to it. I almost envied him having such a name. Much more interesting that Geoffrey Foster!

What did I think I had learned? There were *professionals* on board. Nikolai had deliberately led me to believe the description 'scientists' was a lie. It simply reinforced my understanding that the technicians were secret service eavesdroppers.

I also gathered that my stay on the ship was unusual. They were not in the habit of hosting abducted persons, but nevertheless, I was not necessarily exclusively such a guest, either in the past, or even possibly at that moment.

Chapter 19

It seemed as if it had been a long day, and I began to feel drowsy. My mind drifted from acute awareness to mixed up thoughts and perceptions, and then to the point of nodding off.

Suddenly, there was an ear splitting bang. My immediate thought was that we had sailed, without the usual overture of distant rumblings, into the eye of an almighty thunderstorm. The boat shuddered and rocked violently. The light from the porthole in an instant turned from sunshine to an eerie darkness, as dense black smoke engulfed the whole scene outside. I scrambled up onto the top bunk, but there was no more to be seen but the same blackness.

Even more frightening was the urgent intrusion of the alarm, a persistent and piercing klaxon sound. Whenever we had had fire alarm training at the office, it was emphasised that we should make our way instantly and calmly to safety, and not delay to pick up our belongings, but I am afraid to admit, I always ensured without fail to grab my wallet and keys. On this occasion, my first reaction was to retrieve the few personal belongings secreted in the mattress, namely the Swiss Army penknife, biro, house keys and the pocket Dictaphone, although heaven knows why I thought that would help me out of my predicament. I slotted them into the deep pockets of the clean boiler suit I had been given that afternoon.

No sooner had this been accomplished, a key was hurriedly inserted in the lock of the door, which then burst open. Vladimir stood in the doorway with sheer panic in his expression and voice, as he shouted, "Forserti", and some Russian, and gestured to me to follow him immediately.

As we rushed along the corridor, other cabin doors were opening and the occupants, in various states of dress and undress and one with shaving cream all over his face, bustling to make their exit. There were a few who were forcing their way in the opposite direction from the rest of us, and hampering our progress to wherever Vladimir was trying to lead us. The cacophony of Russian and Polish voices added to the air of bewilderment, although no-one quite rose to the heights of Vladimir's distress.

In the mist of all the feverish activity came another loud bang, which increased the general bewilderment in the corridor to the level of Vladimir's utter panic, and the smell of fear was palpable and overbearing.

After a hands and knees scramble up two flights of stairs, we at last reached the open air. It was hardly fresh air, despite the ocean breeze. The black smoke had intensified in density and acridity. It was difficult to make out anything much, except that people were fleeing in all directions, either screaming orders or responding in what to me was untranslatable despair. I had completely lost sight of Vladimir, and it was at that moment it dawned on me that I was not in handcuffs or under supervision. The irony; free, but freedom to do what?

As my eyes became more adjusted to the new situation, I spotted an orangey glow of flames in the smoke, the ferocity of which was increasing the level of chaos around me. Strangely, I did not fully share the feeling of fear of those around me, because the freedom I was now conscious of seemed to outweigh the obvious immediate danger we were all in, but I was at least for the moment not under anyone's control, and able to react to the imperilment in my own way. It brought home to me how precious even a small amount of being in charge of my future was.

The persistence of the alarm was briefly interrupted by an announcement over the tannoy system in both Russian and Polish. It had the result of the mass of humanity moving quickly towards the stern area, but the passageways were narrow and cluttered with tackle of all descriptions, which led to impatience and acrimony, and standoffishness. I could see it culminating in brawls if the exodus from the forward end of the ship was not completed very soon. One fight did break out, but thankfully those surrounding the sparring individuals sensibly physically restrained them and a truce of sorts prevailed. The lifeboats were still firmly in place, which probably meant they were either unusable or we were not in imminent danger of sinking….yet.

The ship was still steaming ahead at considerable speed, such that the smoke was being dispersed alongside and then away from the vessel, leaving the area where people were gathering at the back end, reasonably clear. I was amazed to see how many there were on board; I guessed at least one hundred and fifty, possibly two hundred. What did they all do? There had not been any evidence of fishing, although some of the gear we had stepped over or squeezed past might have been used for it at times, but not enough to suggest it was the main purpose of the so called trawler.

Men were milling about in total disarray and confusion. It was abundantly clear that regular fire drill had not been a feature in the life of this boat, unless most of those now crowding the deck were like me, irregular visitors.

Although the smoke was billowing forth from the bow end was showing no sign of diminishing, the alarm system was turned off after roughly twenty minutes. It had the effect of introducing an element of calm among those gathered. The tannoy system barked out instructions, again in two languages, and we were all directed to form, as space allowed, six queues or lines. Officers appeared with lists on clipboards, and then conducted a roll call, although I was certain my name was not called, I assumed for obvious reasons.

While the officers were comparing notes afterwards, an RAF Nimrod flew over, much lower than the one I had seen earlier. Perhaps it was attracted by the prolific smoke, which was leaving a trail, visible for many miles behind us. Its appearance generated a certain amount of cheering from what I took to be some of the Polish members of the crew, but was quickly put down by the officer class.

We were kept standing in our serried ranks for what seemed an age. Luckily the sea was now relatively calm, otherwise keeping upright would have been impossible. I recalled how ships of the Royal Navy returning from a tour abroad would enter Portsmouth Harbour with all the sailors lining the starboard side, standing to attention. A magnificent sight! How they maintained their positions when in choppy conditions was a marvel to me.

Although it was now early evening, the clear sky (apart from the smoke) with the burning sun, began to have an effect on a number of us, despite the chilling wind off the sea. Most, like me, were wearing boiler suits of a sort, which kept the sun's rays off all but our hands and heads, but my hair was thinning on top, and my balding patch felt vulnerable. I put my hands on my head, but realised it made me noticeable, which I did not want particularly. Drawing attention to myself might remind someone that I was not handcuffed. I assumed that those responsible for my whereabouts and control, were preoccupied with the emergency up front, and had put me to the back of their minds, or individually imagined that someone else was dealing with me. On the other hand, we were all by force of circumstances, imprisoned on this boat in that there was nowhere else to escape to. Fortunately, as it happened, I was not alone in being challenged by a diminishing crowning glory, and set an example to more than a few others, which left me with a feeling of safety in numbers. In any event, it was not a problem for very long, as the late spring on the cusp of early summer sun moved over to the west and lower in the sky.

However, low in the sky to the east came forth helicopters, three of them at considerable speed. As they drew closer, I could see they had distinctive red noses, and the lettering on the side spelt out what looked Norwegian. Perhaps the Brits had alerted the Norwegian Coast Guard that there was a ship on fire. The RAF would, I was sure, also have warned them that the vessel was Russian. I worked out that we were at most one hundred miles from the coast of Norway.

There was evidently some method of communication going on between the choppers and the ship, as they flew alongside us for quite some time. An attempt was made to lower a coast guard down to the deck by winch, but there did not appear to be any cooperation from those in charge of the trawler. Finally, it was plain to see how dangerous it was becoming for the Norwegian suspended over a fast moving, smoke enveloped vessel, and he was winched back into the helicopter after the fruitless, but noble attempt to offer assistance, a stark example of international ingratitude, even in the face of an emergency. Nevertheless, undaunted, the helicopters remained alongside us until there were clear signs that the blaze was being brought under control. It increased my respect for Norway enormously, and I hoped that Britain would have responded in similar vein, even though relations between our country and Russia were far worse than those of the Norwegians and Russians.

It was well into the evening before we were shepherded inside the ship, below where we had been standing for the last few hours, into what must have been a large storage area, although now devoid of any significant cargo. The acrid stench of the smoke took some getting used to, as it had, as expected, permeated every part of the vessel.

We were invited to sit, or perhaps we weren't, but I copied what everyone else was doing. Several men were detailed to fetch food and water, which was welcomed with gusto, especially the chance to rehydrate. The food was some sort of spicy sausage, and accompanied by dry bread; perhaps not what I most wanted at that moment, but it was sustenance nevertheless. My tastes were catholic on the whole, as was I felt my general attitude to life, taking it as it came; a tendency to acceptance rather than proactivity. Wrongly or rightly, I judged that life presented enough challenges to cope with, (with the help of faith and prayer), rather than agonise over the need to go looking for them. However, I greatly admired those who did. On the scale of complacency and enthusiasm, I dipped slightly on the inactive side of the fulcrum, or leaned towards compliance rather than rebellion, even cowardice rather than courage, although I had my moments. Perhaps it was time to have one or more of those moments if I were to improve my present prospects of survival. Perhaps the disruption the ship was experiencing was an opportunity waiting to be grabbed. Just for this moment, I would eat and keep my head low, and wish not to be noticed.

It was therefore at first, a sense of bitter disappointment when I felt a poke in the back, albeit discreet. I turned, and in sheer amazement saw Gillian, our eyes meeting in a flash of recognition. Absolutely incredible! She was alive! Thanks be to God!

She looked well, if a little stressed, understandably. Her right index finger pointed upwards towards her mouth, indicating I was to keep quiet and not to display any reaction.

I tried my best to follow her instruction, but my heart raced with excitement. At that moment, she was the most beautiful person in the world. I was sure Karen would understand my sentiment. It cast a completely different complexion on the situation, and brought a jolt to my downcast frame of mind.

Her gesture had signalled her wish not to communicate in any open way, but the fact that she had made me aware of her presence, indicated that we had much to make known to each other somehow.

I got on to my feet and walked to join a queue for the latrines, for as much as anything to have an excuse to move to a better position to keep an eye on her on my return, without attracting any attention. From my new vantage point, I was able to observe that she was not the only woman on board by any means, which was an advantage for her in that she like me was not particularly distinguishable from the rest. I also used the opportunity to see if Jack was among the gathered throng, but I could not pick him out.

Later, when blankets were being distributed, it was clear that we were not going to be moved elsewhere any time soon. How I wished I was multi-lingual. To be in such a situation where so much was going on and to understand so little of it, was frustrating in the extreme; and to cap it all, now in one area where there was no language barrier, communication was off limits. A table thumping moment, if I but had a table to thump!

Once most of the shipmates had settled down for the night on the floor, I pondered the communication with Gillian problem, and then it struck me. The potential means of making verbal contact with her <u>were</u> actually at my disposal. They were right there in my pocket. When I had last called at the office on the Wednesday morning to take work home, I had routinely slotted a fresh cassette into my Dictaphone. The combination could well be a life-saver, if only to keep our spirits intact; at the very least a means of staying sane.

In this part of the ship, the level of noise from the engines was much more pronounced than in my cabin. I deduced that they were situated just underneath us. In addition, the height of the hold we were in, contributed to an echo chamber effect.

Once I had discovered that the prescribed blankets were large enough not only to sleep on, but wrap around one's body, at a push, twice over. I settled down with my head under the blanket, and was able to dictate quietly enough into the Dictaphone without being overheard, the noise from the engines drowning out any possibility of that occurring.

I briefly summarised what had happened to me over the last four or five days, and my impressions and assessment of the present predicament, our position and where we might be heading. I also asked how she was coping and what she had gone through.

My plan was to drop the Dictaphone surreptitiously into Gillian's pocket the next day, if the opportunity to do so arose. She would immediately understand the purpose of this, without the need for me to find a means of explaining it. She hopefully would be able to repeat the exercise, only in reverse. It would be highly risky, but what was there really to lose?

The floor of the hold was metal, filthy, hard and cold, and what was more, it reverberated to the rhythm of the engines. My nostrils objected to the stench of the fire to the point of nausea, and my knee throbbed. I was fearful of the fire breaking out again, and the damage caused by the explosions (if that is what the bangs were) eventually causing the boat to sink. Clearly it was the same for everyone there, so why feel sorry for myself? Perhaps it was that I had had no choice at all in being there. I was however, excited by Gillian's presence and the prospect of making proper contact with her. I slept like a log!

Chapter 20

I was awoken by Vladimir the following morning, shaking my arm and calling 'Forserti' in a semi-hushed tone. Luckily, my hand, still clutching the Dictaphone was beneath the blanket. I pulled enough of it over me to enable me to transfer the Dictaphone to one of the pockets of the boiler suit, without the manoeuvre being noticed. I vowed in future not to allow myself to drop off whilst holding the thing.

Vladimir beckoned me to follow him, to my surprise not applying any hand cuffs. I was led to an area where my cabin was, although into a mess room opposite the showers next to my cabin. It had seemed to be too good to hope that I would remain *below the radar* indefinitely, but I sensed that a rigorous restriction on my freedom was not anyone's priority at that time. The relaxation, it appeared, was further confirmed when Gillian entered the room with her keeper close behind her.

At first, we ignored one another, pretending we were complete strangers, but it quickly occurred to us this was a nonsense, and we greeted each other with warmth and relief. Nevertheless, we gauged that conversation was unwise with the minders present. Not only that, we would both have been aware of the likelihood that every part of the ship was bugged, even

228

if the chaos on board meant that there was little monitoring at that time, but we would have been ill advised to act on that assumption.

From the moment I had been roused by Vladimir, I could not fail to notice the stability of the ship had been affected by something overnight. Either the sea was rougher, or the damage had shifted something or affected its navigation.. Added to that, the sound emanating from the engines was somehow different, but I could not quite put my finger on it.

As Gillian and I stood in the mess room, we struggled to stand still, but not to the point of being thrown about by the motion of the boat. However, it gave me an idea. If I slightly exaggerated the effect, I could inch my way closer to Gillian. She was on my left, and the Dictaphone was in a left hand pocket of my boiler suit.

Every so often, the ship seemed to encounter a larger wave than the rest, or we were taken by a gust of wind. I reckoned that if during one of those episodes, I feigned losing my balance, I could bump into Gillian and use the antics of regaining my composure by depositing the Dictaphone into her pocket.

To help matters, we were struck by a particularly large wave. perhaps the wash from a passing ship. We all, except Gilliam who was using a table for support, were thrown across the room. I ensured it was virtually into the arms of Gillian, and thankfully succeeded in executing my plan.

She obviously felt something, while her look of surprise changed to one of acknowledgement, as she grasped the purpose of my amateur dramatics. Fortunately, the two minders were too preoccupied in regaining some decorum to notice. What was noticeable was their embarrassment at their susceptibility to have succumbed to movement beneath their feet, as their sea legs should have withstood it.

This all happened in the space of about ten minutes. I began to wonder, and I was sure Gillian did also, what we were waiting for. The minders kept looking at their watches.

It turned out that we had been waiting for the showers to be unoccupied, so that we could have the opportunity to freshen up and wash the smoke smuts from our hair and faces, but sadly clean clothing was not on offer. After all, it was not a five star hotel.

Breakfast followed back in the mess room. It took a great deal of resolve not to break into conversation with Gillian. However, during breakfast, she contrived to return the dictaphone to my pocket in a much more refined and subtle way. She simply looked quizzically towards one of the port holes, which encouraged the minders to do the same, while she slipped the machine into my right hand pocket with her left hand, brushing against my arm for acknowledgement from me, as I had also been taken in by her ruse. A slight raising of my right eyebrow was sufficient response, as an almost imperceptible nod from her suggested *received and understood.*

This happened in the nick of time, as Bully Officer appeared accompanied by someone I had not seen hitherto. He was well dressed in similar fashion to my interrogator of the day before. That was where the similarity ended.

There were no civil introductions. Bully grabbed Gillian in a brutish manner, while the new interrogator poked a finger in my chest, saying in no uncertain terms in a thick Russian accent, "You will answer my questions with truth and no smart Alec talk".

I said nothing.

Gillian gave a little cry, as it was clear Bully was hurting her with a vice-like grip.

"Yes?" the interrogator shouted in my face.

Again I said nothing, but pouted.

Yet again, Gillian cried out, only much louder.

"You have been investigating Midland Counties Plumbing and Lining Supplies Limited?"

I said nothing.

He continued, "No matter, we know you have".

"Then why ask me?"

He slapped my face. "No smart Alec with me. Understand?"

I said nothing.

"Yes?" he barked.

Gillian cried out again, as I noticed Bully was twisting her arms behind her back.

"Why are you investigating Midland Counties Plumbing and Lining Supplies Limited?" he asked, the company's name being pronounced with great deliberation as if he had spent ages learning it off by heart.

More silence from me, but not from Gillian, screeching in pain, and shouting, "Don't tell that sod a thing, Geoff".

"Get her out of here", the interrogator bawled at Bully.

My word, I thought. We have really rattled them.

But then I heard piercing screams from Gillian, coming from the shower room. The minders were still in the mess room, although looking distinctly uncomfortable. I tried instinctively to rush towards the shower room, but the interrogator blocked my path, and spun me round, facing one of the port holes. There was a coast line, heavily built up and close at hand. We were passing docks of a substantial port.

The interrogator stood behind me and caught hold of my arms, and proceeded to give me the same treatment as Gillian had received.

"Have I not made myself clear? You will answer my questions".

He kneed me in the back of my knee, the one which had been injured. I tried to back-kick him, but I was in the wrong position to do so, but he realised what I was attempting, and pushed me to the ground with intense spite. "I repeat", he uttered, gritting his teeth. "Why were you investigating Midland Counties Plumbing and Lining Supplies Limited?"

Another scream of pain from Gillian could be heard coming from the shower room.

Thoughts began to crowd my mind as I lay on the floor, while the interrogator paced up and down the limited amount of space, and kicking me in the ribs every time I made an attempt to get to my feet.

Who was I protecting by not answering his questions? Certainly not Gillian at that moment! Protecting anyone's financial interests was no justification for allowing Gillian to suffer what she was going and might yet be going through in that shower room. Was my resistance more a natural reaction to coercion or a blind and stubborn holding on to a misguided principle? There are times in life where one needs to plumb the depths of reasoning, and consider the effect on others in making judgements about our course of action, especially in situations beyond the realm of our experience. Although this seemed to be mentally stating the obvious, putting it into practice was much harder. It is in times like this that prayer when it comes from the very soul of our being, brings powerful guidance and growing courage and confidence, and greater clarity of thought.

First, I asked myself, what was it I was holding back? In all honesty, it was very little. The searches at Companies House had revealed nothing which was not in the public domain. The extra knowledge we had was that it was continuing to trade which was illegal, or someone was fraudulently using the company name. It was doing business with our clients Rhodes of Waterlooville and of Fareham.

Second, why were these Russians so interested in this illicit business, and why were they so anxious to discover what we knew? The latter was perhaps the crux of the matter. We were damned if we did tell them what they wanted, and damned if we did not. Either way, they were unlikely to let us go. If they did so, needless to say we would explain to the United Kingdom authorities what had happened to us, which could be regarded as an *international incident*, and lead to repercussions, and a worsening of British/Russian relations, which were already bad enough. Despite the enmity between the two nations, neither relished the prospect of their respective diplomats being expelled. On the other hand, if we were permanently in Russian captivity, or worse still, simply liquidated, there may be no trail of evidence for UK investigators to find that which would connect our disappearance with Russia. If I had no scruples and were Russian, I know what I would choose. The outlook was grim for both of us, and probably Jack of whom I still had no news.

I therefore concluded wrongly, as it later transpired, that anything I knew of Midland Counties Plumbing and Lining Supplies Limited involved no state secrets from the UK's perspective, and that I would reveal that relatively inconsequential morsel of information, in order to spare Gillian any more suffering.

However, my moral dilemma in the event was not put to the test. Once again an impending difficulty was *saved by the bell.*

One of the ship's officers entered on the scene. At first I imagined that Gillian's cries had attracted the attention of those outside the circle of bullying and torture, but it then appeared that the interrogator had been called away on some more urgent business.

Gillian was brought back to the mess room soaking wet, and pushed through the doorway by Bully Officer, who then I assumed went in pursuit of the interrogator. Gillian's eyes were red from sobbing, and her face, ashen from the treatment she had received, and what she was expecting to come. I was to hear later what she had actually gone through. It more than justified the decision I had made, but so far had not had to implement.

Vladimir and Gillian's minder were still present, so at best this seemed to be a temporary and brief reprieve. After about ten minutes, they spoke to each other in Russian, and Gillian's minder left. Gillian thought she would put Vladimir to the test by saying something to me, but was immediately shut down by him. He then led us into my cabin, and at first I thought he was going to lock us in together, but that was being too optimistic. Gillian was led out into the corridor, and I was again locked in on my own.

I climbed onto the top bunk to see what of interest in the outside world might be observed through the port hole. We were being accompanied by a flotilla of small official looking boats, and there were some exchanges via loud hailers, which I guessed were part of attempts to intercept the trawler, perhaps because of its damaged condition.

Beyond the reception committee, was yet another coast very close to us, which, as this was on the opposite side (starboard) from the coast I had seen in the mess room, this could only mean one thing; we were sailing through the straits of Denmark, with Helsingor starboard and Helsingborg port side.

I imagined neither Sweden nor Denmark had an absolute right to prevent the trawler passing through, but will have had some responsibilities for any boats in distress. However, it seemed our boat was ploughing on regardless, despite the curiosity it was attracting. I guessed this was why our interrogation and Gillian's subjection to torture had been halted. It was feasible that Gillian's screams could have been heard, especially as one of the vessels was only a couple of metres from us. We were so near and yet so far from freedom!

As we pushed further on towards Copenhagen, we appeared to be making less speed, although there was no let-up in the noise from the engine. I wondered if we were up against a tide running in the opposite direction, making our progress increasingly laboured. The unusual noise I had noticed earlier from the engines was becoming more obvious, and I began to wonder if mechanical problems were to be added to the woes of the ship. Might this work in our favour, or would we all perish at the bottom of the sea? Somehow I felt more secure now that I knew we were in the Baltic, but there was no real logic to it. It was as deep and as dangerously cruel as any sea.

I climbed down and placed behind the door, a tray left over from my last meal in the cabin the previous day, the tray containing a dirty plate, mug and fork. I put it behind the door in the hope that it would distract anyone entering the room, and allow me an extra couple of seconds to hide if necessary whatever I might be doing.

I lay down on the lower bunk, pulling a blanket over me, head and all. In hopeful expectation, I switched on the Dictaphone, with the volume set to its lowest, and listened to Gillian's response. At first, I found it disappointing, both for its brevity and its incoherence. I replayed it a couple of times to check I was hearing it correctly, but there was no question, she was saying, and only saying, "Geoff, Charlie, one of Pete's successors, who was coming to see us on Thursday, one who you may have found perplexing, I do happen to understand what he says and know where he is coming from".

She had erased my message as I had asked, so that anyone picking up the tape would find no context for anything she would say, but this message was incomprehensible even to me. I realised it was code for something. She knew I was a fan of the Daily Telegraph cryptic crossword, and clearly reckoned on my picking up the nature of the message and its meaning.

I began to work on it, one phrase at a time. 'Pete's successors' had a certain ring to it. Of course! She was aware that I was a Catholic, and Peter's successor was commonly held among Catholics as a title for the Pope. The next bit was easy. The current Pope was Karol

Wojtyla, Karol being the Polish equivalent of Charles, hence 'Charlie'. He was due to arrive in the UK on the day after I was abducted, which was the Thursday just gone. So far, so good, but the rest of the message certainly was perplexing. She had accentuated 'you', suggesting me, as opposed to her would find the Pope perplexing, but in what way? She went on to say that she understood where he was coming from. Rome or perhaps originally, Poland? But why would I find that strange and she would not? It had to be something to do with our present predicament. The *penny dropped* . How dense of me not to have understood straight away!

She was telling me she understood Polish, and of course, this would be extremely useful as most on board seemed to be Polish. It was probably fair to say that anyone in Britain who understood Polish at that time, was Polish or had Polish parentage. I tried to remember her surname, but I couldn't recall anyone ever mentioning it. It was indicative of my failure to take enough interest in the people who worked for me; something I resolved there and then to put right as soon as I was *back in harness*. Was that ever likely?

I wiped the tape clean, and recorded a new message, simply asking if she had any news of Jack, and whether she had any idea of where we were heading. I did not bother with devising any code, as there seemed little point. We would be extremely fortunate if we had a third opportunity anyway of exchanging possession of the Dictaphone. It was remarkable that we still had not been searched, or rather I had not been. How the contents of the boiler suit pockets had not spilled out during the spat with the interrogator, I did not know, but it did increase my confidence in that God had an interest in our future.

I returned to the top bunk, and reflected on the visit with the schoolchildren to see the Pope, which had been planned for the next day. I doubted whether my family would now go amid the anxiety over my whereabouts. Gillian must have had family who would have been equally frantic with worry. Certainly Jack's daughter must have been in a state. She was very close to her dad, and looked out for him in many ways. She was the motherly type, who during her time working for us, seemed to take on everyone's problems and concerns – a lovely person to have known.

I wondered where Gillian had been taken. It might have been to the adjacent cabin, so I knocked gently on the partition, but there was no response.

By mid-afternoon I was hungry and thirsty. As no one had brought anything, I assume I was being punished. Much of my time had been spent reclining on the top bunk and looking out of the port hole. Occasionally, I could see the coast of Denmark in the distance, but otherwise the inactivity led to increasing boredom.

At half past four, the boredom turned to fear and panic when the sound of a key being inserted in the door lock alerted me to the prospect of more brutal inquisition. Relief was palpable when the doctor, Nikolai Kuznetsov appeared in the doorway. I had completely forgotten his promise to re-dress my wounded knee.

He again was friendly, but seemed worried by something to the point of being clearly very nervous. While he was with me, I took the opportunity to ask him to look at the bruises around my ribs. He applied some ointment and enquired how I had acquired them. "They were not there yesterday, were they?" I confirmed they were not

"So what has happened? Were you injured during the explosions?"

"Not exactly. Some of your companions on this boat do not have the sweetest of natures."

"You mean they were not very nice?"

"That's putting it mildly".

"It is not permissible for them to do such things. I shall speak to the captain, and he will make certain that the people who have done this to you will know that the ship's doctor is aware. They will not do it again".

"I wish I had your confidence in that respect", I said, but I was not certain he quite understood me.

"Your knee is a little better today; the infection has gone down".

"Something at least is going in the right direction", I remarked. "Thank you for what you have done."

I paused for a moment, and then asked, not really expecting an informative answer, "How is my colleague, Gillian? She was treated much more severely than me. One of the officers was doing something very unpleasant to her in the shower room this morning which was making her scream in absolute agony".

"I do not know, but I shall take a look at her".

"Do you have a lady doctor on board?"

"I understand what you are suggesting. I am the only doctor, but there is a lady nurse who assists me, and she will be sympathetic".

"How is my other colleague Jack, by the way?" I asked on the spur of the moment, almost without thinking.

"As a doctor, I cannot discuss his health without his permission", he replied, but he then realised I had led him into a trap. I now knew Jack was on board, although he was nowhere to be seen when we assembled on open deck the day before.

"What happened yesterday to cause the fire and explosions?"

"You know that I am not permitted to tell you that."

"What is the scale of the damage?"

"That neither", he replied with mild irritation.

"He quickly gathered his equipment before I confronted him with further awkward questions, but as he was leaving he asked, "When did you last have any food or drink?"

"Breakfast time", I asserted.

"I shall ask for something to be sent to you".

We sailed past Copenhagen, visible in the distance, and shortly after that into open sea; well it appeared to be from my limited view from the starboard side of the ship.

No drink or food came, while my anxiety increased rather than subsided, that a repeat performance of the morning's scare tactics was in the offing, despite the good doctor's assurances. From time to time I could hear the shower room being used, but otherwise the only feature was the drone of the engines, and the accompanying mechanical whine which steadily grew more intense.

It had been a warm and sunny day, but as sunset approached, the blackest of clouds began to gather and fill the sky from the south, and the sea quickly went from calm to choppy, as the wind stirred into ever increasing gusts as the clouds rolled on relentlessly towards us.

Chapter 21

At first the distant rumble of thunder could be heard, then becoming more a continuous roar, as sheet lightening flashed high in the sky between one cloud and another, silhouetting the lower clouds of rapidly changing majestic shapes, against a background of a variety of pastel shades and intermittent flares of iridescent pale blue. Then the sweeping rain and hail formed wind drawn curtains across an ever more tempestuous sea.

I thought of the peonies in our garden at home. Every year it seemed, coming into the promise of full magnificent bloom in the early summer, they were cruelly flattened by torrential downpours. Had Britain some of this today? I envisaged drenched pilgrims returning from Cardiff after seeing the Pope. But that was nearly a thousand miles away, where the weather was probably quite different.

There were some very loud cracks of thunder in the eye of the storm, one in particular which immediately followed the brightest of flashes by far, during which the boat was rocked violently. We must have been struck.

After that, although the sea became very rough, it did not appear to affect the boat as much as I would have expected. Perhaps it was to do with the relative shelter of the Baltic compared with the Atlantic, I said to myself in a moment of irrational thought.

Suddenly, as the storm receded a little, there was a commotion outside in the corridor. I recognised the voices of the interrogator, Bully Officer and the doctor. A heated argument ensued, and someone crashed against my door. Then I heard Vladimir, which was followed by much more intensive fighting. I found it impossible to tell what it was all about. Gillian would have known, I thought. It was fearful. I was concerned it would spill into my room, but then the fisticuffs must have stopped. Two of the voices seemed to retreat, but continued shouting back until there was silence. It became obvious that the interrogator and Bully were still just outside my cabin door, because they began talking to one another in a moderate tone.

Fear once more welled at the thought of them now entering the cabin in a wound up state, and setting upon me, but one of them rattled the handle of the door, and then the two of them went off down the corridor speaking to each other in a subdued and matter of fact manner, as the sound of their voices faded from my hearing completely.

As darkness fell, it was at first impossible to sleep. Although we were past the worst of the storm, the thunder rumbled on for hours and at times gave the impression it was paying a second visit. It was hot and humid. There was the ever present worry of the thugs returning, but eventually all became quiet, apart from the engine noise and the accompanying whine, which ironically lulled me into a peaceful sleep.

In the early hours of the morning, long before first light, I dreamt of being in a hospital ward, screened off by curtains, but being surrounded by a collection of serious faces, none of whom I recognised. One of them belonged to a priest, who was administering Extreme Unction. Someone else was reciting the Rosary. Then an alarm sounded, and they all deserted me. That was the dream, but the alarm was real. I awoke sharply. From the corridor came the sound of people scurrying about and shouting. I assumed that once again, there was a fire on board. The engines were much quieter, and then I worked out that only one of them was running, but there was still the mysterious whine.

I switched on the cabin light, but it was dimmer than it should have been. It was clear the boat had developed a list to starboard, as the floor was noticeably sloping downwards in that direction. Someone rattled my door and shouted to me through it, but gave up trying to open it, as of course it was locked. I pulled on my boiler suit, but what was I to do? We were sinking, and I had no means of escape. All I could do was to shout for help at the top of my voice, which encouraged passers-by to rattle the handle, and then move on.

It dawned on me that the whining I had been hearing was from the bilge pumps, and that we must have sprung a leak resulting from the explosions on the Sunday, but with an engine apparently now down, there was insufficient power for the pumps to keep up with the ingress of water. This was my calculation of the situation, but my knowledge of boats, and especially trawlers such as this one, was sadly deficient.

I looked around the cabin to see if there was anything I could use to break down the door, but there was not. The door was very solid anyway. However, the dividing walls between the adjacent cabins were much flimsier.

I studied the bunks. The whole unit was bolted to the floor for obvious reasons. We were on a boat after all, but I recalled when I was a child at home, my brother and I slept in bunks. The top one was not bolted to the lower, but simply slotted into it by means of spikes in one fitting into recesses in the other. In every situation, however bad, there is space for faith and a little prayer.

Needless to say, the tapered spikes were tightly jammed in the recesses, but there is nothing like desperation to provide a rush of adrenalin to find untapped latent physical strength. The bed springs of the top bunk were not fixed and were a little awkward but with effort, relatively easy to remove. Iron members running the length of both sides, slotted into the bed ends, and were detached with a little persuasion from one of my shoes redeployed as a hammer. Vigorous rocking of one of the bed ends loosened the spikes in their recesses, and I was able to lift it down on to the floor. I then wielded the bed end, which was quite heavy, spike end first against the wall, making an impressive gouge. The next blow created a split running between the now two points of impact.

I frantically pounded the wall with further blows of increasing ferocity, until the studding came away by my pulling on it and using the iron side members for leverage. Eventually, there was a hole large enough to climb through into the adjacent unoccupied cabin. I ensured all my belongings, such as they were, were in my boiler suit pockets, and clambered through the gap. It was identical to the cabin I had just left, except for one thing. Much to my relief, its door was not locked.

As I went out into the corridor, I was almost mown down by a tide of humanity returning from the right, I guessed because their way had been blocked in that direction. I allowed myself to be swept along until we arrived in the hold where we had spent the previous night.

The agitation among my fellow shipmates was turning to panic, a state I had to admit, I too was on the verge of possessing. I looked for Gillian, but without success, although I thought I saw the back of Jack, but I was far from sure. Men were climbing the stairs leading to the upper decks, but several were returning, I guessed because there was no way through to the open decks. I shouted, "Does anyone speak English?" but it resulted in nothing but a few stares.

Despite not knowing what the problem was, I decided to return to my cabin and collect the two long iron members of the top bunk which I brought back to the hold. They were immediately snapped up and taken upstairs, along with other bits of furnishing people were bringing from the messes and cabins. Someone had found a sledgehammer, which prompted a cheer.

There followed a great deal of hammering and crashing from aloft, until at last a way had been cleared through to somewhere. All the occupants of the hold moved upwards to the next higher interior deck, and it was there that I found Gillian. It should have been a moment of great relief, but it was more of one of shock. She had a cut to her face, a bruised lip and grazed hands. "The bastards!" I remarked. "Has the doctor seen you?"

"No, but just at this moment it looks worse than it feels. My mind is on the present emergency".

"Have you picked up on what's going on? I worked out from your riddle that you understand Polish".

"Yes. My parents were children of Polish immigrants. I shall tell you about it later. In the meantime, we are standing in the part of the ship where all of the intelligence work goes on, well here and the deck above. The Russians were trying to keep everyone else in the lower decks, but as you can see, the Polish crew have overpowered them with whatever they could find. The Poles are debating whether to force open the doors to the outside deck, but there is so much chaos outside, most think we are better off inside and together for the moment, but some are saying we must get the doors open now in case this thing sinks".

"It is listing starboard, so I assume <u>that</u> is very much on the cards, as we take on more and more water".

"That's not why it is listing. One of the damaged gantries was struck by lightning during the storm a little while ago, and it's now leaning over the starboard side. As you can imagine, those things are quite some weight".

"But I do think the boat is taking on water, as I am sure the bilge pumps have been going non-stop for the last twenty four hours or more".

"Those explosions on Sunday were caused by one of the workmen with a cutting torch up front, accidentally setting light to some oil tanks, hence all the black smoke. The hull was damaged just below the water line. The pumps were coping until one of the engines packed up. With one engine out of commission, the power for the pumps is diminished, as it is for everything else".

"Do you know where we are?" I asked.

"We are heading east of course, and its several hours since we passed Bornholm on the port side of us. It's a Danish island, half way between Sweden and Poland".

"I'm impressed Gillian that you know all this. Have you an informant?"

"No. I have just kept my ears open and listened to the chit chat, just like you told me to do at Rhodes".

"Gosh! That seems a lifetime ago. I'd like to hear the rest of your story, but later, as it looks as if something is going on further down the corridor. Just one thing though. Have you any news of Jack?"

"You asked me that on the tape. I had no idea he had been taken. No, I've not heard a dickie bird".

"He is definitely on board, or has been", I asserted. "I got one of the English speaking Russians to admit it".

We both made our way along the corridor to where there was some animated conversation going on. Gillian listened attentively, but without betraying any clue that she understood it. There was a mixture of Polish and Russian being spoken, but whatever it was about left the Poles with smiles on their faces, and the Russians anything but, as they retreated, banging doors as they went. I turned immediately to Gillian and beckoned her into a quiet spot. "What was that all about?" I asked.

"The crew who have already kind of threatened mutiny.... I'll tell you all about that later....have insisted that they are going to take the ship into Gdansk, because its condition is now so unsafe. The Russians want to hobble on to Kaliningrad, but with only one engine functioning, the boat will have sunk before there is any chance of reaching it".

"Why are the Russians giving into the Poles?" I asked.

"The Russians on board haven't a clue about running this tub, and are totally reliant on the crew to bring it safely to port, and it's my guess that they do not wish to antagonise the Poles any more than they have to, in view of the Solidarity unrest during 1980 in the Polish shipyards, and the influence the Pope is having in Polish affairs".

"I imagine the Russians are aware we have escaped from our cabins. It makes me wonder if being here among the crew, we are protected from those thugs who set about us on Monday morning. How did you escape, by the way?" I asked.

"I didn't have to. A number of the crew heard my screams from the shower room".

"I'm not surprised. I should think the whole ship could".

"I did ham it up a bit", she said.

"I bet you didn't. Those screams were real enough. I could hear some of the punishment they were meting out".

"Well anyway, after Vladimir dropped you off in your cabin and locked you in, he was surrounded by about ten crew, who took me to their quarters which were elsewhere, that's where I have been until an hour ago. One of the lady members, a cook, has been with me all the time, and dressed some of my wounds from the beating".

"Apart from a visit from the doctor, I have been locked up all of this time with no food but a little water the doctor left with me. I haven't been to the loo, but haven't needed to".

"I overheard some of the crew discussing your plight last night. Apparently, the doctor and Vladimir had gone along to your cabin taking you some food, but were intercepted by the thugs outside your door. There was a fight between the four of them. Vladimir and the doctor were arrested and thrown in the slammer. The interrogator was overheard to say he wanted you kept locked up in your cell, even if the worst happened and they had to abandoned ship. They were saying that they no longer had use for either of us, but they needed to get rid of us somehow. They couldn't risk having us blurting out to the world what they had been up to, and how neat it would be if we went down with the ship. That was what the fight was all about; the doctor and then Vladimir wouldn't stand for it".

"So the two thugs must be pretty desperate to get hold of us now", I remarked.

"I guess so, but they will have no cooperation from the crew".

"What about Vladimir and the doctor? We wouldn't want them to go down with the ship".

"The crew had said they would break into the slammer and free them if we were in imminent danger of sinking. However, I have my doubts whether in the heat of the moment, with everyone trying to save their own skin, anyone would think to rescue them".

"Heavens, Gillian! I'd hate to have you as a prying neighbour, listening in on everybody's business".

She grinned, although because of the damage to her face I could tell it was painful.

"Could you gather from what the crew were saying, how long it will take us to reach Gdansk?"

"All I could pick up was that Kaliningrad would add an extra two to three hours, but my guess is that we are about an hour or so from Gdansk, so long as we are able to maintain our present rate of progress".

I wondered how she knew all this. She appeared to have a wisdom, knowledge and confidence way beyond her years. She had an intelligent face; her looks were attractive but not outstandingly beautiful. However, her cobalt blue eyes seemed to drill into the very depths of your mind, which was most disarming, and tended to make you automatically avert your gaze when speaking to her, although when she spoke, your own eyes locked on to hers and you were transfixed.

The corridor had several rooms or offices off of it, some of which spanned the breadth of the ship. They were all locked and in darkness, but the dim lamps of the corridor cast enough light into them to enable us to see there were banks of computers and other electronic equipment. When I had been standing on the open deck two days before, I had noticed a tall mast just fore of the funnels, bristling with antennae and discs, all far too much sophistication for fishing.

In one of the rooms, it was possible to see right through to the windows on the starboard side of the boat, out of which we could just make out the occasional lights on the coast of Poland. It provided a measure of reassurance in the event of inundation.

"Have you had anything to eat recently?" I asked Gillian.

"I am not especially hungry, if that's what you want to know".

"I've had nothing since breakfast on Monday morning", I countered.

There was a vending machine in the corridor which dispensed chocolate and bags of what I imagined to be some sort of crisps. With no expectation of the machine relinquishing any of its wares, I tried pulling on a knob, but its stubbornness to move sent out a clear message, *no cash, no give.* Nevertheless, a crew member approached, and unceremoniously struck the glass front with one of the previously commandeered pieces of metal furniture. The glass shattered completely allowing us free reign for the goodies inside. One bar of chocolate was all I needed to quell the pangs of hunger. Gillian succumbed to temptation and helped herself to a bag of crisps, but her facial expression was not one of pleasure, more one akin to disgust.

As the mood among the men calmed down, and there appeared to be no imminent risk of the ship sinking, we decided to go back to the deck below, as we were concerned about the fate of Vladimir and the doctor, and had little faith in the forethought of their compatriots. Gillian had a rough idea of where the slammer was located. Despite the brutality she had endured the day before, she negotiated the steep stairs with more agility than I could muster, and moved much more quickly than my painful knee would allow me to. I called for her to slow down, but she gave me a look as if to say, *'Stop feeling sorry for yourself, and put a bit more effort into it'*. Perhaps she was too polite to actually say it. It had the intended effect, as I realised I was becoming too engrossed in my own problems.

However, it was important to keep up with her, as I could easily lose her in the labyrinth of corridors on the lower deck. She was merciless, but I think with good reason. Whatever lay before us would undoubtedly demand alertness, cool-headedness and determination, and she had obviously detected a certain indolence on my part.

We hurried past my cabin. For no particular reason I pocketed the key sticking out of the lock. Further along the corridor, we were confronted by a locked door barring our way, which must have been the problem for the crew earlier on, when they returned past my cabin. The door had a glass panel, but it was too dark to see anything of moment. Gillian rattled the door as one does. I was about to insert the key I had just taken from my cabin door, when we heard voices from beyond the door, and quickly retreated into a cabin close by. As we hid behind its door, spying through the gap on the hinged side, someone came to the corridor's locked door and peered through it, said something in Russian to a person standing behind him. They also looked through the glass panel, and both stood back, proverbially scratching their heads, and then called down the corridor on their side presumably for means of unlocking the door.

While we were hoping for a moment when they might desist from peering through the glass panel so that we could tiptoe back along the route we had taken, we were plunged into complete darkness. Although it gave us the opportunity we had wished for, it was impossible to make our retreat in silence, as we stumbled along the corridor, lined with debris from the previous ransacking of cabins by the crew, grabbing whatever was available for breaking open locked doors.

We had just turned a corner in the corridor, when we saw the beam of a torch playing on the wall of where we had just been. Although it would not have picked us out, it was clear that the Russians had opened the locked door and were heading our way. They had a clear advantage over us in having torchlight to guide them, and it would only be a matter of moments before they reached us. I sensed that we had arrived at the cabin adjacent to mine, and turned into it, pulling Gillian in at the same time. We were able to use some of the reflected light of the, by now, several dancing torch beams, to scramble through the hole I had made during my escape, into the cabin which ironically had been my prison. Our pursuers were making so much noise, it drowned out whatever sound we made. I hurriedly placed the bed springs across the hole in the hope it would provide some discouragement to them climbing through it. For once, I was grateful for the fact that the cabin door was locked, and I had the key in my pocket.

Our hearts pounded as a torch was shone into the adjacent cabin, but none of those in pursuit bothered to enter it. A comment was made, and they then continued their chase in the direction of the hold. Unless they had some sort of weaponry, their progress would come to a full stop when they were confronted by the mutinous crew. That thought brought us some respite from our immediate fears.

It was at this point that we both noticed the ships main engine had fallen silent, the panic of the last few minutes having taken all our attention. It was taken for granted that the blackout and the sudden inactivity of the engine were linked.

We considered whether this would be a good opportunity to continue our mission of rescue. If we moved with caution, we may be able to find the slammer without being observed. The hitherto locked door stood a likely chance of being open. After all, why would the Russians have locked it in the dark? As there was no sign of them coming back, we stealthily made our way back into the corridor, and along to the door which had been locked. As we had reckoned, it was indeed open. It was a moment of serendipity when I sunk the key from my cabin into the lock, and discovered it fitted and worked. "Surely", I said to Gillian, "all the locks can't be the same. Why have them, if they were?"

"Don't go trying them all out. There isn't time. Be alert to the danger we are in, for goodness sake".

"Yes Ma'am", I responded, taking the admonishment on the chin. "Do you think we should lock this door, so that it at least impedes their return?"

Gillian thought for a moment, and then answered, "I think it will confirm to them the fact that we are down here; and in any event, they must have on them the key which was in this door. Come on. We are wasting time".

Progress was a little easier as moonlight was more in evidence. The sky must have cleared. We found the slammer in just a few minutes, but it was open and empty, and its key in the lock. Out of curiosity, I tried the key in my pocket, but this time it did not fit. "Geoff, just stop obsessing over that wretched key", Gillian whispered loudly.

We then heard the Russians coming back down the corridor. There was no option. We had to lock ourselves in the slammer. As the cohort reached the door of the cell, someone tried the handle. Some discussion ensued, and a torch was held up to the spyhole, as a shaft of light was cast upon us both. We figured that they would not have been able to do that and see into the room at the same time, but nevertheless, we had to assume that at least one of them would have peered through the hole and spotted us, as there was sufficient moonlight entering the window set high in the cell wall.

They probably did not have a key, as of course we had the one which had been in use, and so they moved on. It was eerily silent now that there was no running engine and no artificial light. I looked at my watch in what light there was, wondering why there was no sign of sunrise, and was surprised to discover it was only five minutes past two.

We waited in case the troop intended returning to open the cell door, but after twenty minutes, we supposed they were satisfied that their prisoners had been securely locked up by someone in charge. I suggested we explored further in the direction of the fore end of the ship, but Gillian said, "Look Geoff, we have achieved our objective of ensuring the doctor and Vladimir were not trapped in here. Let's be sensible, and head back to where we were in the company of the crew. Why push our luck any further for the sake of your innate curiosity?"

I agreed reluctantly, feeling a little put down, but she was right of course. Even so, as we unlocked and crept out of the slammer, I started off in the other direction just for a quick peep.

"Geoff", she whispered harshly, "where do you think you are going? Just get on and lock the cell door, bringing the key with you, and head back towards the hold as we agreed a moment ago".

She was being very forthright, and I began to think, may be, I was not taking the overall situation seriously enough; too casually perhaps. Certainly, she was no wallflower, and I should count myself fortunate in that my companion was so clear-headed.

We were just approaching the top of stairs to the corridor where we had left the crew, when an engine started up again, and the lights came on, although dimly as before. While we had been away, the crew had broken into the room where we had seen the computers, etc. and several of them were looking out of the windows. What was instantly noticeable was how much the boat was now listing. We joined two of the crew at one of the windows. They knew who we were, and one of them addressed us in broken English.

He explained that we had shipped a good deal of water while the pumps had not been running, and the men had concluded that it was inevitable that the trawler would sink. The pumps might delay the final moments by half an hour or so, depending on when the water reached the engine room.

We could see the lights of the coast very clearly now, and must have been only three or four miles offshore. The English speaker told us that we had just passed Gdynia. All being well, we should reach Gdansk in the next twenty minutes.

We stood and watched out of the window as we sailed past lights of a continuous built-up area, and various ships, most moored up, but one or two on the move. The increase listing was now observable in its progress. We were completely helpless, and could only hope and pray that we would dock and get ashore before the boat went down.

Gillian continued to listen in to the conversation now spurred on by fear and panic. She gathered that, because of all the damage, only one lifeboat was serviceable, and that had set off with a party of Russians during the blackout.

One glimmer of hope was that some tugs had arrived, and were deployed on the port side, two with lines now attached. They were pulling on them apparently trying to drag the boat into a more upright position, and with luck bring the starboard side up so that the hole was above the waterline but most of the crew thought they were wasting their time. Another tug was towing the boat to augment its progress and pilot it to the nearest quay. Gillian then heard that a lifeboat was evacuating people from the forward area of the ship where the Russians were, but it was a painfully slow progress as they were having to climb down rope ladders, a number of them frozen half way down with fear.

Inch by inch we came up to a jetty on the starboard side, but we could see that the overhanging gantry was hampering the docking. Our hearts sank when it was revealed that the boat would have to be turned around so that it could be moored up on its port side, and that it would be a delicate time consuming manoeuvre.

While this was being performed, the evacuation had to be suspended. A fourth tug arrived with pumping gear. Hoses were hurriedly put in place by a number of the crew who had broken through the locked doors at the aft end of the corridor.

Headlights were dancing along the length of the quay, as we watched police vans and cars, a couple of ambulances and a fire engine, arrive on the quayside, all with sirens sounding and blue lights flashing. The police emerged from their vehicles, and busied themselves putting up cordons. Another police van arrived. The driver sprang from his cab, and opened the back doors, to release four large police dogs.

Finally, two large black cars drew up in far less dramatic style, and quietly parked in the shadows. Their occupants remained in the vehicles. A policeman walked over to them as if to tell them to move on, but seemed to get short shrift from one of the drivers. The policeman, shrugged his shoulders and returned to his cordon duty. Another more senior police officer approached him. They spoke for a few moments. The officer, looked towards the cars, threw his arms up in despair and walked back to where he had come from.

"Security men, KGB perhaps, or the Polish equivalent", muttered Gillian.

"KGB", interrupted the crew member who had earlier spoken to us in English.

"Jack!" exclaimed Gillian suddenly.

"Where?" I responded, looking around the room.

"No, I've not seen him, but that's the point. What if the Russians have lined up for him the same fate they think they have for us? What if he is languishing down below, locked in one of those cabins?"

"Oh my goodness! Yes, that is very possible. Do you think we could enlist the help of some of these chaps in a search. You see what you can do, while I get going downstairs and make a start. It's unlikely that any of the Ruskies are down there now. They are all busy saving their own skins."

In spite of my painful knee, I raced down the steps and along the corridor, looking in every cabin and room of any description, calling out Jack's name as I went. There was already about an inch of water on the floor. All doors *en route* as far as the slammer were open, but beyond that several were locked. I discovered that the key to my cabin fitted a couple of them, but no sign of Jack.

I could hear the search party Gillian had managed to enlist, coming along the corridor, and then once again we were plunged into darkness, but this time the engine and the pumps kept going. I guessed that the incoming sea water had fused the lighting system. However, we were a little further north and much further east than Buckinghamshire, and daylight was making its first tentative appearance of the new day. Not yet three o'clock by my watch, but it was still set on UK time.

We reach the fore end of the corridor, turned around and returned the way we had come, but breaking open the still locked doors as we went. By now the inch of water on the floor was more like four or five, lapping over our shoes. The third cabin we forced open justified our reasons for the search. Jack was sitting on a lower bunk, hardly noticing our arrival, and certainly not leaping to his feet and greeting us like long lost relatives. Even if he had wanted, he could not. He was manacled to the bunk by his ankles. The search party conferred, and sprang into desperate action. They dismantled the bunk in much the same way as I had mine, but at quadruple the speed, until all that was left in place were the bed end of the lower bunk. One of the crew was a hefty chap, arms as thick as a flagpole. With one wrench, the bed end was ripped away from the floor to which it had been bolted, and the manacles slipped of it. They were still attached to Jack, but that was the lesser of our concerns. Jack was in a bad way. He did not know who we were, and became extremely agitated as we coaxed him out of the cabin and along the corridor.

The water level was now accelerating rapidly, and by the time we reached the hold and the foot of the stairs, it was almost up to our knees.

At the top of the stairs, we turned right into the corridor, along a short way, and right again into the room with the computers. We sat Jack down on the most comfortable chair we could find. His pallor was ghostly, and his eyes vacant. He seemed unable to speak, almost as if his brain was unable to function. Someone brought him drink from the vending machine, but he looked at it in puzzlement as if not knowing what to do with it. "We can't let him back in Russian hands, if this is what they do to him", asserted our new found friend, the crew member who could speak English. He informed us that his name was Dominik, and then left the room and headed aft as if on a mission.

I tried to speak reassuringly to Jack, but could not get through to him. Gillian spoke to him. He turned towards her and looked up into her eyes, but said nothing. He kept staring at her in puzzlement, clearly struggling to work out who or what she was, the way a baby of a few weeks will.

We were both at a complete loss as to what to do now. Whatever plans we made would have to factor in Jack's state of mind, health and the fetters around his left ankle.

The ship was listing more than ever to starboard now that the tugs were no longer straining to keep it upright, as starboard was now on the seaward side. Dominik returned and explained that some help may be available if we followed him. He kindly took Jack's arm and more or less carried him uphill to the doorway, and helped him along the corridor until we reached the top of the stairs again. The exit to the outside deck had been opened. Dominik led us through to the open deck, but not before I glimpsed down the stairs, and to my horror saw that the water level was a third of the way up them. It meant that my cabin and Jack's would be almost completely under water, and our fate sealed had we not managed to escape from them.

We scrambled down to the starboard side where one of the crew of the tug pumping water from the boat, was manhandling an extra hose into a hatch. Dominik introduced him as Tomasz. He had arranged with him that we would be taken off the boat on to the tug, and hopefully be able to somehow make a get-away.

Tomasz, removed his jacket and put it on Jack. He gingerly held on to him as they both climbed over the side and down a rope ladder on to the tug. In the meantime we hid behind the cowling over a ventilator shaft, until Tomasz reappeared with two more jackets for us. First, he guided Gillian down to the tug, but much to my chagrin, a police launch came alongside, and paused. Luckily, Gillian had gone inside the tug before their arrival. An official in the launch asked Tomasz something while he was making his way back onto the ship. I remained hidden behind the cowling. Whatever Tomasz said in reply appeared to satisfy them, and they went on their way. It emphasized however, how much attention the ship had attracted, and the area around bristled with officialdom. Dominik's parting words to me had been that he and the crew faced arrest for mutiny on the high seas, and imprisonment, but wished us well in <u>our</u> bid for ultimate freedom.

Chapter 22

Once we were all on board the tug, I agreed with Gillian that now we were away from the trawler it was appropriate for her to use her Polish to communicate directly with the populace, but perhaps we would just wait until the pumping was over. We did not have long to wait. Pumps from the quayside had been brought into action, but it was considered dangerous for the tug to remain alongside, because of the risk of the ship capsizing on top of it.

Gillian began the conversation by asking Tomasz how much Dominik had explained of our situation. The fact that the trawler had been in trouble had been known for a couple of days, as it had been on the television news. There had also been speculation in the West that the crew had refused to cooperate with the mastership of the boat, had 'mutinied', so the headlines had read, although the reasons had remained a mystery. Dominik had apprised Tomasz of the incompetence of the management during and after the storm, and the disgraceful treatment we had received.

"Surely", we asked, "the crew were well aware beforehand that the trawler was used for nefarious operations and not just innocent fishing?"

"You mean spying on the West?" responded Tomasz, Gillian translating for me. "Officially, our government does not see it as illegitimate, although we the people are not so sure nowadays".

Very diplomatic, I thought. This led me to think that our next move should be to contact the British Consulate in Gdansk. Perhaps Tomasz would know where it was, or be able to phone them. Gillian asked him, but he did not know off hand, but would make enquiries when the tug returned to base.

Tomasz, who we learned was in fact the skipper, and his crew retrieved the hoses from the trawler, and then moved the tug away from the vessel. We sailed over to and came alongside one of the other tugs. All agreed that the work of the tugs was done, but our seaborne journey was not yet over. The base for our tug was in Gdynia which would take another half hour at least to reach. Tomasz thought that it would be a better place for us to land anyway, as the security forces might be searching for us in Gdansk. He was certain that we posed a serious risk for the Soviet authorities, as it was they who had taken us. Yet we also would be an embarrassment to Jaruzelski's Polish government, which had imposed martial law a few months before, perhaps in the mistaken idea it would appease the Soviets. Poland was after all a Warsaw Pact country, although the relationship between Poland and the Soviets was very strained, as indeed was the relationship between the Polish government and its people.

By the time we had arrived at Gdynia and docked in a small shipyard it was mid-morning. The first thing Tomasz did was to fetch some bolt cutters and remove the handcuffs from Jack's ankle. By then he was showing signs of improvement. The tug crew had worked hard to persuade him to drink tea and coffee, and to eat chocolate, which he did with relish after reluctantly accepting the first piece. It was Tomasz's opinion that he was diabetic and dehydrated. Gillian confirmed he was indeed type one diabetic, and would disappear every so often while they were working at Rhodes, to administer his own injections. He always kept a Mars Bar handy in his lunch box. However, Tomasz said he wouldn't put it past some Russians on that trawler to have used drugs or even poisons on him, but Tomasz proved to be very anti-Russian, which would have coloured his opinion, although I conceded that in this instance he was probably right.

We were led into a small office on the quayside, attached to a storeroom full of tackle and equipment, water proof clothing, boots, etc. We removed the jackets he had lent us which had protected us from recognition during our escape from the ship.

We were introduced to Tomasz's wife Marta, a heavily pregnant lady with a permanent smile. Gillian asked how long to the happy event. Two months, she was informed, but there were three other bairns being looked after by her mother, while she dealt with Tomasz's paperwork. I was very impressed by Gillian's Polish. She spoke it with a fluency and complete lack of hesitancy, and no-one thus far had shown any indication of incomprehension.

Marta began making phone calls, the first to the British Consulate in Gdansk, but a pre-recorded message informed her that it was closed until the following Monday, but no reason was given. It was probably staffed by one man and secretary, and both were on holiday. Marta asked Gillian to leave a message anyway on the answerphone. "That's that", I said with exasperation and resignation. Perhaps we should make our way to Warsaw.

Gillian suggested it to Tomasz, but he thought it a bad idea. Since the introduction of martial law, it was better to keep away from the capital without identity papers, visas and documents. He had a cousin who lived in a village forty kilometres west of Gdynia, and worked for a farmer who had a sizeable farmhouse. There, we could lie low for a few days, while the inevitable search for us hopefully cooled off.

I asked Tomasz through Gillian if the trawler would be allowed to sink at its moorings. He answered that there was no way of stopping that from happening. It was shallow where the boat was, and would not have sunk much lower than it was when we left it. It was nearing high tide then, but it would be resting on a submerged bank of mud, and at low tide the boat would be largely drained. "That's a pity", I remarked. "The Russians would discover we had not perished in the lower deck cabins after all, which means we should be in no doubt that they would come looking for us. At least for the moment they would expect us to be in Gdansk".

Marta slipped out to buy us some food to take away with us, as she and Tomasz were very nervous about sheltering us any longer than could be helped.

It was arranged that they would take us in their van as far as the city's outskirts, beyond the likely risk of being caught out at the several check points within Gdynia. They knew where they would be and how to avoid them. Normally they were casually manned, but it was better not to take any chances.

Marta typed out several phone numbers for us which we would need or might find useful, and the address of Tomasz's cousin. The list also included a local doctor and a priest. She phoned a friend to ask for details of local bus services. They thought they would be safer than trains, where inspectors frequently doubled up with identity checks as well as tickets.

Marta took us to a friend's café a few doors away, and bought us a simple lunch, which we ate in a back room, away from potential public gaze. The meal was accompanied by beer, which was very fortifying, even if the taste, to put it kindly, was interesting. We felt it unwise to let Jack have any. Instead, he drank some homemade apple juice, which I suspected was a watered down version of cider, having sniffed it.

After we had had our fill, we returned to Tomasz's premises, where we were directed into a yard at the rear and ushered into the back of a somewhat rusty faded blue van. Marta presented us each with a rucksack in which she had very generously deposited some clothing and the food. A variety of boxes and sacks were piled up around us, in order that we could not be seen from either the back door windows or the driver's cab.

We set off west by what was now mid-afternoon, Tomasz driving and Marta to his right in the passenger seat. We were stopped only once, on a road near an airfield. It all seemed very casual as Tomasz had said, until Gillian was unable to control a sneeze, possibly aggravated by dust from the sacks. Marta had the presence of mind to instantly pull out a handkerchief, and perform a second mock sneeze. The security officer was not totally convinced and peered in our direction. Tomasz, equally as quick as his wife at improvisation, pointed out that his wife was pregnant, and the large bump was putting pressure on her bladder. She needed a toilet urgently, and with no such facilities to hand, it was imperative they got home urgently. This allayed the man's doubts, and he detained us no further.

We travelled another mile or so and pulled into a modest shopping centre with car park and bus bays. "This is as far as we can take you", Marta said apologetically. She had an appointment at the maternity hospital for a routine check-up. Tomasz proceeded to give Gillian some money, which we were really in no position to refuse, except to insist that it should be no more than the bare minimum we were likely to need, and to express our regret that there seemed to be no way of repaying it. They assured us they had had given us enough for our bus fare to the town of Lebork, and a taxi from there to where his cousin lived.

We thanked them profusely for all their kindness and wished Marta well with her confinement. Both he and Marta said how proud they felt to be helping us. After some handshakes and hugs, and a tear or two we walked across the car park to the bay for our bus to Lebork.

Jack's health had steadily improved during the day, but he still found it a struggle to cover the distance from the van to the bus stop.

As we walked, Gillian suggested that as she would have to do all the talking, which would be as little as she could get away with without arousing suspicion. I would pretend to be profoundly deaf and mute, and if necessary she would improvise some sort of sign language, and hope that no-one else we encountered would know the recognised forms.

Whilst we were waiting for the bus an elderly lady tried to engage Jack in conversation. Gillian immediately intervened and explained that he was suffering from dementia, and we were taking him to a relative, after a spell in respite care. Gillian was tempted to expand on the severity of his mental state, but thought better of it, as he was in no position to defend his sense of dignity or reputation.

The wait for the bus was about a quarter of an hour. It was packed with boisterous schoolchildren, which was to our advantage as it meant that Gillian could whisper instructions to accompany the sign language, without being overheard. She struggled a little with buying our tickets as the driver needed to know what stop we wanted in Lebork, as it was a fair sized town. "Town Hall", I suggested to her, keeping my teeth clenched and mouth shut as if I were a ventriloquist. She had to be a bit generous with the fare, as the driver did not have enough change, at least, that was what he claimed.

At the second village we came to, almost all of the schoolchildren got off, their exuberant chatter no doubt being about much the same as it would have been among schoolchildren in Britain. The elderly lady who tried to communicate with Jack at the bus stop was sitting in the seat in front us. She turned round in her seat and made a second attempt, but Jack just stared vacantly at her. I wondered if he was acting. If so, he was making an excellent job of it – a performance deserving of an Oscar. Gillian apologised on his behalf, but the lady remarked how sad it was when life robbed one of one's mental powers. Getting old was no fun. She had watched as her late husband had gone from being the light of her life, to being a cabbage, as she put it. When it was clear to me at least that Jack was straining not to laugh, his shoulders giving the game away, I was relieved that he was regaining a little of his old self.

My attention was drawn to a newspaper someone had left on one of the seats on the opposite side of the aisle. I reached across and grabbed it as the picture on the front page was of a trawler. It had listed so far as to be on its side, the over-leaning gantry apparently preventing it from capsizing completely. Gillian snatched it away from me. I could not understand why at the time, but it would become clear to me later.

She resumed her conversation with the elderly lady, who seemed determined to chat. I was grateful as it meant the other passengers eyes, which I sensed had been on Jack and me, now turned to the two women. I relaxed a little, and gazed out of the window. We were going through a mainly agricultural area, not particularly scenic, but it was interesting to see how the use of horses was still in evidence in pulling carts and farm machinery. The afternoon was sunny and the temperature comfortable. It was relatively easy for a short while to forget how precarious our predicament was as I began day dreaming, helped by the lack of sleep we were enduring.

After about an hour, we entered a substantial town having passed through several hamlets and villages, some quite pretty and vaguely Germanic in appearance. As we ventured further into the town, the bus, as might be expected, stopped at shorter and shorter intervals. Eventually, Gillian rose to her feet and gathered up her holdall, and I followed suit, also picking up Jack's things. This all happened without a word being said.

As we alighted from the bus, I glanced back at the passengers who had been behind us. Most of them seemed to be watching us as we stepped down onto the pavement, and they must have thought how strange we looked, all three of us wearing the boiler suits issued to us on board the trawler. Out of recently adopted habit, I checked the contents of my pocket. The Dictaphone, biro and penknife were still there, but I hoped that except for the biro, these items would now be redundant in getting ourselves back to the western side of the Iron Curtain.

Our next challenge was to find a taxi. The choice of getting off the bus at the Town Hall was a good one. For one thing, the square in front of it and the accompanying shops were bustling, and we felt less conspicuous. Everyone gave the impression they were focussed entirely on their own business, and three people wearing identical boiler suits was all part of the daily round.

We found what passed for a taxi rank, but there was a queue of would be passengers. We joined it, but after five minutes not a single taxi had appeared, and we began to wonder if the queue was for something else. A lady with two children aged around seven or eight asked me something. I shrugged my shoulders, but she was not going to give up that easily. She repeated the question, only louder. Luckily, Gillian came to the rescue and gave an answer, which she did not seem too happy about. One of the children asked Gillian another question, and the answer made them and others in the queue look quizzically at Jack, followed by much mirth. She later confided that she had told the child that the boiler suits were our disguise. We were nasty British spies, and that Jack was the Grand Spymaster. "That was highly risky", I chided.

I looked at Jack who seemed to be full of confusion again. I wondered for a moment if he was practising his drama skills. If he was, he was very convincing. Gillian was looking concerned as well. She spoke again to the lady with the two children, and then signalled to us to leave the queue and follow her. Jack almost collapsed and we had to virtually frogmarch him around a corner into a quieter spot. We asked him if he feeling unwell again, but he simply looked at us with the same vacant stare as before.

Gillian informed me that her last question to the lady with the children was whether there was a taxi office nearby where one could be booked. There was indeed, but it was five minutes' walk away. She would go and sort it out, and have the taxi brought round to us. Would I stay where we were and look after Jack, as clearly he was in no state to walk anywhere?

While she was gone, I asked Jack if he was seriously diabetic, but there was no sensible response. He struggled to ask me something, but could not think what it was or could not find the words to use. I rummaged around in my holdall and found some chocolate, which was offered to him, but he did not respond. It was extremely unnerving; all I could think to do was to push the chocolate up to his lips. After several moments, he opened his mouth a little, enough to shove some in. I made chewing actions to encourage him, and he seemed to cotton on. A couple of passers-by spoke to me, I presumed asking if Jack was all right. All I could think to say was the universally understood 'OK', but they looked very unconvinced. It was getting extremely awkward, as more and more people were stopping and making enquiries. One or two phrases were being repeated. I began to respond by holding my hands to my ears to signify I was deaf. One gentleman repeated what he had just said by shouting at the top of his voice. It alerted a policeman some distance away, who began walking in our direction.

Luckily, Gillian appeared and explained to the little group which had congregated around us that I was profoundly deaf, and that raising one's voice would be of no benefit, and most of them nodded in comprehension.

The gentleman and I helped Jack into the taxi Gillian had ordered, which had just drawn up. Gillian thanked him profusely, making a semi-curtsy the charming way Polish women often do, and climbed into the front passenger seat. As we pulled away, the policeman arrived on the scene, but we had already moved into the stream of traffic. "That was a close run thing", I muttered inaudibly.

The route out of Lebork was northwards towards the coast. The taxi driver knew the area we were heading for fairly well but not the farm itself. He apologised in advance that we might have to drive around a bit, or ask at the nearest village, to find it.

Gillian explained to the driver, so she told us afterwards, that she was escorting the gentlemen in the back of the car to the farm for a respite holiday. We had disabilities and lived in a special needs home just outside Warsaw. One of us had been deaf from birth, and the other was in a state of advanced dementia. The driver was somewhat anxious about Jack's demeanour, but Gillian put it down to the long journey they had made that day, having set off at five o'clock that morning. Gillian, I thought was very good at improvisation, and enjoyed downplaying our abilities. I later told her I would keep all this in mind when discussing the staff Christmas bonuses with my partners. That earned a mild kick in the shin from her, mercifully not on the injured leg.

As we reached the proximity of the farm, the taxi driver mentioned that the security had been particularly tight at the check points in Gdansk that morning. Word was that some escaped prisoners were on the run. He was beginning to pry into where exactly the special needs home was, and what trains we had caught. This accounted for Gillian's increasing agitation, and why she was so relieved that we had come across the farm almost at once without the need for prolonging the taxi ride.

When we drew up at Tomasz's cousin's house, Gillian hurried us out of the taxi and shooed us up the garden path, flapping her hands as if she were a school teacher directing children to get a move on. She returned to the driver to pay him the fare as quickly as she could, not giving him a chance to ask any further questions, but to explain, she later told us, her impatience by telling him *she was up to here with us, and how difficult we had been all day. The home should have provided her with a companion to help her with managing us on such a long journey.* I promised to extend my threat regarding her Christmas bonus to the next round of salary reviews. Her reply was, "Who says I shall still be with the firm by then? There are greener pastures, you skin flint".

"You insolent young whippersnapper! You should be more respectful towards your bet……..", I said stopping in mid-sentence, not wishing to dig an even deeper hole for myself, even though it was only banter.

"Betters, you were going to say….and who might they be?"

I winced, grinned, and then stuck my tongue out at her.

Back to the arrival at the cousin's house. Before we reached the front door, he came out to greet us and welcomed us inside. The house was neat and tidy, but frugally furnished. He pointed to himself and said "Nowak". We shook hands, and I indicated that I was Geoff, and my companion who was in such a sorry state was Jack. As Gillian entered the lobby, he again introduced himself by pointing and saying, "Nowak". He was quite shocked and a little disarmed when she responded in Polish. Apparently Tomasz and Marta had not explained that one of us was a Polish speaker.

We were invited to sit at a table, while Nowak warned us that not all Poles had Western sympathies, especially in the countryside. His own wife, who brought us a fruit drink and did so without saying a word, was not the epitome of hospitality. Nowak whispered to Gillian that she was not at all happy with our being there, and that was why he had asked his employer to take us in.

Gillian and Nowak chatted for a short while, and then he led us to the farmhouse after he had seen the farmer drive past the cottage on a tractor heading in that direction. Jack really struggled walking the two hundred yards or so, Nowak lending some support as it became clear he hadn't the strength in his legs to remain on his feet unaided. My own knee was becoming very painful and so I was not much use to him.

Nowak introduced us to the farmer and his wife, Bartek Felinski and Sabina, and retreated as quickly as he decently could. I actually felt sorry for him because I was sure he was in for an earful when he returned home.

Bartek and Sebina were quite different. He lost no time in telling us in English that he served with the RAF during the Second World War in 53 Squadron, based in 1941 in Cornwall, flying Blenheim and Hudson bombers against enemy shipping and submarines off the French coast. After delivering us a pocket history of his post war career whilst we remained standing in the hallway, he ushered us into a large sitting room, and invited us to sink into deep and enormous armchairs. Jack fell asleep immediately or passed out, we were not quite sure.

Bartek returned to the subject of the war and regaled us with his experiences in England, Wales and Northern Ireland during that time, but Gillian and I began to flag, having had little or no sleep in the previous twenty four hours. Bartek could see we were battling to keep awake and not appear rude. He apologised profusely for 'going on'. Sabina mildly rebuked him. However, they both made every effort to make us feel welcome. She had prepared a traditional Polish dinner, and assured us we would enjoy it.

While Sabina busied herself in the kitchen putting the final touches to the evening repast she had promised us, we gave him a brief account of what we had been through over the previous few days. He was horrified and it was with some difficulty he felt obliged to inform us that although in all other respects we were most welcome, it was too dangerous for us to stay for more than a couple of nights. Our being there presented them and us with the considerable risk of discovery if we were too long in one place.

He had been in Gdansk that lunchtime, and there was a great deal of hue and cry over some escaped prisoners from a ship. From what Nowak had told him about his cousin's phone call, and what we had just revealed, it was obvious that we were the fugitives the authorities were seeking. Goodness only knew how we got away with avoiding them, especially in our boiler suit garb. Because of his well-known British sympathies, he was certain it was only a matter of time before the police would be knocking on his door. Gillian went as white as a sheet as she recalled the taxi driver's inquisitiveness. Her story of our being inmates of a special home near Warsaw hardly matched our sartorial appearance.

Over dinner, which was absolutely delicious, we discussed the most urgent matters. Apart from the threat of being discovered, Jack's health was the immediate problem. He was unable to partake of the meal, but fitfully dozed in one of the armchairs. Sabina was particularly concerned. She made him a hot chocolate drink and gently coaxed him into swallowing some of it, but had more success in plying him with sugary drinks, although we were not convinced it was any longer making much difference. Bartek felt they had no choice but to call the local doctor, who promised he would call during his evening rounds.

By now Gillian and I, despite the wonderful hospitality we were receiving, were feeling very depressed. We desperately wanted to be back with our families and friends, and carrying on with our normal (sort of) lives. Bartek's warning had pulled us up short, as we grew more aware that we were far from being out of danger. Our almost charmed experiences that day were unlikely to be repeated in the subsequent days, as it was abundantly clear that our new found freedom was considered a serious enough threat to the authorities for them to have organised such a *hue and cry*, as Bartek had put it.

After dinner he made numerous discreet phone calls. I could tell by the tone of his voice, and the expression on Gillian's face, that he was becoming increasingly frustrated and desperate. Then the doctor, Lech Adamik, arrived. He asked if we would leave the room while he examined Jack, with Bartek and Sabina in attendance.

After about half an hour, Bartek called us back into the sitting room. "I'm afraid we have a very serious problem. Jack needs to go to hospital, Because of your circumstances, it will have to be a private clinic where too many questions will not be asked, and a level of discreet anonymity can be maintained. Doctor Adamik says that Jack is in a semi-comatose state. He has been given insulin, but the doctor says he suspects there is an underlying condition which needs investigation.

"Not good", the doctor said shaking his head, "Not good".

"The doctor wants to know what happened to him while at sea", Bartek said. "He seems very traumatised and delirious, quite apart from the effects of diabetes".

Gillian and I explained that we did not know. We had not seen Jack until the last moments before we left the ship. He had not been in any fit state to tell us anything.

We had been badly treated ourselves, and I for one had been drugged during the early stage of our abduction.

Quite apart from the treatment Jack needed, and the risks of discovery that entailed, there was the question of how the fees of the private clinic would be paid. There was also the difficulty of how we would get payment across to them. It would then be for us to pursue the matter with the British Government to ascertain what forms of redress may be possible. However, that was the least of our concerns at that moment.

Dr Adamik tried to phone the clinic, but discovered that the line was dead. Bartek checked the connections, found no fault, and concluded the problem was external.

Kowak (Tomasz's cousin) arrived and let himself in. He was in some distress and almost in tears, informed Bartek that his wife had walked out on him, or rather had driven off, taking the family truck, after a row over helping us, even though it was only to have acted as a go-between. She or more likely the taxi driver must have reported our presence to the police, as they had arrived on his doorstep a short while ago and asked if he had seen any strangers of foreigners. He said he had not, but still being in a state of shock over his wife's exit, was unable to sound convincing. However, the police left after making it clear that he must inform them of any sightings or suspicions. He had come to warn Bartek and to report that his phone line had been cut off. Bartek then remembered that when he had been using the phone earlier, there had been the occasional click, and he now suspected that someone must have been listening in on his calls.

Bartek said to Nowak that he was sorry to hear his wife had deserted him, but with a little insensitivity perhaps commented that they had all seen it coming. She had originated from south of Warsaw and hated living in the agricultural part of the north, and feared Nowak's cousin's sympathy with the Solidarity movement.

Bartek and Sabina concluded that it simply was not safe for us to stay at all, not even for one night in their house, as it was inevitable that before long the police and others would be banging on their door, and no doubt insisting on searching the place from top to bottom. However, they would not just throw us out. They would sort out a change of clothing for us and destroy the boiler suits in the log burner. Dr Adamik would re-dress my leg wound, and then drive Jack to his surgery and give him some more treatment, and provide him with a supply of insulin to take with him. The idea of a clinic was abandoned, as it was considered to place Jack in greater danger than taking his chances with us.

In the meantime, Nowak would lead Gillian and me across the fields to the village priest's house. Sabina promised us that he was a lovely man who would always welcome strangers, even without warning, and had a network of loyal parishioners who would do anything for him, although some might require a little gentle coaxing. Dr Adamik said he would contact the priest, Father Janusz Janowicz, from the surgery, and make whatever arrangements seemed appropriate after treating Jack. Bartek cautioned Dr Adamik that the phone may not be the safest means of communication, and so the doctor agreed he would think of an alternative method.

We all lent a hand in changing Jack's clothing, but were horrified to see the amount of bruising on his limbs, by no means all of it attributable to constant insulin injections.

Bartek's final advice to the doctor was to take one of the field tracks back to the village, even though the ride would be somewhat bumpy. There was still about enough daylight to do so without using headlights. Headlights bouncing across the fields would make them more conspicuous that going by road.

A little while later, after exchanging hugs and warmly thanking Sabina and Bartek for their kindness, we set off in the dark with Nowak towards the village along overgrown footpaths, keeping close to hedgerows, It was about two kilometres' hike. We eventually arrived at Fr. Janowicz's presbytery, a somewhat dark and austere abode, but in stark contrast to his personality.

We could not have been made more welcome, even before Nowak had explained our circumstances. We were to discover he was the same to everyone, rarely judgemental, except for some reticence in dealing with the authorities. He was younger than I had anticipated, in his mid-forties, abundant jet black hair, bushy eyebrows and of a sunny disposition. He put me in mind of the bishop in *Les Miserables* who gave sanctuary to Jean Valjean, whilst still in his unreformed state.

Gillian explained to him that Dr Adamik would be in touch about Jack. He decided he would pre-empt any communication from the doctor, and promptly walked round to his surgery, which happened to be only a few doors away. He invited us to help ourselves to coffee, fruit juice or vodka while he was away. We chose vodka in the hope that it might perk us up, as we were both dog tired.

As we sipped, we glanced at various photos and pictures hung about the room, including a number of drawings and paintings by children, usually of farm produce and animals, and one of a haystack overlooked by a smiling sun, but strangely there were none of tractors which British children loved to portray.

Gillian picked up a breviary, the title of which she translated as *Liturgy of the Hours.* She thumbed through it for a while, then put it back where she had found it, open on the same page. There was much I wanted to ask her, but felt too tired to do so. I reckoned it would best keep until we were both rested, besides which I noticed she was beginning to shiver, I guessed with anxiety rather than feeling cold, as it was still quite balmy from a warm early summer's afternoon. A clock in another room softly chimed eleven.

Fr Janowicz returned after about half an hour. He said that Jack had been taken to one of his parishioners who was a nurse, and if any questions were asked of her by unwelcome officials, she would say that Jack was her elderly father, who was passing through his final days in this world. He was in reality a great deal better, largely cognisant, and beginning to accept sustenance. Janusz, as the priest insisted we should address him, explained that he had also visited his friend Szymon, the Lutheran pastor in the village, to confer between them how they would help us.

He noticed the vodka, and congratulated us on our wise choice. He then sensitively invited us into the church to pray with him for guidance through our difficulties. It was at this point Gillian and I discovered that we were both Catholic, although I wondered considering her Polish origins. When Janusz was informed, his smile widened for moment.

The church was illuminated only by the sanctuary lamp and three candles in front of a statue of Our Lady. The smell of burning candles and the faint aroma of incense filled me with a sense of God's perpetual closeness and presence. Gillian had some change from the taxi, which she placed in the candle box. The clatter of the coins finding their resting place rang throughout the building and startled Janusz, who had started to pray in silence.

We settled together in a pew, and also prayed in silence. After a few minutes, Janusz began to pray in a loud whisper while Gillian translated for me. "Almighty Father, we come before you and ask for your grace and blessing, and the guidance and protection of your Holy Spirit, throughout this night and the coming day, in the name of your son, our Lord and Saviour Jesus Christ. Amen" Janusz and Gillian then recited the Lord's Prayer and Hail Mary in Polish, while I did so in English.

We returned without a word to the presbytery. Over a cup of coffee, Janusz spoke of the conversation he had had with the Rev. Szymon. The following day they would use their respective networks to find in their midst, their fishermen contacts, who might be persuaded to take us across to the Danish territory of Bornholm as soon as possible, hopefully in the evening of the next day. It would be a risky journey of about one hundred and forty kilometres and would take roughly seven hours. In the meantime the two reverend gentlemen had agreed it would make sense if we were split up, as in the event of one of us being caught, there would be a chance of two of us remaining free. In view of the fact Pastor Szymon lived with a wife and children, it might be more appropriate if Gillian stayed overnight with them, and I remained with Janusz, who knew a little English. We were sure we would get along.

After escorting Gillian to Szymon's manse and his return to the presbytery, Janusz showed me into a small bedroom, which in addition to the bed, was simply furnished with a chest of drawers, a wooden bedside lamp carved curiously in the shape of a wellington boot, and a crucifix hanging over the bedhead. After some brief prayers with which to wrap up the long day, I crashed out and slept without interruption for around five hours.

Chapter 23

The new day began when I awoke as a clock downstairs struck five in the morning. Fr Janusz was already up and speaking on the telephone. I hoped it was not about us in case the line was being tapped. Momentarily, I reflected on and in the cold light of day, wondered if we had been right to be so eager to trust him. What if the phone call was to the authorities arranging for our arrest? However, that would not have made any sense. Janusz would have turned us in on our arrival. Besides which, I was totally in his hands and had no alternative but to put my faith in him completely. After all, I had nothing to lose, but everything to gain. A spirit of hope and optimism would give us all strength to get through what promised to be a very difficult day.

Janusz reassured me that the call, in case I felt alarmed, was to his mother who lived in the village, to check she was all right, and would she like him to collect her for daily Mass at six a.m. She had declined, which was just as well, as she might have been put in a difficult position had she been interrogated later in the day. Nevertheless, he invited me to join him. The Mass would be said in Latin, so I should be able to follow it. In a rash moment I asked if I could serve, as I used to be an altar boy in my youth, and could still remember most of the Latin responses. I was then concerned that my eagerness had overtaken my common sense. The congregation might be suspicious. He told me not to worry. There would be only a handful of very elderly villagers, and they were quite used to visiting clergy serving at the early Mass. There was no need to fear they might engage me in conversation afterwards, as they always trotted off quickly with no more than a nod and a smile at the priest and his visitors. It could not be more different from the warmth of our Methodist friends at Buckingham, but then it would be unusual for them to hold a weekday service, especially at six a.m. There was no cause to pass any judgement whatsoever.

After Mass and communion, we sat for almost an hour at breakfast swapping life stories and our respective upbringings. There were some amazing similarities. Such was the universality of the Catholic Church with all its virtues and failings. We both shared a deep respect for the then current Pope. Janusz's English proved to be very adequate. I asked how so. He loved languages at school, and made it his business to be reasonably fluent in Latin of course, but also in Russian, French and English.

At nine a.m. he tried calling the British Embassy in Warsaw, but could not get beyond an answerphone. He had the same result from several attempts over the next hour, and so we both concluded that was not going to be an effective avenue open to us, besides which enough time had been wasted, and there was much to do.

The clothes Sabina had given me were ideal. They fitted well. Luckily my height and build were very average.

The Rev. Szymon called round to say he had thought of a number of connections, identified a couple of fishermen with boats who were prepared to make the trip to Bornholm, one of whom was a Danish speaker, but they both had warned they had spotted a number of boats they had not seen before, patrolling up and down the coast. The Danish speaker had received a visit from the police who reminded him of his duty to report any approaches he received for smuggling people out of Poland, although they gave no indication of whom they had in mind.

Szymon, an older man than Janusz, was I had been told, a keen cyclist and very fit for his age. Unless he had passengers to ferry, he cycled to all his local appointments, except this one which was just across the road. In fact I had seen Gillian at the window of Szymon's manse, but resisted the temptation to wave. Szymon picked up a newspaper on Janusz's kitchen table, and pointed to an article attached to a photo of a very sad looking trawler in Gdansk docks. Janusz looked at it and translated it for me. It was fairly brief, but said three British spies had infiltrated the boat, had inveigled and manipulated the loyal Polish fishermen working on a friendly Russian trawler into committing mutinous acts during a violent storm, whilst legitimately fishing off the Faroe Islands. There was no speculation or mention as to how we were supposed to have made our way onto the boat. Both clergymen agreed that it would be all but the most gullible or inveterate Soviet-minded who would believe the article had much truth to it, but there may be quite a few, especially working for the authorities who would accept we were Western agitators; hence <u>our</u> need for extreme caution.

Szymon suggested the two of them drive over in Janusz's car, (his own had a flat battery and other problems), to see the Danish speaker first, and the other fisherman if it was felt necessary afterwards. It was gratifying to know we had a choice. In the meantime, I should lie low, and not answer the door to the presbytery or the telephone on any account. Janusz's housekeeper was expected to call round, but she would let herself in. He had already warned her I was in the house, but would she not mention it to anyone. If I were bored, there were some books in English in his study, and I was very welcome to help myself to them.

Szymon informed me that Gillian was in his wife's care and playing the role of his wife's niece. They were getting on "like a burning house". I smiled warmly.

I took up Janusz's invitation and ferreted among the books in his library and was surprised to find "Risk", a Dick Francis novel. However, it was a French translation.

Although my French was now very rusty, I was reasonably familiar with the story, and thought it would be good exercise for the brain to follow it in the French version.

Once or twice, I paused and wondered if I dare risk popping across the road to see Gillian, then considered how reckless that would be, and would display a flagrant disregard for all the brave efforts which were being made on our behalf. Nevertheless, the temptation was strong.

Eventually, I tired of reading the French which proved more difficult than it ought. It was probably due more to exhaustion and anxiety. I found a book on British history written in English, but by a Polish author. It was fascinating, clearly written from a Polish perspective of the British. We came across as a race who went our own way, oblivious of the Europe on our doorstep, which was a bit rich, since we declared war on Germany in 1939, supposedly because the Nazis had invaded Poland. The book had been written before our entry into the Common Market, so that impression may have changed since then, perhaps. At times it seemed as a nation our heart was not in the spirit of the Union, despite the result of a referendum not long after our entry. Perhaps it was just a matter of it taking time to adjust. Ten years after all was not a long enough period for the accumulation of the dust of centuries to be brushed aside, and the stubbornness against facing change embodied in such phrases as *'if it aint broke, why mend it?'*

Our clergymen friends reappeared around one o'clock lunchtime. The basic arrangements had been made. We would be ferried across to Borholm after dark that evening by the fisherman, Piotr Gasiorowski, who could speak Danish, but Jack, Gillian and I would be taken to the boat at different times from our separate locations well before the boat's departure. Piotr would collect me in his van from the presbytery at 6 p.m. and his two mates would independently collect Gillian at 7:30 and Jack at 8:30, those times being much in keeping with the routine they followed when fishing through the night. Piotr liked to allow about three hours for essential housekeeping and checks, and loading provisions and gear before setting out.

It transpired that Piotr and Janusz knew each other from years ago as they had been brought up in the area and had been at school together. They had been quite some time away in making the arrangements because of the reminiscing between the two of them. I thought to myself that if nothing else, this exercise had at least brought two old friends together again.

The time dragged between then and 6p.m. when Piotr arrived at the presbytery exactly on time. Before we left for the boat, with Janusz's help, we ran through all the instructions for me to follow, as although Piotr knew Danish, he had no English apart from the odd word he had picked up from the subtitles of American films he had seen, mainly Westerns or musicals. He made me put on a boiler suit/ overall, and then rub dirty grease into my hands. He wrapped a plaster around my thumb and rubbed grime into that as well. The final touch was to wipe a few smudges of it on my face. In the event of any unwelcome visitors, I was to pretend to be busy in the engine room compartment. There were some spanners I could use, but at all costs I was to remember anything I loosened with them, so that Piotr could double check afterwards that everything was properly tightened and shipshape. Unwanted curiosity was highly likely as boat patrols had been up and down the coast all day, but Piotr had been familiarising himself with their course and timing, and had worked out the exact moment for us to set sail. Nevertheless, he would still need to monitor the patrols for any variation in their pattern.

Szymon was particularly keen to cycle down to the quay once we were all on board to bless our venture and bid us farewell. He would ride back once we had disappeared into the black beyond, and confirm our departure with Janusz.

Piotr had arranged for one his mates to take his own boat out and anchor five kilometres offshore. In the event of undue attention on us by a patrol boat, Piotr would make a prearranged signal to his mate with the spotlight attached to our boat, and the mate would send up a flare to distract the patrol. Hopefully, it would allow Piotr time to disgorge his passengers on shore for us to hide in a nearby boathouse. If we had already set sail, it was hoped that the patrol boat would change course for the decoy friend.

All went to plan. There had been no interference from the patrol boats, and at just after 8:45, the second of Piotr's crew arrived with Jack. He was still very frail, but his mental state was stable, and he managed the odd quip or so as he was helped aboard the boat. I carried his holdall to the boat and asked him if his insulin was inside. As he did not know, I checked, but it was not there. It had clearly been left at the nurse's house where he had been staying. The van in which he had been brought to the boat, was searched in case Jack had dropped the medication, but there was no joy there. Krzysztof, the crew member jumped in his van and sped off to the nurse's house to retrieve it. There was no way we would risk Jack's health again without it.

The latest time we could set sail by Piotr's reckoning was 9:45pm. The tide was going out, and 20 minutes after that our way would be blocked by sand banks at the entrance to the tiny harbour. The other problem would be that a patrol boat was due to pass by at 10:00, so we really had to be under way fifteen minutes at least beforehand. By 10:05 we would be trapped by the sand banks, therefore timing was all of the essence.

The journey back to the village was just over three kilometres. It would take Krzysztof in his van about five or six minutes to get there as the lane was narrow, twisty and rough. He had gone about five minutes, when the Rev. Szymon arrived at the jetty on his bike. He said he had just encountered the van rushing along in the opposite direction and guessed there was a problem. He waited for a few minutes while it was explained to him, and then set off at 9:05 on his bike back to the village to find out where Krzysztof had got to.

Everyone's patience began to wear thin as anxiety levels rose. We were elated when Krzysztof's van reappeared and skidded to a halt on the gravel of the harbour parking area. However, even greater panic took hold when he informed us that he did not have the insulin. He explained that when he had arrived at the nurse's house, a police car was parked outside. He sat waiting nearby in his van for the car to go, but there seemed to be no sign of that happening. Then Szymon arrived on his bike and saw the problem. He told Krzysztof to return to the quayside and explain the delay. Meanwhile, he would call on the nurse, police car or not, and ask for the insulin. If the policeman seemed puzzled in any way, he would simply say it was for his wife, and hoped the nurse would understand the subterfuge.

All <u>we</u> could do was wait for Szymon. I made a mental calculation that it would take him about eight minutes to cycle back from the village. I glanced at my watch. It was 9:35. Szymon's blessing would have to be extremely brief. At 9:45 the light from a cycle lamp was seen wriggling in the darkness towards us at great speed, and once more our spirits were lifted, this time not in vain. He threw his bike to the ground and came running along the quay in great excitement with the medication held aloft. The man was completely out of breath, and must have used every ounce of strength. We each gave him a pat on the back as he reached us. He just had time to say that at first they could not find the insulin, and the policeman even joined in the search and it was he who found it in the bathroom. He was puzzled why Szymon's wife's insulin was in there, but thankfully did not pry any deeper.

The boat's engine had been running since before Szymon's return. He said a hurried prayer, but gave a heartfelt blessing as the boat was released from its mooring, and its engine revved to full power. As we left the harbour entrance, we heard a loud grating noise. The boat slowed dramatically while the engine almost stalled, but then sprung back to life again as we regained our speed. The little harbour badly needed dredging, but the small fishing community were struggling for funds to pay for it.

Ten minutes later our worst fears of what seemed the inevitable materialised. The two or three minutes delay in our departure looked as if it had cost us the success we had hoped for in our escape. Racing towards on our port side was a patrol boat gaining on us at alarming speed. Then, far off to our rear on the starboard side a flare rose high in the sky, illuminating the sea like a lightening flash, only lingering much longer. The patrol boat immediately changed course and headed off behind us, its lights completely consumed by the darkness after six or seven minutes. The decoy had worked.

We all caught our breath and settled down, and dared to hope that we had overcome the last major obstacle to freedom. Somehow, although we had a long journey ahead of us, we hardly minded what the sea might throw at us. The sea was moderately calm, which helped placate our anxiety on that score.

As we ploughed on westward I reflected on the fact that it was then two days since we last passed through these same waters, going in the opposite direction, with no discernible prospect of being free again.

The fishing boat we were travelling in was not dissimilar to the one which had taken me out from the Cornish coast to the trawler. Then we were also heading west. I shuddered at the thought of all the fears and what had actually happened in between.

Chapter 24

We were confined to a small cabin, but this time the three of us were together, homeward bound. Jack was sound asleep, Gillian just staring motionless, apart from the rocking of the boat, towards the wheelhouse. She was deep in thought with fixed expression, hurting, the hurt of unspeakable violation to her body and mind. My earlier plans to catch up with other's stories seemed inappropriate at that moment. *Let our minds catch up and cope with our own experiences first*, I mused. Mine were as nothing compared with hers and Jack's. What was it all for? What <u>was</u> it for?

I moved closer on the bench to Gillian and tentatively put my arm around her shoulders. There was an initial quiver from her, and then she wrapped her arms around my waist and buried her face into my chest, and wept quietly, her upper body shaking in defiance of the composure she was desperately trying to maintain. Krzysztof came through from the wheelhouse en route to the engine compartment. He crouched down before us and asked Gillian in Polish if we wanted a drink, I presumed. I shook my head, but her voice muffled by my clothing, requested coffee in English. Nevertheless, Krzysztof understood. When the drink arrived, she slowly unwrapped herself from my arms as she accepted the steaming tin mug. "Sorry about that Geoff", she whispered.

"Not at all! I needed it as well".

Gillian spent the best part of the rest of the journey leaning forward on the bench, her elbows on her knees, holding the mug in both hands, and staring at the floor in complete silence.

I moved up to the wheelhouse and stood staring out to sea. It was as smooth as glass reflecting a perfect image of the moon, held in a crystal clear unpolluted sky, and a panoply of seemingly highly polished stars, outshone by an occasional planet. The boat's wake cut a glistening silvery furrow through an otherwise undisturbed sea. What a contrast to the state of our emotions over the last few days, the comforting hand of our creator waving his blessing over our troubled lives.

Every so often we could see the distant lights of passing ships, posing no threat but offering a kind of reassurance there was a normality of a purpose without malevolence, which we now could again hope be a part of.

Just before the night began to give way to the first glow on the starboard side of the coming day, there could be seen static strings of far off lights on the horizon before us, signalling our approaching landfall. A chart was produced and pinned up on a board. Piotr beckoned and showed me where they were heading for; a small harbour near a place called Snogebaek on the east coast of Bornholm. I called Gillian up to the wheelhouse as an interpreter was required. There were a number of questions we needed answers to. Was Piotr familiar with the area of disembarkation? The answer was no. Had he made contact with anyone on the island, and if not, was there anyone he knew? Again the answer was negative. Had he intended accompanying us until some sort of contact was made? He would initially as he was aware none of us spoke any Danish, but he would have to be setting back within an hour to allow some time for fishing. He did not relish the thought of being intercepted by one of the Polish patrol boats, without some justification for the trip. The last thing he wanted was any entanglement with any authorities, be they Polish or Danish, or come to that, Russian.

Gillian was showing obvious disappointment, and insisted Piotr took a look at Jack as he was our main concern in getting help as quickly as possible once we were ashore. The ability to communicate would be key to this. Jack was gently woken. Apart from understandably feeling 'a bit groggy', he appeared at that moment to be reasonably compos mentis, and accepted a mug of strong black coffee. Whether this was the right thing for him or not we had no idea. Gillian helped him with his injection which was due. We persuaded him to walk up and down to check his balance. It was not the best, but we were on a boat after all, so the validity of the test was inconclusive. We had to accept that it was not going to be easy.

It was just touching six when we entered the harbour. Snogebaek proved to be a small fishing village. At first there were no free moorings, but we spotted one boat preparing to leave. We waited patiently a few yards off shore with the boat's engine ticking over in neutral. Despite the early hour, there was a moderate amount of activity among the fishing vessels, as we moved in to take the place of the first boat to move out, but some locals sauntered over to us waving arms as they approached, which suggested we should not be there. Piotr on whom we were relying completely for communication had some difficulty in understanding them as they seemed to be speaking something other than Danish. In the end he picked up enough words to realise that the mooring was private and not available to visitors. Some of the words were not as polite as that, but he got the general drift. He explained to them in simple terms as possible why we had arrived. And they appeared to be appeased, as long as it was a very short stay. However, there was nothing they could do for us, or more likely wished to, probably suspecting that we were illegal immigrants, which I suppose we were of sorts.

We must have appeared a motley bunch as we alighted from the boat and made our way along the quay, the three of us and Piotr. Jack looked for all the world like a drunk. We were very much aware that without Piotr's help, we would be regarded as inebriated British holiday makers, attracting very little sympathy.

Snogebaek would have had little in the way of facilities which would help us, especially at that time of the morning.

Piotr tried to find a café or somewhere open. But progress with us in tow was painfully slow. Having found a bench to sit on, we agreed that he would go off and scout for something open or of help, while we sat and stared in silence at the sea and distant horizon. Eventually he returned and reported that he had found a lady, who happened to be a town councillor, walking her dog. She would take the dog home, and then come and find us and see what she could sort out for us.

The lady councillor, a middle-aged no nonsense kind of woman, approached a few minutes later accompanied by two policemen. A police car also appeared on the scene after a moment or two. I expected them to be friendly, but they were not exactly bubbling over with delight. They unceremoniously bundled us into the car, while Piotr stood helplessly on the pavement, imploring the councillor to explain to the police we were in need of help, not arrest. He said in Polish to Gillian he had done all he could. His Danish had not been as good as he thought it was. It was important for him now to leave us, but he felt any misunderstanding would soon be resolved and that the police would realise we were not vagrants, criminals or intoxicated penniless Brits, although it was true that we were without any Danish currency. All we could do was hope that he was right.

Our best hope was that at the police station, always assuming that was where we were being taken, there would be someone who spoke English or even Polish.

A police station was indeed our destination. We were at first thoroughly searched, the only time anyone had thought to do so in all the time since I had been captured. The police sergeant found my Dictaphone very suspicious, but paid little attention to our other meagre possessions. Even the penknife aroused no interest. Gillian had absolutely nothing except a comb, and Jack had his insulin, the only item which for a moment slightly modified the brusque treatment we were getting.

The councillor reappeared and there followed some earnest discussion between her and the sergeant. I gained the impression that she was pleading our cause but he was having none of it. Whatever she said, it seemed that he was determined to lock us out of harm's way in the police cell. To be fair, they brought us mugs of decent coffee and pastries. Our delight was obvious – no language barriers there! Nothing happened for another couple of hours until we were taken into an interview room where a suited gentleman sat across from us at a table, while a policeman stood guard by the door.

The gentleman spoke to us in Danish, but it was of course beyond our comprehension. The one word which Gillian and I locked onto was one that sounded like 'advocate'. We concluded that he was a duty solicitor. It seemed he wanted to help us, but English, Polish and mine and Gillian's school French were beyond him. He held out his arms and hands, and shrugged his shoulders in despair.

We were then led to a police car in the yard behind the building, probably the same car we had been in before. We set off eastwards. We assumed we were being taken to a larger town where there would be the facilities to deal with us, including interpreters. However, as we approached the quay where we had come ashore, we noticed Piotr's boat was still there with a group of police apparently standing guard over it. The car came to a halt at the entrance to the quay, and we were shunted along to the boat and hustled inside it.

Piotr was protesting, and told Gillian the boat had been detained until we were back on board, and now he had strict instructions to return to where we had come from, or at least out of Danish waters. We felt as if we were back at square one. Piotr was ordered to set sail and not return to Bornholm, although all the duress was strictly verbal, not physical.

By this time Gillian was in tears, those of utter despair and exhaustion. I was in a filthy temper. She and to some extent, I felt Piotr should have been much more persuasive about our plight, but it was difficult for me to comment, as I had no knowledge of what he had said to the councillor or the police.

Once clear of the harbour, Piotr brought the boat to a near standstill while we all allowed ourselves to calm down, and gather our thoughts. Gillian and I had a three way conversation with Piotr, and suggested we try again at landing on Bornholm, perhaps at a port of some size if we could find one. Piotr was anxious to return to Poland even if it entailed bluffing his way with us on board past any patrol boats, but after much persuading, he agreed to allow one hour to find somewhere to dock on the south coast of the island. Surely, I suggested to Gillian, the charts he had in the wheelhouse would be of some help. We could not understand his reluctance to produce them, but eventually he did so, albeit with less than good grace. Perhaps he was ashamed of the antiquity of them, dating back to the early part of the twentieth century. I noticed they were German. Possibly he had stolen them in the long and distant past.

Nevertheless, Gillian put him through the third degree about his disinterest in the charts, and it emerged that he did not wish to get tangled up with the Danish authorities in any way, as he would later have to explain himself to those in Poland, where there was the risk of his landing up in prison and his assets, including the boat, confiscated. We were perhaps being a bit selfish, although understandable given our circumstances. Even his actions so far could lead to long term consequences for him and his family. It was time to show him and his crew at least a modicum of gratitude. I offered to make a round of hot drinks for us all, which was gladly accepted.

We found from a map that the main town on Bornholm appeared to be Ronne to the west, about twenty miles away. To help Piotr out of his predicament, we suggested that he dropped us off where ever he could and set sail for Poland before anyone had a chance to take in what had happened. We would avoid giving anyone specific information about him, his crew and the boat. If it ever came out that he was involved in any way, we would admit that we had forced him at gun point with a weapon we had stolen from a farmhouse, and disposed of it in the sea after he had dropped us off.

It seemed our attempts at freedom were dogged by obstacles all the way, but nevertheless so far overcome by timely good fortune.

The shore line around Ronne was rocky and much of it made up of reclaimed land. At first it seemed we were spoilt for choice as there were a number of small constructed inlets either side of a large busy enclosed harbour accommodating boats from small yachts up to sizeable ferries. We needed somewhere which was quiet and not enclosed, as a quick getaway was essential for Piotr. At length we found a quayside about a mile beyond the town, with a few yachts and fishing boats not too dissimilar to Piotr's, close to a church.

We had the uncomfortable feeling that the police over the last hour had been following us along the coast, as here and there the coastal road could be seen from the sea. Now and again we had spotted a police car; too often for it to have been a coincidence. We guessed they were determined not to allow us to make landfall.

However, we had not seen them for a while. Piotr picked his spot; not the best, but time was running out for him. He explained that he would come alongside the mooring he was heading for, but not tie up. The top of the gunwales were at about ground level. We were to jump off as soon as we were close enough. He would then pull away at full speed. He had draped a blanket over the stern to cover the boat's registration details painted on its hull, but it was flapping in the breeze and draught created by the momentum. It did not seem very effective to me, but then desperate measures are necessary in desperate times, and any little thing can help.

In the event, at the moment we were instructed by Piotr to jump, although the boat was so close at times bumping the quay, it was still slightly in motion. Gillian and I held Jack between us as we leapt, but it proved to be a foolhardy move and clumsily and dangerously executed, all to save Piotr a few seconds. Jack's feet were insufficiently elevated to mount the quay, and he slammed into its side, and dropped into the water between the boat and the quay, dragging Gillian in with him. I lost my grip on Jack, but just made it onto the quay, fighting to maintain balance as I teetered on the edge, my right leg still in a great deal of pain.

The boat had fled in seconds and was already forty yards off shore and heading away from us with its engine at full revs. No one was looking behind. All I could see was the back of their heads. There was no chance of them helping us now.

Gillian proved to be a strong swimmer and managed to keep Jack's head above water. I reached down to grab him, but the quay surface was too high above the water line. How stupid we had been not to have donned lifebelts, but there was no time for self-recrimination. I signalled to Gillian to make for a dinghy moored nearby, but she was quickly running out of strength, not helped by the fact that both she and Jack were fully clothed. I wanted to jump in to help, but I had never learned to swim properly, and the likelihood was that Gillian would have to save two of us from drowning. I jumped down into the dinghy, and immediately realised that climbing into a dinghy from the sea would tip it over.

We worked out that if Gillian could bring Jack alongside the boat, I would hold on to him while he treaded water, and she would swim around to the other side of the boat and climb in and provide the counter-balance as I hauled Jack over the side and into the dinghy. Gillian found that clambering into the boat was easier said than done, but after several attempts she made it in very ungainly fashion, rocking the boat violently, making it difficult to maintain my hold on Jack.

However, try as I might, Jack was a dead weight made heaver by his waterlogged clothing, and I had not the strength to lift him into the boat. It was no good Gillian inching across to help as it was obvious the boat would tip and water would rush over the gunwales.

We then realised that forty yards away the moorings came to an end, and beyond was the natural rocky shore. Using the mooring rope, Gillian climbed up onto the quay, unfastened the ropes from the mooring posts, and dragged the dinghy backwards to where the moorings were replaced by the natural shoreline. We were surprised how deep the water was when Gillian attempted to wade around the stern. As Jack and I were towards that end of the dinghy, Gillian and I reckoned that if she could swivel the back end around so that we were on the shore side, between us we should be able to haul Jack up on to the rocks.

It proved to be much more difficult than we expected, but after using every ounce of strength, we eventually succeeded, but by then Jack was in a very bad way. Poor Jack! It seemed his body had taken just about all it could, and to make matters worse, the precious insulin had been lost.

Chapter 25

Within moments a small cluster of residents from the houses opposite the quay had huddled around us, one lady in particular trying her best to communicate with Jack. He gave all the appearance of having drowned. Someone had phoned for an ambulance, which arrived in minutes, but not before the residents had brought piles of blankets and towels and wrapped them around the three of us, as Gillian and I shivered uncontrollably. They spoke to us incessantly, but of course, we could only answer in English or in Gillian's case, a bit of Polish. However, we could not make ourselves understood, nor could we understand them, except through a very limited amount of sign language.

Jack was carried into the ambulance, while we as walking wounded were urged to join him. On the way to the hospital, Jack was given oxygen, and periodically encouraged to expel any seawater he had taken in. One successful morsel of communication was the need for insulin. For now, our main hope was that Jack was in good hands, and his survival was back on the cards. Our next priority was to be able to make ourselves understood.

Our arrival at a hospital was joined by a bevy of police officers, eager no doubt to discover who we were and the circumstances leading to our drenching. We had the feeling that they and all concerned were under the impression we had dived into the sea to save a drowning man, as they appeared to be expressing gratitude towards us. The one thing they had realised by now was that we were English.

Once inside the hospital, Gillian and I were ushered into a treatment room, while Jack was wheeled off for more intensive care.

We were seen by a doctor who could speak English. His priority was to get us out of our wet things into something temporary and dry. We would have the opportunity of a shower later and some fresh clothing from somewhere, as yet to be determined, but for the moment a hospital gown and an over-blanket would suffice.

We were medically examined and my knee re-dressed, and then invited to explain how we came by our injuries. Mine was simple – I had stumbled getting out of the back of a car but Gillian's account was more problematical without revealing much more than we felt we should. She said she was beaten up but didn't wish to go into detail, except with the proper authorities. The doctor accepted this, and said that the police were setting up an interview and interpreter at the nearby police headquarters. Nevertheless, he for medical reasons wanted to know what had happened to Jack to find himself in need of rescuing from the sea.

We admitted that we had been travelling together, but had become embroiled with some very unpleasant people, and after a complicated story, had finished up in the sea. Jack had been particularly roughly treated, his condition compounded by his diabetes. He had been unwell for several days. The doctor asked, "Apart from the diabetes, are you aware of any other illnesses, etc Jack suffered from?" We were not.

Apart from what was obvious, we were given a clean bill of health, but could expect some repercussions from the trauma of our experiences, but Jack was likely to need some overnight observation in the hospital.

Some reasonably suitable clothing for us was rustled up from a hospital charity's storeroom, and after enquiry on my part, I was reassured that the good people who had lent us blankets and towels would have them returned to them washed and dried.

Gillian and I were then whisked off to police headquarters for more comprehensive questioning.

The interview got off on the wrong foot as far as we were concerned. It began by us being accused of illegal immigration from Poland. Where were our papers and passports? Police in another part of the island had turned us away in the early morning, and yet we returned to have another go at landing, this time at Ronne. What proof did we have we were not Poles who had learned to speak English well? The interpreter was local and was unable to confirm that we spoke English without any trace of a foreign accent.

We tried to explain that we were victims of an abduction from Britain, but it seemed our interrogator had a fixed agenda and was not going to be side-tracked from it. Our most serious crime was not to have passports or papers of any sort. We suggested he must be aware of reports of a stricken Russian trawler which had sailed through Danish waters the previous weekend, but he waved his hand dismissively.

Exasperated, Gillian and I agreed we would no longer co-operate with him if he continued to show no interest in what we had to say about the events of the last ten days. We concluded all we could do was to insist that we were put in touch with the British Embassy in Copenhagen.

At first, he resisted entertaining compliance with the request, but then appeared to gain confidence in the notion that the British would also regard our protestations as far-fetched, and have nothing to do with us, and thus justify his determination to have us 'repatriated' to Poland.

We on the other hand, were equally confident that the Brits would not let us down.

The policeman eventually got through to an official at the Embassy and told him he was holding suspected illegal immigrants who claimed to be British. The initial response was that these persons should call at the Embassy for some forms to be completed. Alternatively, they should provide an address to which the forms could be sent for completion and return.

I got up from the chair and angrily walked around the desk where the policeman was sitting and shouted, (hoping that the person on the other end of the phone would hear), that we had been abducted from Hampshire and Buckinghamshire without our passports by Russian criminals last week, but had managed to escape. We were now stranded in Bornholm without money and papers, and were desperately in need of the Embassy's help immediately.

The official suggested to the policeman that perhaps he should put me on properly so that I could speak to him directly. The policeman after some hesitation reluctantly handed the receiver to me.

I explained that there were three of us, one of whom was seriously ill in hospital. If he (the official) cared to contact the authorities in Britain, I was certain he would discover that we would have been reported as missing persons. I gave him our names and he agreed to make some enquiries and call back.

After he had hung up, the policeman told us he could not sit around waiting indefinitely until the Embassy rang back, and said he had no choice but to detain us in a holding room. Someone would let us know if and when the Embassy called.

Several hours passed while we waited. During that time we were treated well by the staff of the police headquarters, who plied us with plenty of coffee, tea and pastries and even a glass of larger. We asked for news of Jack, but none was forthcoming.

Eventually, well into the evening, a policewoman beckoned us into an interview room, and signalled to us to pick up a telephone receiver on a table in the middle of the room. Apart from this and three uncomfortable looking chairs, the room was completely devoid of any furniture, and without windows, except for what looked like a large mirror but I suspected it was of one-way glass enabling the room to be seen into from the outside, but not vice versa.

Gillian and I huddled round the telephone receiver (there was no speaker facility), as we spoke to a lady from the British Embassy in Copenhagen.

"I am Madelaine Macintosh from the Security Services at the Embassy. Before we go any further, would you confirm you are on your own? Simply answer 'Yes' or 'No', please.

"Yes", we both replied.

"Good. I would rather you did not discuss our conversation with anyone, even family, and avoid as far as possible providing the police or any other authorities with information about your experiences over the last week. In the meantime, I am arranging transport to bring you here as soon as possible. I have already spoken to the police commander where you are, and he has agreed to release you to a Laurence Bonham when he arrives in approximately two hours' time".

"Phew! What a relief!" exclaimed Gillian, while my own thoughts mulled over the possibility that this may be a trap. We had at least two hours to think about it.

Gillian asked Madelaine what arrangements if any had been made for Jack. "We are working on that. It very much depends on how well or otherwise he is" She then hung up.

Gillian and I debated my fears that we were about to be ensnared, but we rapidly came to the conclusion that it was highly improbable. Realistically, was there any other choice open to us?

I suggested that this would be the first opportunity for us to relate to one another each other's story during the past ten days or so, but Gillian felt it unwise in case the room we were in had listening devices. All would be revealed in due course.

At around 10 that evening, after attempts to sleep sitting up with our heads buried in our folded arms at the table, we were interrupted by a cheerful and jolly policewoman, who appeared equally excited as we were at our release into the care of Laurence Bonham, who accompanied us to a waiting taxi. We were whisked off to a local airfield, where a helicopter awaited us. The journey to Copenhagen was made in silence, mainly because, despite the noise of the helicopter's engine, we succeeded in what we had failed to achieve in the police station; sleep!

The flight of about 90 miles lasted less than an hour, but long enough for us to feel significantly more alert when we landed. An Embassy car took us from the airport to the Consulate, where we were greeted by Madelaine Mackintosh, who proved to be a very gracious and kindly lady. She had thoughtfully laid on a light meal, very welcome hot drinks and a glass of something stronger of our choosing to finish off with.

Much to our relief, she said there would be a debriefing mid-morning on the Friday which would allow us time to catch up on lost sleep, and hopefully help us to face the ordeal with fresh minds. Although our respective families had been given no information on what had happened to us, she confirmed that they had been reassured we were safe and well, which perhaps was a slightly rosier picture than the true state of our mental health and to some extent, our physical condition.

Chapter 26

At 7:30 on the Friday morning, Gillian and I enjoyed a hearty breakfast in true English fashion in the Embassy dining room of fried egg, bacon (had to be Danish), mushrooms and limitless offerings of toast and coffee. Neither of us had slept soundly, as our eagerness to recount our stories would not abate. It was as if our heads would not allow our bodies to rest until we had divested ourselves of the pent up emotions, resulting from keeping our own counsel during recent days, because there had been no-one we dare trust completely, the two clergymen, Tomasz and the Felinskis perhaps coming the closest. It had also been essential for us not to give into being swept away in a tide of despondency.

It was a bright sunny morning with only the merest hint of a chill in the air when we took the opportunity of a couple of hours free time before our debriefing, to wander among the blooms of an early Scandinavian summer in the Embassy grounds, the scents of blossoming flowering shrubs, covered in honey bees carrying swollen sacks of nectar, their humming chorus rising above the orchestra of city traffic, the percussion of distant hammering from a construction site, the clamour of refuse lorries accepting the detritus of a civilised way of life, accompanied by the shouts and whistles of the cohort of attendant bin men. After the fears and horrors of the last few days, it all combined to sound like heavenly music of freedom, extracting an overwhelming sense of relief from deep within our very being. A wisp of smoke from a nearby chimney seemed to symbolise the incense from an offering up of the whole experience of that moment in thankfulness to God.

We were warned that the debriefing was likely to be exacting and tough at times, as the handful of interrogators included a gentleman from MI6 in addition to Madelaine Mackintosh, two Embassy staff, immigration and Foreign Office officials, and note takers, although the interviews would also be tape-recorded. We should expect the proceedings to last at least until lunchtime.

Gillian asked when we were likely to be returning to the UK. We were told that it could be that day, but we were not to get our hopes too raised, as it depended on the outcome of the debriefing, and what security arrangements could be put in place in the time available.

I asked if there was any chance of speaking to my wife at this juncture. Although I was told that she had been 'reassured' we were safe, I knew Karen would be assured of nothing until I had spoken to her. There was some gentle resistance for security reasons, but finally reluctant consent was granted for a five minute call with the proviso that on no account was I to reveal where I was or give any details of the abduction at this stage.

It was a very poor connection making our conversation stilted and repetitive in struggling to verify that our words had been heard and understood. Nevertheless, she seemed to take comfort from the little I had managed to convey. A modicum of her sense of humour returned when I asked if she and the kids were okay and whether they were missing me, to which she replied, "May be".

I responded with, "I am desperately missing you too", but I thought that was lost in the crackle on the line.

"When are you likely to be back?" she asked.

"No promises whatsoever, but it could be this evening".

"Good, I'll put the kettle on then".

My five minutes were up.

Chapter 27

Up to that point Gillian and I had been very restrained, and still had not spoken to each other of our separate experiences up to the moment we had met on the Sunday afternoon in the midst of the confusion and medley of the crew, etc. in the smoke-filled hold of the trawler.

We were led into an oak-panelled boardroom without windows, but illuminated by a large central magnificent crystal chandelier, the room's crowning glory. The room was traditionally furnished, the main feature being an immense typical boardroom table, the surface luxuriously inlaid with marquetry and green leather inscribed with gold leaf, the leather and designs repeated in the chairs surrounding the table

Along one wall were a series of finely fashioned sideboards graced with objets d'art, except for one which was bedecked with ornate tea and coffee cups and saucers, sugar bowls with silver tongs, coffee and tea pots, cookies neatly arranged on serving plates, and various accoutrements promising lavish refreshment during the progress of the morning's inquisition.

While the 'players' entered by way of a choice of three doorways, I glanced at the paintings and photographs, one hung on almost every panel, illuminated by green shaded strip lamps. Apart from those of our present Queen and Winston Churchill, the only others which caught my attention were of Hans Christian Andersen, 1805 – 1875, presented by Margrethe II, Queen of Denmark, and a beautiful portrait of herself dating from 1980.

After introductions, the proceedings began with a series of questions aimed at formally confirming we were who we claimed to be. I noticed amongst the plethora of papers by now scattered across the table, were certified copies of photographs of Jack, Gillian and myself, presumably obtained overnight from family and acquaintances, which on the face of it seemed to render the lengthy questioning pertaining to our identities somewhat superfluous, but who were we to challenge long established procedures?

It was agreed among the questioners that Gillian be invited to tell her story first, as she had been abducted before me, and it would help 'if they were to receive the facts in chronological order'.

Before she started, I enquired into Jack's health, and we were informed that after a comfortable night he was very much improved and would be fit enough, God willing, to accompany us on our return journey to the UK. The plan was to bring him to the Embassy after lunch, and 'be processed, sorry debriefed', in much the same way as ourselves that morning.

Gillian began by asking me if it was in order for her to divulge details of the investigation work into the Rhodes businesses, which I agreed was highly relevant and essential background information. Her description of that part of her testimony was succinct, but to my mind sufficient for the moment. She continued, *"Twelve days ago, on the Monday, we, that's to say Jack and I, worked frantically to gather and put in order all the information for the meetings scheduled on the following day (Tuesday). It was a bit of a scramble as there was so much of it, but we just about managed. Our problem had been gaining access to the one Fax machine at the Waterlooville depot, as the office manager protested that it was necessary to keep it available for his own staff for constant communications with customers and suppliers. It was obvious to us that he was fed up with Jack's and my presence and our enquiries, and resentful of our use of his precious Fax machine, which admittedly I had monopolised that morning in getting a considerable amount of paperwork over to Geoffrey, which ideally he needed to see before the first meeting on Tuesday at Southsea, most of them being documents I had no permission to remove from the client's premises.*

In the afternoon I had phoned Companies House about a company we had come across in the course of our investigation. They called me back later that afternoon with what they referred to as interesting information, which they would fax over to me. I asked if they would refrain from doing so until after 5:30, as I really did not want the Rhodes staff seeing it. It was almost six o'clock before it come through. I hurriedly forwarded it on to Geoff as the information it contained was highly pertinent to our investigation. It was about the legal status of one of Rhodes' principal suppliers of material destined for the Ministry of Defence.

I think it was about 6:15 when I finally left. I decided I would head straight back to our Southsea office, and deposit all Jack's and my working papers including the Companies House fax, in a lockable filing cabinet in Gordon MacNeal's room, in view of their potential sensitivity. The Southsea office was still open at 7 o'clock when I arrived, as the office cleaners had not finished their work".

The MI6 man interjected at this point and asked Gillian what she had done with the key to the filing cabinet. Could it eventually have fallen into the hands of her abductors?

Gillian replied and continued, *"The system Gordon operated for the cabinet was that only he and one of the other partners had a key to it. When it was empty it was kept unlocked. It could be locked without a key by pressing in the keyhole button just above the top drawer, but obviously required a key to unlock it. When someone required access to retrieve their papers it meant that they would have to ask Gordon. The arrangement had its downsides, but had the benefit of being simple.*

After leaving the office, I stopped off to buy some fish and chips as I felt too exhausted to cook anything for that evening. Home is a ground floor maisonette in St Ronans Road, Southsea, where I live on my own. It is not far from the office – about ten minutes' drive.

While I was unlocking the front door I noticed a trodden in cigarette end by the doorstep which unnerved me a bit, but then dismissed it as having been left there probably by the postman or paperboy.

However, a greater sense of alarm struck me as I opened the door without the usual resistance from the newspaper and post piled up behind it. They were there, but already pushed to one side. The only other people with a key were my sister and the landlord's agent. I tried telephoning both, but got no reply from either; it was out of hours for the agents anyway.

I noticed a faint smell of tobacco, strong enough though not to be masked by the fish and chips. Neither my sister nor I are smokers, but then I considered that the landlord's agent might be. Perhaps it was he who had put out his cigarette on the doorstep, may be not realising or not caring that the smell would be on his clothing, which would linger inside for hours afterwards.

I thought little more of it as I settled in the kitchen to eat my fish and chips. Then I heard what sounded like a suppressed sneeze in my spare bedroom, but was too petrified to investigate.

Trying desperately to convince myself that I had imagined it, I nevertheless phoned my sister but there was no reply, then tried Jack's number as he lives only five minutes away, but he too was out. I left a message on his answerphone, which must have sounded garbled because of the rising panic taking hold of me.

No sooner had I put the receiver down when a strong arm gripped me from behind and pinned me to the back of the kitchen chair I was sitting on. A second person, a man, appeared in front of me as I began to scream for help. He tied a gag around my mouth. Then he menacingly produced a hypodermic syringe, tapped it and injected me with what must have been a strong anaesthetic of some sort, as I passed out immediately.

I later came to momentarily as I was being bundled into a fishing boat moored up in the Camber, that's a non-naval dock in Old Portsmouth. The next I remember was being in a cabin on board the Russian trawler, the one Geoff was brought to three days later."

Gillian was struggling with her speech and began to shake uncontrollably, unable to continue. Madelaine called the Embassy's resident nurse for help, while I wrapped an arm around her shoulder in the vain hope of calming her down. She began sweating, becoming very red in the face, and panting for breath. At one point she shouted, puce with anger, "How dare they have treated me the way they did? It was barbaric". She then broke down in tears.

The nurse encouraged her to take deep breaths and then release slowly. She kept this up interspersed with blowing into a paper bag, and thus breathing in the carbon dioxide from it. Gradually, she became more composed. The nurse prescribed sleeping tablets, and suggested that the interview should be suspended for a couple of hours, despite Gillian's insistence that she should continue.

It was agreed that we should have a break for refreshment, and then resume with my testimony instead, Gillian, if she was feeling up to it continuing after lunch, but before Jack's interview.

I began by giving some background to the reasons for our investigation at Rhodes, i.e. low achieving gross profit margins at Fareham. We had found some low-level fraud, and were beginning to make a breakthrough in finding an explanation for the apparent poor performance there. I had been partially briefed on the Monday morning on Gillian's and Jack's discoveries. The intention of the meeting at Southsea with them on the Tuesday morning was to go through all their notes and observations with them, and reach some conclusions for discussion with Donald Rhodes in the afternoon. Neither meeting of course took place due to Gillian and Jack's disappearance.

Unfortunately, Gillian's efforts in faxing the Companies House information to my office at Buckingham on the Monday evening had to some extent been thwarted. I was unaware she had done so. I imagined she had intended ringing me during that evening which would have given me the opportunity of collecting the fax then and thinking overnight about its implications and consequences, either that or collecting it early the following morning before leaving for Southsea.

I said to the MI6 man that our abductions were clearly connected with the contents of that fax, as the company concerned was Midland Counties Plaster & Lining Supplies Ltd, the one Oleg during the inquisition on the trawler was so keenly interested in. The MI6 man nodded slightly, which suggested he was not awarding me any Brownie points for stating the obvious.

By the time I had brought everyone up to date it was lunchtime. Despite the hearty breakfast, I could have eaten an ox. Gillian re-joined us, and the whole party ate with us. The conversation was about families, holidays and pastimes, studiously avoiding the topic of the morning. It was actually a relief, as it took our minds away for the first time from the ordeal of the last fortnight.

After lunch, Gillian, now very composed, told us of her horrendous treatment in the days leading up to encountering me on the Sunday. *"When I came to on the Tuesday, I found myself in a squalid windowless room or cell, dimly lit by a single lamp bolted to the ceiling. The room reeked of bad fish. I was lying on a metal bench, wrapped in a filthy blanket. The wall was badly stained with what I assumed was fish blood, and the floor was soaking wet. I later discovered that it was where they gutted fish used for consumption on the boat.*

It must have been for about an hour that I kept shouting, 'Is anybody there?' It was to no avail. Then the ship ran into heavy waters, which made me retch violently, but there was little to bring up, as I had had nothing to eat or drink since the fish, chips and Coke of the night before, and even then I had hardly touched them when I was interrupted.

I tried to arrange the smelly blanket as best I could to make it comfortable to sleep on the bench. There was a pile of hessian bags heaped next to a sink, the top ones of which were fairly dry. I used these to create a mattress and pillow. After a while I acclimatised myself to the smell and dampness of the room and the scratchiness of the improvised hessian pillow, and managed some sleep.

It must have been several hours later when I was awoken by voices outside the room. My stomach and head were aching because of my low blood sugar level. The door was unlocked by one of those thugs we saw last Monday morning, who beckoned me to follow him. I was led to the cabin next to the one you were in Geoff *when you arrived. Compared with where I had been for best part of a day, the new cabin seemed quite homely, and it had a porthole. I would now at least be able to know whether it was night time or day. It <u>was</u> night time.*

I should make it clear that up to that moment I had no idea where I was, or who was holding me. I had guessed Russians were involved as the occasional voice I had heard sounded Russian. Once in a while I caught some Polish being spoken, which had provided me with some minimal clues such as the vessel we were in was a trawler. I am a fluent speaker of Polish, by the way.

I asked the thug what was going on, and for something to eat and drink. He signalled that he did not know or perhaps want to know what I was saying. Instead he spat at me. I put my hand up to hit him, but he grabbed my wrist and threw me to the floor. He then went out of the cabin and slammed the door in my face. I tried the door, but of course it was locked.

No food or drink was forthcoming. I eventually fell asleep after feeling giddy through lack of nourishment. At some time in the middle of the night I was pulled off the bunk and made to stand up straight, while that nasty interrogator who confronted us on Monday morning…..," Gillian paused and looked towards me for confirmation that I understood whom she meant. I nodded and she continued, *"……paced in circles around me. He then stopped in front of me, staring into my eyes* in a most intimidating way, and told me in English that he hated the English. 'But you can nevertheless speak our language'. 'Don't be smart with me', he said.

He then proceeded to tell me he knew my name was Gillian and that I had been working with someone called Jack. We had been carrying out an investigation in the account books of Rhodes building supplies. I said nothing, but he shouted, 'I am correct, yes?' I continued to say nothing. He then kept asking me what we had found, but still I would not answer him. He became increasingly frustrated, grabbed my forearms and shook me violently, so much so that my face caught his shoulder and I passed out.

I must have been unconscious for a while. When I came round, I was again on my own, lying on the floor and soaking wet. It is my guess that water had been thrown over me in an abortive attempt to revive me. It was getting light, but I had no means of knowing the time as my watch must have been taken from me on the Monday night or I had dropped it whilst drugged. All I knew was that it was Wednesday morning.

A couple of hours or so passed before I again had my fears aroused by the rattle of a key in the door lock. This was when I met Vladimir for the first time. It transpired that he was to be my 'jailer' and provide a minimal amount of care you might say. He was not a bad sort, and certainly not a thug. However, he spoke no English and I no Russian, but we managed a certain rapport when he was accompanied by a bowl of warm milk and porridge, and a tin mug of metallic tasting water for me. After two days of nothing, even this was most welcome.

He left me for a few minutes while I drank and devoured the breakfast with the eagerness of a dog. When he returned, he tried to handcuff me, but when I resisted, he imitated the act of washing. I realised I had no choice but to trust him. This was the point where I warmed towards him. Someone at last showing a degree of humanity! He led me a short distance along the corridor outside the cabin to the latrines and shower room, which no doubt Geoff will have referred to in his account. My hand cuffs were removed, and I was allowed the freedom to use the loo, (by this time I was busting as gravity worked on the water I had just drunk), and was given some soap with which to wash, and a boiler suit and underwear to replace my smelly office clothes, now soiled because of the lack of access for so long to essential facilities. How these things can be an absolute luxury when you have been deprived of them for several days!

Vladimir had the decency to wait outside in the corridor until I knocked on the washroom door to signal I had finished. He also spared me the indignity of reapplying the handcuffs on the short journey back to my cabin, although he was duty bound to lock me in.

However, the improvement in my well-being was short-lived, as that evening the interrogator (whom the crew *referred to as Ivan) and his thug paid me another visit. He began by saying in a very hammed-up American gangster accent), "Tonight, you sing for your supper", and then laughed at his own twisted humour. He looked at the thug, as if to say, 'why aren't you laughing?' The thug responded with a loud laugh, so false it came across more as derision.*

'Tonight you will tell me what it was you were investigating at Rhodes. What did you find out?' Again I said nothing.

He repeated his questions more threateningly, but I was the more determined not to answer. The thug lit a cheroot. At first I thought it was to calm his nerves as the tension in the cell heightened, but then the full horror of the significance of his action became clear as Ivan pushed me on to a chair and held me tightly in it from behind. The thug approached me and pulled up part of the trousers of the boiler suit I was wearing, sucked on the cheroot until its end glowed brightly, then held it less than inch from the inside of my exposed leg. I screamed. The thug with his free hand hit me across the face.

My inclination was to wriggle, but then I realised that was what they expected, as in so doing I would catch my thigh on the tip of the cheroot. Instead, I made my whole body as rigid as possible. Ivan, still with his arms clamped round me, then shook the chair. The shock and excruciating pain from the burn of the tip of the cheroot forced such a piercing scream from me that it seemed to take them by surprise.

'Shut your mouth, you screaming cow, and answer my questions', he shouted ferociously in my ear. How I could be expected to do both simultaneously, I did not know.

All the commotion had drawn attention from elsewhere in the boat, as there were excited Polish voices outside the door, which incidentally was locked from the inside.

Ivan shouted through the door in Russian with words I assume meant, 'Go away', to put it mildly, but the calls from outside became more persistent. Finally, Ivan and his friend, unlocked the door, barged their way through the crowd which had gathered, and hurried away.

Vladimir appeared on the scene and persuaded the crewmen somehow to leave, which they did reluctantly, muttering that they suspected I had been subjected to torture, which they were not prepared to tolerate if it happened again. One of them said he would report the incident to the captain. I decided it was not yet the moment to reveal to anyone that I understood Polish, as I reckoned that I stood a better chance of finding out more of my circumstances from overheard, unguarded conversations of the crew.

I spent most of the Wednesday night awake because of a constant headache and the soreness of the burn to my leg which kept chaffing against my other.

On the Thursday morning when I arose from the bunk, I examined the burn which by now was much more painful and was showing signs of being infected. After breakfast, again brought to me by Vladimir, I was taken to the washroom, where I bathed the wound in cold water not so much to bring relief which it did not in the least, but in the hope that it might reduce the infection.

It was an awful day in many respects. The wind buffeted the boat, and the waves tossed it about as if it were a cork. I was in constant fear of Ivan the terrible paying another visit. As it happened, I saw no more of him until Geoff's and my encounter with him and his thugs the following Monday, which no doubt Geoff has already described to you.

At one point in the mid-afternoon the ship's engines quietened during a particularly squally bit of weather, and there seemed to be quite a lot of movement in the corridor. After a while, I thought I could detect some activity in the adjacent cabin. I now realise of course, that this was Geoff taking up residence in there.

I saw no-one again that day until Vladimir brought me an evening meal and mug of lukewarm tea, at least I think that's was what it was. Putting all pride aside, I showed him the burn which looked ghastly. For a moment he looked sympathetic, but then shrugged his shoulders, leaving me with the impression that he was not going to do anything about it.

However, later that evening the pain became so unbearable that when Vladimir returned to collect the crockery and cutlery from my meal, I pleaded with him using sign language to find help, muttering the word doctor. That seemed to sound some resonance with him, and he disappeared for a short while. He returned accompanied by someone I had not seen before. I think he was Vladimir's immediate boss. He was another unpleasant character, but apart from a habit of pushing and shoving me whenever he moved me from one place to another, he was not physically violent. We never discovered his name, but Geoff later would refer to him as bully officer or just Bully. He appeared to be suggesting Vladimir was making a fuss about nothing, but then Vladimir signalled to me to show his boss the burn, to which I conformed. The boss was dismissive, but Vladimir to give him his due, was insistent that some attention was essential. The boss simply walked out on us seemingly washing his hands of the whole matter.

Again to Vladimir's credit, he did not follow his boss's example, but made sympathetic signals and sounds, suggesting he was going to do something about it. He was gone for at least an hour, by which time I had lost faith in him as well, but much to my surprise a doctor arrived, equipped with medical bag and the ability to speak English. A brief examination of the burn and my overall condition convinced him I needed transferring to a sick bay, which is where I spent the next two days until being returned in handcuffs by Vladimir to the cabin late on the Saturday night or early hours of the Sunday morning. He was distinctly off hand with me compared with the Thursday evening, and I wondered if he had got into trouble with his superiors over the compassion he shown towards me.

The time in the sick bay had enabled me to regain my composure, even though on one occasion Ivan the terrible had tried to gain entry, but was rebuffed by someone with greater authority than him. I overheard a Polish lady say to a crew member that it was the captain that insisted the sick bay was out of bounds for Ivan. This was only a few hours before my discharge from the sick bay. Nevertheless, all my earlier fears returned, and became heightened still further when Vladimir removed the cuffs and locked me once again in the cabin.

I could not sleep, and tossed and turned and dreaded the inevitable forthcoming attempts at further interrogation and physical persuasion. I have always tried my damnedest to be emotionally strong, but that night this really got to me, and I just could not stop myself sniffling and crying, despite realising that the brutes somewhere on the other side of my door could hear me, they would feel they were winning the war of attrition. I felt so ashamed at my loss of control.

Suddenly, I heard a muffled voice from the adjacent cabin asking in English if there was something they could do to help. My immediate thought was that it was Geoff, but it was too indistinct to be certain. At that moment Vladimir and Bully entered my cabin, and the latter gestured the throat cutting threat, and stormed out. Vladimir shook a fist at me which looked more like a sop for Bully's benefit, than a warning to me. He then retreated and turned the key in the door lock. I heard him go next door and remonstrate with its occupant, presumably you Geoff.

The following morning there was a contretemps of some sort in the corridor, and Vladimir and a colleague bundled me out of the cabin and took me to a cabin in another part of the ship. There I stayed until the alarms sounded that Sunday afternoon. I was released and like everyone else was left to my own devises. I eventually joined the throng on deck, and then down into the hold where I spotted Geoff. I am sure he has told you the rest of the story".

Chapter 28

The MI6 man, who remained nameless throughout the enquiry, had a few questions. He was interested in the identities of the Russians we had encountered, and coaxed from us descriptions which in the end sounded feeble and vague, and to some extent contradictory. I was fairly good at recognising people when I saw them, but hopeless at remembering their appearance well enough to describe it. I was better at recalling mannerisms.

He produced a folder of photographs, and asked if we could identify any of the characters portrayed. Oleg was among them, but the rest meant nothing to either of us. He then showed us pictures of trawlers. It was difficult to be certain whether any resembled the one we had been held in, as we had only seen it from the boat itself, and then what we had seen on deck, well most of it was a scene of devastation. The best I had had of a distant image, was from the Cornish fishing boat while it was aligning itself to come alongside, but due to the mountainous waves and the lashing rain, I had only managed the briefest of glimpses of the trawler.

He then showed us an aerial photograph taken from a great height of a vessel with dense black smoke billowing from it, but there was enough detail for it to be ours. He confirmed that the photo had been taken over the North Sea off the coast of Norway on the previous Sunday afternoon. It seemed pretty conclusive. I was surprised to notice that even then, the boat had a distinctive list.

He closed his folder, and thanked us for our help. He managed a faint smile when Gillian graciously thanked him for his interest in our account of what we had been through. He said the whole incident was a disgrace and would have repercussions, and that we could expect further questions in due course from the British intelligence services. In the meantime, would we avoid divulging more than was absolutely essential relating to our abduction?

Jack was interviewed without our presence. He later told us it did not take very long as there was so little he could recall because of the effects of the drugs the kidnappers had used. Like Gillian and I, he had been injected the moment more or less that he had been seized, in his case in the car park at Waterlooville. The one thing he was certain of was that the whole affair centred around our investigation into the Rhodes companies and its connection with 'that bloody Midland Counties Plaster company'. As far as he was aware, he had given them no information, not that there was a lot he could have said, as the plaster company was Gillian's baby. When the three of us were together on our own, Jack said that even before the abduction, he was beginning to suspect that there was something that smelt about the contracts of supply to the Ministry of Defence, and that the fire at Fareham was somehow connected.

That evening we were flown back to the airfield at Northwood, Middlesex by a special flight arranged by the Foreign Office. We were accompanied by two security people from the Embassy who were surprisingly quite chatty, perhaps more so than they should have been when it came to discussing their work. They told us that our escapade as they called it was all very hush hush, that Thames Valley and Hampshire police forces were involved, but there had been nothing in the media about it. 'Don't expect a heroes' welcome when you get back', they warned.

Chapter 29

Two cars awaited us at Northwood, one for Jack and Gillian to head south to Portsmouth, the other to take me home to Gainsthorpe. I was not certain who had provided the cars and their drivers. Mine did not utter a word during the whole journey back to Buckinghamshire. I thought perhaps he was under orders not to.

Karen may have sounded cool on the telephone earlier that day, but not so when I walked through our front door at 11:30 that evening. She flung her arms around my neck and we hugged for ten minutes or more in the hallway, but hardly saying anything to each other. Then MaryAnn came down the stairs half asleep and joined us in the hug. "Daddy we were so worried about where you had gone. We've missed you so much".

"I shall tell you about it in the morning. There'll be no school as it will be Saturday."

"Can I make you and mummy a cup of tea?"

"That would be lovely", I enthused.

"I didn't know she could do that", I said to Karen.

"She's been making lots of them while you've been away. It's helped her to feel she has been doing something to help during the torrid time it has been."

"Do you want to talk about it now?" I asked.

"Perhaps when MaryAnn has gone to bed".

MaryAnn came through to the lounge with the tea.

"Mummy, there's no sugar left".

"Don't worry darling. We'll get some more in the morning. You go and get some sleep now. You should be able to now that Daddy's back with us".

"She's beginning to seem quite grown up", I commented after she'd gone upstairs.

"I think we have all grown up quite a bit in these last ten days", sighed Karen.

"I can't begin to imagine how you must have felt when I didn't return with the kids that Wednesday".

"I was frantic. It has all been further compounded by coping with three lots of police".

"Three! How so?"

"Thames Valley and Hampshire concerning your disappearance, and the local bobbies at both Gainsthorpe and Buckingham about Joe".

"Joe! Bernadette's husband?" I exclaimed… Karen nodded. …."What's he been up to?" I asked.

"Well, it all happened the day after you vanished. He came round here that evening in a rage. It was awful.

He clearly hadn't heard about you. I don't think Bernie knew at that stage either as she had not been at school on that Thursday. The kids were still up. Anyway, without giving me a chance to say anything, he sounded off about how we had let him down, how he had regarded us as friends and yet we had not warned him of what was going on between Bernie and another unspecified teacher. She had decided to come clean with Joe as she couldn't cope with the deceit any longer, and it would only be a matter of time before he would hear about it from us or other friends".

"I suppose he was right there", I commented.

"I tried ushering him into another room", Karen continued, "as the kids were clearly upset by the language and tone he was using about Bernie and us. He accused me of being a conniving stuck-up bitch. I tell you Geoffrey, I just could not take any more of it, already panicking because of you, and then to be spoken to like that. I screamed at him to get out, and go and cool off. As he stormed off down the drive on foot, he shouted further obscenities at me, and I told him in no uncertain terms to get lost, words to that effect anyway. There was a couple walking up the lane at the time who heard it all, and are causing me grief at the moment. Joe has not been seen since."

I sat opened-mouthed, shocked, but as much anything trying to grasp how Karen must have felt at that time.

"What does Bernie have to say about it all?"

"Well she is as distressed as I am, but with the added sense of guilt. She blames me to some extent for not being more sympathetic towards Joe, saying I should have tried to calm him down, but I was hardly in a fit mental state myself just then."

"Have you tried talking to her about it? It strikes me you could be supportive to each other".

"You only know the half of it. Did you not see the police hanging about when you got back?"

"I thought they were something to do with the security we should be having because of my experiences".

"I do not think so", she said with assertion. "They have been here on and off this week only partly for my protection, but mainly to ensure I do not swan off myself."

"I think you will find they have now been replaced with security men to guard us", I said.

"Anyway", she continued, "that couple I mentioned who were walking down the lane are saying to the police, the media, half the town and anyone else who cares to listen, that I was using threatening language when Joe 'ran off, making his escape'.

"Are they anyone we know?"

"Not that I can recall. At first, the police thought that Joe's and your disappearances were connected as I seem to be the common link, but since the intervention of the diplomatic service in your case, they have been a bit more open-minded."

"So what line are they taking now with Joe's disappearance".

"Oh, I am not off the hook. On the following day, the Friday, there were police crawling all over the place, around the farm, the school, the town, looking for clues in connection with you and Joe. That day, I was taken into and held at Buckingham for questioning. I had to phone dad to bring mum down to take care of the kids, although Kathy next door met them from school and playgroup, and had them until mum and dad arrived.

The police wanted to know why Joe had come round to ours, why he and I were so angry with each other, they suggesting we had had a lovers' tiff. There was even some thought of questioning the children, but one of the policewomen present said, thank goodness, that would only take place as a last resort, and would be conducted by a specialist unit.

I was held for twenty four hours, and then released for lack of evidence to charge me with. I was warned not to leave Gainsthorpe without their permission. I am afraid I did not endear myself to them when I asked if I needed their consent to use the telephone or go to the lavatory."

"This sounds so preposterous, and all on the strength of that silly couple's exaggerated account."

"To be fair, I did shout some pretty nasty things at Joe in the heat of the moment".

"I take it there is no further news of Joe as yet?"

"Not that I am aware of".

"What have the press and media had to say? I imagine that because of the double disappearances, they are having a field day".

"They certainly are, but there has been hardly any mention of yours, and none in the last few days. The mysterious diplomatic people, whoever they are, told me this morning you had been found, but that it should be confidential. There is an embargo on the press for reporting anything at all on the subject, as a D-notice had been issued, whatever that means. Today, interest has waned in the news and speculation has shifted to the possibility that Joe has simply walked out on the Bernie and the kids, which is what I have believed all along". She paused for a moment and then asked, "Geoff, what has been going on?"

"This is going to sound absolutely crazy, but I am not allowed to discuss it even with you. What have you been told so far?"

"Only that you have been in Denmark, and have been looked after by the British Embassy there, I assume in Copenhagen. What were you doing there? How did you get there and why? I suppose it is something to so with Donald Rhodes, that strange business with the car following you, and your colleagues who did not turn up for work. Do you happen to know if they are okay?"

"I am sure it is in order for me to say yes to what you have guessed, but no more, because the matter is in the hands of MI6, not that they will admit that is who they are. The Embassy let slip that that little bit of information. It seems to be a murky world the diplomatic and security services operate in".

"It seems ridiculous that you cannot tell me anymore of what has happened to you. Do they really think that I am going to quietly accept that?"

Chapter 30

The following morning (Saturday), I received a call from the MI6 gentleman we had seen in Copenhagen, who informed me that a meeting had been arranged in London for Jack, Gillian and me for 10:00 on Monday morning. We would be collected at 8:30 from our respective homes. Would we please bring our passports with us? I asked, slightly tongue in cheek, for an assurance we would not be whisked away abroad somewhere. If he smiled at that thought, he certainly did not betray it in his voice. I took the opportunity to check with him that there was no objection to my being seen in public, for example in church. It was not a problem as long as I gave nothing away about the abduction. I asked if he had any suggestions as to how I should explain my absence. It had to be good as a good number of acquaintances knew what Karen had been through during that time. He said that a complete but temporary loss of memory might work. When I said that sounded corny, he replied that it was not essential for them to believe you if they were not close family. It was probably easy for him as he was used to having to be secretive, and his friends would know that. I would try out his idea and if the looks were too disbelieving I would add that I was now receiving treatment with the right drugs, but there was still a large chunk of memory to be retrieved.

In fact, at church on the Sunday, the only person to show a hint of doubt was Father Nugent, who commented that he was aware that Karen and I had been through a lot in the last fortnight which we would, with God's grace, wish to forget. He reminded me to give him a call anytime if I thought I needed his help or simply to talk over things. I said there was every chance I might do just that.

Gillian and Jack looked somewhat shaken when we met on Monday in offices on the Embankment near Vauxhall Bridge. Apparently they had been chauffeured by a former police driver at breakneck speed to cover the 72 miles from Portsmouth in an hour and a half.

We were shown into a room high up in the building, with a window which had a splendid view overlooking the Thames, not that we allowed much opportunity to sight-see, as the four interrogators, including our 'friend' from Friday, lost no time in getting down to business.

They had before them Jack's and Gillian's working papers from the cabinet in Gordon's office. They had clearly been very busy over the weekend.

The gentleman taking the lead introduced himself as Mr S. and his colleagues as Messrs B, W and our 'friend' Mr G. Mr S assured us that no offence was intended, but we may at some stage be asked to sign a document under the Official Secrets Act, but hoped that it would not be necessary, as long as we understood that we may be asked to treat everything discussed during the meeting as confidential for the time being. We would be informed when that restriction could be lifted, but it would be after any investigation was over.

As in the British Embassy in Copenhagen, we were shown a series of photographs and asked if we recognised any of the individuals portrayed. Gillian and Jack shook their heads but one of them I had no difficulty in identifying. It was the one my initial kidnappers had referred to as 'Boss'. Mr S said with a look of satisfaction, "That comes as no surprise". Clearly he had been encountered before.

I asked if Mr Rhodes was aware that they had requisitioned the papers on the desk. He was not aware, but that would be discussed in due course.

Mr S made it clear that apart from having clear statements from all three of as to our treatment, etc. throughout our capture, which incidentally was to be taken up with the Russian Embassy, they were interested in the work that Jack and Gillian had been carrying out on the supplies to the Ministry of Defence and their source, and everything we had gleaned about the buyer Roy Burnside. Gillian said it was all in the notes she had left in her file, even the tittle tattle she had overheard from the staff. He was not much liked. I was able to add the little I knew about his involvement in the fire at Fareham, and his fight with Evan the lorry driver. "His surname is Thomas according to the schedule in Gillian's file", interjected Mr S. I explained that Roy and Evan had apparently fallen out over some disparaging remarks Roy had made about Evan's wife, according to Donald Rhodes.

Mr S went on to say that they suspected there was another reason for the fall out. Were we aware that Evan was exclusively the driver for all the Ministry deliveries arranged by Roy? We were not. Were we aware that Evan was the only person with a pass into the two forts in Gosport? That was news to us, although it was not something we had thought to enquire into. I began to wonder what this was leading up to. I was also surprised, with just the weekend intervening between the Friday meeting and this one, that they had uncovered such information.

Mr G, our Copenhagen acquaintance, began to elaborate. After digging Gordon out of bed in the early hours of Saturday morning, they, by whom I assumed he meant himself, Mr B and Mr W, escorted Gordon to his Southsea office and retrieved all the Rhodes papers from his cabinet. In the ten days that they had been lying in the cabinet, Gordon had not noticed it had been locked. The MI6 men must have been very persuasive, as an accountant as a rule does not give up clients' confidential papers readily, especially at that time of the morning and at a weekend.

One of Gillian's listings contained the staff National Insurance Numbers, and through their connections, Messrs G, B and W had traced Roy's and Evan's addresses. Armed with that information, they were able to tail the duo throughout the weekend and were still doing so. "Incidentally, we have had people following the movements of the three of you night and day since you arrived from Denmark, but in your case for your personal security and safety", assured Mr G. That answered one of the questions I had intended to raise.

Mr S intervened and decreed that as we were getting into the realms of how their organisation operated, we had reached a point where it was necessary for us to sign the Official Secrets Act documents. Once that formality was out of the way, Mr G continued.

Roy had spent most of the weekend watching television, apart from a half-hearted effort at cleaning his car. I remarked that he was not long out of hospital and would still be recuperating.

Evan on the other hand seemed to be moonlighting, doing deliveries for a poultry farm just outside Petersfield. He had a wife and family and apart from a hurried trip to a supermarket in Fareham, spent most of his free time in a Bridgemary pub. Mr B befriended him there on the Saturday evening, plied him with drink until his tongue became very loose.

It was not difficult getting him to talk about his work with Rhodes and relationship with Roy. He had discovered that Roy was pulling a fast one on Rhodes. He, through his own company, was supplying Rhodes with all the plaster supplies destined for the Ministry of Defence, and was clearly pocketing the profit through inflating the wholesale prices of the supplies by his own company to Rhodes. Evan, rather than reporting the matter, decided to blackmail Roy. This had been carrying on for about a year, when Roy began behaving oddly. He wanted to accompany Evan on some of the deliveries into Fort Rowner and Fort Abbotshead, telling Evan he was on the look-out for opportunities of expanding business. On each occasion he was barred from entering these Gosport establishments, and was left at the security gates. On one such occasion it was raining torrentially and he asked the security guard if he could shelter with him in his Kiosk. The guard took pity on him and took him in. Roy afterwards told Evan that they discussed the refurbishing projects going on within the forts, Roy making great play of the fact that they presented him with the prospect of gaining contracts for future supply of all sorts of building materials.

Evan said this did not ring true somehow as Roy often bemoaned Donald Rhodes' constant 'nagging' to use every opportunity to drum up new business, when he Roy was supposed to be a buyer not a salesman. Evan decided he would up the pressure on Roy, and demanded a higher rate of blackmail money, but Roy resisted.

Some days later, when they were both at the Fareham depot, Evan tried again to lean on Roy for more money, and told him he thought Roy was up to something other than just new business at the forts. Roy flew into a rage and tried hitting Evan with a shovel. Evan retaliated and in the confusion knocked Roy flying, tipping over a paraffin heater. They then got into a 'punch up', resulting in Roy catching his head on a concrete lintel. The heater set light to the depot.

Evan in his drunken state went on to explain to Mr B that they had since made up, and he had now got his own way; Roy has agreed to meet Evans demands. He was thinking of up-dating his car.

Mr G went on to say that they had reason to believe that Evan Thomas was correct in his suspicions of Roy Burnside. Having reviewed all our papers and gathered additional information since, the security services suspected that Roy was not only subjected to Evan's blackmail. Others, perhaps having discovered that Roy was using a defunct company to cream off his employer's profits, were suspected of putting pressure on him to carry out activity putting the safety of this country in jeopardy.

Mr G had examined the copies Gillian had made of the Ministry of Defence contracts. Although they specified the materials Rhodes were to supply, no hint was made of what they would be used for. Nothing unusual in that! It was possible that foreign government agencies were keenly interested to know, and were putting pressure on Roy to find out. This was all supposition at the moment. Our security services had no proof or identities of these nefarious persons, but were anxious to uncover exactly who was involved. Of course they had a pretty good idea from the abductions we had experienced.

Mr S looked at me and said, "This is where you come in. We feel that to bust Roy's little operation will set the cat among the pigeons, and in the aftermath whoever his handlers are will be exposed".

I was horrified at the suggestion, and said that I was not prepared to put my family at any greater risk than they were already.

He assured me there was no risk as my part was simply to arrange to meet him 'in the course of our investigation on Donald Rhodes behalf, to clear up some anomalies'. The mere prospect of such a meeting should be enough to cause alarm in the handler's camp. "Mr B and Mr W with a team of others will be in the shadows the whole time watching him wherever he goes and whom he sees. He does not know it, but he has already been bugged. Our men will continue to watch over you and your family until all this is over".

I made it clear that I was nevertheless very unhappy with what I was being asked to do.

"Look at it this way", Mr S said, "in doing what we are asking, you shall be reducing the threat that exists while those concerned remain at large. All we are asking is that you telephone him perhaps from your office to make the arrangement, to set a date and time, but not to go through with it. As he is under our observation the whole time, we shall let you know when he is in his office at Rhodes and therefore able to take your call, without the bother and risk of you having to leave a message for him."

"What if he wants to know what the anomalies are? Do I give him any examples?"

"No. Just say that you will be dealing with them face to face".

I asked if Donald Rhodes would be aware of our reappearance. He was and had been told that the backstory was *sub judice*. He seemed to accept that, but has been asked not to spread the news.

I also enquired after the progress if any in apprehending any of the individuals who had kidnapped us in the first place. I was told that it was essentially a police matter, but some noises were being made at a diplomatic level as regards those thought to be Russian. The Cornish fishermen had been tracked down that morning and were being held for their part in the matter. Mr S said he would be in touch with the police in Cornwall as soon as our meeting was over. As of that moment, the fishermen were the best lead they had.

His parting remark as we were leaving was that our shipwreck in Gdansk harbour had made for interesting reading in the Polish press, along with the hunt for British spies. He then spoke with a smile to Gillian in fluent Polish.

Chapter 31

On the way home, I pondered over the request to arrange the meeting with Roy and decided I would discuss it first with Karen before committing to what on the surface seemed quite straight forward, but I knew that she would be extremely uneasy about it, and possibly think of risks which had not occurred to me. It played on my mind to an extent that I paid little attention to the journey itself, until the driver suddenly swung the car sharply to the left into a side street off Ealing Broadway, and then left again into another road consisting of Victorian terraced houses, where we stopped abruptly. His companion in the front passenger seat leapt from the car and hid behind a large van close to where we had just turned off. After a few minutes he returned to the car and said that we had appeared to have shaken 'him' off.

I leaned forward and asked them what had happened. The companion explained they suspected that we were being tailed ever since we had left the Embankment by a Ford Granada. We continued along the road we were in and back into Ealing Broadway, but heading the way we had come towards central London, where our driver chose another route back to Buckinghamshire via the M1.

As we sped north along the motorway, the driver expounded on the ways of detecting if one is being followed either on foot or in a vehicle. Experience had given him a second sense, but of most importance was observation of the myriad things we take for granted. Someone following is constantly playing catch-up, especially in busy traffic in built-up areas and town centres, which means their speed is erratic. It was second nature for him to have his eyes on his mirrors as much as looking through the windscreen. On motorways, he tended to make his own speed erratic, and watch for anyone following suit. One of his favourite moves was to come off at a junction and go straight back on in the same direction, although an experienced follower will be wise to that trick and not come off but speed ahead so as to be well in front of his prey, and then at the next junction copy your manoeuvre. It can turn into a game of cat and mouse for those in the same business, so to speak.

However, my main concern was that despite all the security in place, our pursuers were still active and alarmingly cognisant of my movements at least. Once I had reached home I immediately phoned Mr S, who had given me his number to call him at any time I felt the need. He was aware of the problem as the driver had already reported the matter. He accepted it was a worry that 'these people' knew I was back in circulation'. I queried why they felt the need to follow us when they already knew where I lived. He said it was probably a habitual insatiable urge to know exactly where the object of their observation was at any time. He agreed it did not make a great deal of sense. However, in his opinion, it had become imperative for me to make that phone call to Roy as soon as possible. I promised to get back to him that afternoon with my decision.

Karen returned from school with the children and one of the security men in tow. "How did the meeting go this morning?" she asked.

"Fine, but there is a problem". In the spirit of my promise before the abduction, I spoke to her about the incident on the way back from London that morning. Not only that, I hoped that she would be decisive in her answer to my revelation and Mr S's request. I expected a categorical 'No', but instead she was adamant that I got on with the phone call without delay and not 'faff' about. The sooner Mr S's plan came to fruition and the 'bastards' were flushed out and behind bars, the better for all of us. She perfectly understood how precarious our present position was, and doing nothing was just as precarious as 'setting the cat among the pigeons', as Mr S had called it.

I phoned him immediately, and he promised to phone me back as soon as he was able to establish that Roy was in his office.

Karen and I sat by the phone for what seemed like an eternity. When it rang I shook with nervousness from the sheer moment of it all. "Yes, he is there now", said Mr S urgently. "Best of luck, and let me know as soon as you have spoken to him".

I called Rhodes' number and spoke to the receptionist. "I think I saw Roy come in about twenty minutes ago. I'll put you through. It's Mr Foster, isn't it?"

Half a minute later, the receptionist again, "Can you call back tomorrow Mr Foster, as he is unavailable at the moment?"

"That will be too late. Is he not there?"

"I'll try again"....

"Mr Foster, I'm sorry about that, but I am a bit pushed this afternoon", Roy uttered in a falsely apologetic tone.

"It won't take long. I simply wanted to arrange a meeting with you in the next few days, so that I can wrap up the report Donald Rhodes has asked us to prepare. You probably know that we have been examining all aspects of the business with an eye to improving its systems and making them more efficient. The only senior person we haven't interviewed yet is yourself. I understand amongst your range of duties is that you manage the Defence orders. Some of my questions will revolve around that, but I shall look at other aspects of the buying operation. I had in mind coming down to see you this coming Thursday. Will that suit you?"

"Does it have to be this week?"

"I am under pressure myself I'm afraid".

"What about Friday?"

"Okay. Shall we say 9:30 a.m.?

"Fine. Will Donald be in the meeting?"

I hadn't anticipated that question. "No", I answered without time to give it any thought.

"Good, I mean right, okay. See you then".

The deed was done. I hoped from that moment on the whole business would now be in MI6 hands, and we perhaps could have some peace.

That hope was dashed when I phoned Mr S and confirmed the arrangement had been made. "Good! Friday gives us enough time for what we have to do. Needless to say you can forget the appointment. Roy will be in custody by then. However, in view of this morning's incident, you and your wife will need to be extra vigilant."

I was unable to sleep at all that night. The following morning, after Karen and the children had left for school accompanied by her 'personal bodyguard', I was preparing myself some breakfast, and happened to glance out of the kitchen window which overlooked the back garden. Christina's toy car, a large moulded plastic thing she could climb into and push along with her feet, was in the middle of the lawn. I muttered to myself about the times Karen and I had told the children to put their toys away in the shed once they had finished playing with them. Without a second thought, I went out into the garden to deal with it when I felt a heavy blow to the back of my head, and then oblivion.

Chapter 32

The next I remembered was the sound of MaryAnn screaming, as I gradually regained consciousness and took in my surroundings. She was strapped to an old wooden chair. A gag was being tied around her mouth, while she struggled to free her arms, while a familiar face was cursing her and threatening to punch her in the head. The thug was the Russian gunman I had nicknamed Boris on the trip to Cornwall two weeks previously. I could hear other voices from outside the building which appeared to be a breeze block shed or barn. It had an air of semi-dereliction, and a very damp mustiness about it.

Through the disorientation and thumping pain of my head, I shouted at the thug, calling him a disgusting coward, picking on a little girl to exercise his brutal instincts (not quite the words I used). This time I could not see a gun, but he had armed himself with a knife, which he waved in MaryAnn's face as a threat to quieten me.

My anger intensified, but I had to keep the lid on it, as I just could not run the risk of him carrying out his threat. "What the hell is it you want?" I shouted at him.

"You shut your mouth. We wait until boss comes, then you find out". He pulled up another chair and sat on it next to MaryAnn, who was shaking uncontrollably, too much so to cry. I tried to move towards her to provide some consolation, but Boris signalled with the knife for me to get back in my corner, squatting on the dusty floor and leaning against the wall, with my feet bound together by a leather belt. I glanced at my clothes which were covered in mud and suggesting that I had been dragged into our present location.

Boris did not seem to mind my reassuring words to MaryAnn that we shall be rescued and the bad man will be captured by the police very soon. Perhaps he thought that what I was saying would stop MaryAnn from further screaming, which was clearly irritating him.

Another gang member came in from outside, carrying a hot drink from a flask for Boris. He had left the door open, which enabled me to recognise where we were. It was not far from home; the gravel quarry near Marsh Gibbon where we had first stopped and left my car on the way down to Cornwall.

MaryAnn looked at the two of them and turned to me, saying, "They snatched me from the girls' toilets when I had to go out during the science lesson."

"How did they manage that?" I asked, but Boris curtailed any further discussion by waving his fist in her face, while the flask carrier came over to me and copied Boris' pathetic gesture, and then returned outside, allowing the door to slam shut.

Judging by the indistinct chatter outside, I surmised that there were at least three of the gang in addition to Boris. Suddenly a strong gust of wind blew open the door which crashed against the wall outside. I could see that there were indeed three of them, two leaning against a Mercedes people carrier, and one standing in front of them, all smoking cigarettes. Two, I recognised, one I didn't. There was no Martin, however. Perhaps, I thought cynically, he was still trying to find his way out of the woods where I had left him in Cornwall!

Nothing much happened apart from my being led to the bank behind the shed for a call of nature at one stage, and being re-bound on my return. MaryAnn who had stopped shaking beforehand, was now quivering once again. She said that she thought they had taken me outside to shoot me. Relative calm was restored.

The hours ticked by while the early drizzle gave way to brilliant sunshine. MaryAnn and I were too scared to feel boredom setting in, but the same did not apply to our present company. Silence reigned while I imagined the outside crew had retreated into the vehicle perchance to snooze. Even Boris' eyes glazed over at times, but the slightest movement on my part brought him to an instant state of alertness.

Just before half past two in the afternoon, a vehicle drew up outside, skidding on the gravel as it did so. A car door slammed, as some commands were tossed at the sleeping beauties in the Mercedes, and they except one, and the new visitor marched and joined us inside the shed, slamming the door behind him. It was as I suspected, the one they called Boss, and whom I had recognised in the MI6 rogues gallery.

Without any provocation, he came over to me and punched me in the face. Luckily he had not positioned himself very well, and it was more of a glancing blow. He made it quite clear that now was the time to start talking. He began by asking me about the wretched plaster company, but had hardly started when there was a shot outside, and the doors of the shed burst open. Armed men shouted at the Boss and his gang to hold their hands behind their heads, while they were pushed to the ground face down, and handcuffed. Our ordeal for the present was over, as MaryAnn and I hugged each other, she consoling me as much as I her.

We stood outside in the sunshine as the gang were bundled into a police van which seemed to arrive from nowhere. Its departure was equally speedily executed, the whole removal taking no more than a couple of minutes.

Another van (unmarked) arrived which had probably been lurking a short distance away. Our rescuers, who were wearing bullet proof vests but no uniform, invited us to join them as they clambered into it, all with hardly a word spoken. We headed back to our house where we were dropped off, while the rest of the contingent except one, continued I assumed on their return to base. He followed us indoors, and introduced himself as being the one in charge of the armed unit, called in for a special operation by the security services.

The house seemed to be filled with police milling about; two policewomen and a doctor were comforting Karen, who had obviously been heavily sedated as she struggled to take in the fact that MaryAnn and I were there. One of the policewomen explained that Karen had collapsed at school after learning that MaryAnn was missing, and was still in a severe state of shock. The policewoman offered to make us all a cup of strong sweet tea, which was accepted eagerly.

The head of the armed unit, who invited me to address him as Andy, informed me that when Karen's bodyguard (her terminology), returned to the house that morning after accompanying her and the children to school, he had discovered his colleague, who had been guarding me, unconscious on the driveway with blood pouring from his head. (I automatically put my hand up to feel the large and sore bump on my own). Karen's man called for an ambulance and the police, and went searching the house and gardens for me, but felt duty bound to return to his colleague until help arrived.

He phoned his headquarters in London, and that was when Andy and his men were hurriedly assembled and instructed to get down to this part of Buckinghamshire. While the unit was on its way from London, news came in of MaryAnn's disappearance, and a team of police dogs and their handlers were rustled up from Oxford. They were able to establish that MaryAnn had been taken away in a car from outside the school gates. A passer-by thought it looked suspicious and called the police from the phone box opposite the school. She described the car as a large people carrier which she was fairly certain was a Mercedes. Road blocks were set up around the area, and a fleet of police cars scoured the roads and country lanes until the Mercedes was spotted at the gravel quarry some hours later.

MaryAnn interrupted and asked where her brother and sister were, and was told they were with our neighbour. She wanted to join them, and I could see no reason why she shouldn't. She had calmed down considerably and I imagined was keen to tell them all about her ordeal.

Andy, equally keen to continue his account of the rescue, explained that while they were racing towards the quarry he received radio instructions that they were to take up positions under cover around the shed where the Mercedes was parked, and wait for the arrival of a suspected ring leader of the abductors, who was being tailed and thought to be heading their way. At the speed the suspect was travelling it would take him around another about ten minutes. Five minutes later Andy and his men were in place at the quarry, and within a matter of moments watched the ring leader arrive and enter the shed, and then they moved in. He was chuffed by how smoothly that part of the operation went. I asked him whom exactly he and his unit worked for. The answer I got was simply 'security'.

Chapter 33

In the weeks which followed, life became just a little more settled for us, but still had its moments.

Karen remained under police orders not to leave the country (not that she had any plans to) as their enquiries into Joe's disappearance continued. She found it particularly galling given all the stress she had been under while there had been no news of my whereabouts during the time I was missing. I had even taken the matter to the Chief Constable, but he said it would be inappropriate for him to interfere in the investigations. He promised to satisfy himself that all the procedures were being correctly followed by his officers, and that the evidence they were working on was of substance. He later assured me that it was, but it did little to placate Karen.

We discovered that Bernadette and Brendon were also under similar suspicion which helped Karen feel slightly less that she was being unfairly treated. I had to keep telling myself that it was right for the police to pursue every avenue, but wondered if they could have handled the case with a shade more sensitivity.

One of our most worrying problems was MaryAnn. Although at first she appeared to cope well with the abduction, as time went on she began to have nightmares, some so very real to her that she would quake for hours even once fully awake. Our doctor suggested that the trauma was partly down to the possible onset of puberty, but we felt it was unfair on MaryAnn to leave it there. With considerable pressure from us, we managed to obtain specialist medical help for her, and after an initial period of little progress, she began to recover and focus her energies on her love for animals, especially dogs, although it was several years later before we had one.

Following the apprehension of the gang of kidnappers, the security people (I never knew whether they were MI6, MI5 or the Fraud Squad) were all over Rhodes' accounting records, etc. and it was a couple of months before Gillian and I eventually had a meaningful meeting with Donald. Sadly, Jack's health never fully returned to normal, and after a few weeks back at work, he found he was unable to cope. He was on sick leave for several months, but in the end had to accept early retirement, mostly because of mental health reasons.

Much of our work, the reports Gillian and Jack had produced, and the outstanding queries we had accumulated leading up to moment of the abductions, had been superseded by the forensic work carried out by the security investigators. Donald had had countless sessions with them. The investigators had amassed a massive dossier on Roy's Rhodes and hitherto unknown extra-mural activities, and on a not too insignificant part Evan had played in them.

Donald had been become very cooperative when the investigators were able to quantify in great detail the actual illicit profit Roy had creamed off. He had now been replaced by a very competent lady he had 'head hunted' from a competitor.

As had been suspected, the Russians had got wind of the refurbishment of what had been Gosport's supposed derelict Forts of Rowner and Abbotshead, and were keen to find why. According to undisclosed sources, observers working for the Russian Embassy were recording the contractors and suppliers vehicles visiting the forts, and an agent from the their Embassy approached the companies who owned the visiting vehicles for inside information. None of the companies, including Rhodes would play ball.

The agent one day tracked Evan and struck gold when he followed Evan into his favourite lunchtime pub, loosened his tongue with drink, and discovered that the supplies Evan delivered originated from Midland Counties Plaster & Lining Supplies Ltd. The Russians made enquiries at Companies House and discovered the anomalies as we had done. Roy was approached by an Embassy handler and systematically blackmailed into gathering as much information as he could as to the purpose of refurbishments at the forts, but without much success it was understood. Roy had cooperated with the investigators once he realised the game was up, but he was not, in the event, to escape prosecution.

The whole matter led to the expulsion of a number of Russian diplomats and Embassy staff, followed by the usual tit for tat ejection of our own people from Moscow.

Many years later, I learned that Fort Abbotshead had been used to temporarily provide secure housing for Russian diplomats who had defected to the West. I also discovered that the person overseeing the refurbishment of both forts was none other than Dave Jenkins, with whom I was at School in Southsea, and who was married to Susannah, the lady whom I had known from my days working at Fareham, the kind soul who invited me into their home on the day of the fire at Rhodes depot. This renewed acquaintance later developed into a friendship between our respective families.

Chapter 34

Two years after the abductions, we received the sad news of the passing of my friend Bob Willetts. The cancer had finally taken him at such a relatively young age. At his funeral I reflected on the many reasons I had to be grateful for our friendship since our school days, but the most precious was his part in bringing Karen and I together, for organising the holiday during which she and I first met, his forbearance of our swooning over each other for much of that holiday while he was left to fend for himself, and the help he had given me in tracking Karen down in the months following. (An account of this features in my earlier book).

The search for Joe and the police suspicion of Karen's, Bernadette's and Brendan's involvement in his disappearance rumbled on for several years. In time, the police action fizzled out, although it officially remained an open case. Local interest waned, and friendships which had been tarnished were gradually restored. The travel ban was lifted after a year, which meant we were able to enjoy holidays in France, Austria and Italy.

One day, years later, ours, Bernadette's and her family's and Brendan's lives were shattered when a television documentary to 'commemorate' the 10 years since Joe's disappearance was broadcast. It was billed as,

'Results of forensic research by investigative journalists and new evidence have come to light into what had happened on that fateful night, when he vanished without trace'.

The programme was written and presented in a sensationalist style by a self-accredited criminologist, whose research had traced Joe's family back in Ireland. It transpired that on the day of his disappearance Joe had phoned his uncle who lived in Co. Kerry. The uncle claimed that Joe had always looked up to him and used him as his mentor. Joe in great distress had told him he had just learned of his wife's infidelity, and that her friends had colluded in keeping it secret from him. He was feeling very let down and a laughing stock of their community. When the programme presenter asked the uncle if Joe had sounded suicidal, the uncle said he was not the type to even consider it, besides which he would realise the strength of the support he would receive from his family back in Ireland. Joe would always return to his roots in times of trouble.

The programme correctly stated that my car had been traced to a nearby quarry, but went on to claim that there had been a cover-up because attention had been diverted away from the strong likelihood that my car had been used for carrying Joe's body from the scene of his murder to his final resting place, somewhere in the quarry. The diversion used, the programme maintained, was some 'dubious story' about the car owner, a

388

Geoffrey Foster, having been abducted on the same day as the killing (my abduction was actually during the day before), a story which had never been authenticated in the public domain. MI6 could have of course refuted the wild speculation, but chose not to, presumably on the grounds of national security.

The programme went on to use spurious 'evidence' which despite what it claimed, was merely hearsay and inconsistent with the known facts, and at times obvious to the discerning listener, at odds with the reasoning used by the programme itself.

The programme became a hot topic within the town and particularly our circle of friends, and opened up old wounds and revived much of the hostility we had suffered in the months following the events of 1982.

However, the programme was largely discredited by the local police and media, and in time the furore once again died down, although much damage had been done to our standing in the meantime.

Chapter 35

We now move on another eight years to the day in year 2000, and the scene described at Gatwick in the opening chapter of this book.

I had been watching the screen showing the status of incoming flights, and noticed that a flight from Jersey had landed. I was expecting Andy Harper to have been on it. With luck he would be in the arrivals area within the next quarter of an hour. There was just enough time to call Donald on my mobile to find out where he was. It was just possible he had been waiting at the wrong terminal. He hadn't. He was at a prize giving in his fifteen year old daughter's school near Petersfield. I asked if he had forgotten our meeting at Gatwick. Without any apology, he said he must have done. It was not in his diary. Could I postpone it to the following day? Mustering every ounce of patience I was able to, I reminded him that Andy Harper had flown over from Jersey especially, his plane had just touched down, and I had left home at eight o'clock that morning, having inconvenienced another client by postponing her appointment originally fixed for that day.

With some reluctance he suggested we met for lunch in Petersfield, but I objected that it was too far from Gatwick. It would be a double journey for me as I would have to take Andy back to the airport afterwards. I countered with Petworth, but that was too far for him, especially as he would have his wife with him. In the end we compromised on The Spread Eagle Hotel in South Street, Midhurst at 12:30. He would make the booking.

Andy and I found each other with very little difficulty, and set off for Midhurst without delay. On the way down I provided him with Donald's background as I knew it, up to the point at which we had parted company in the mid-eighties.

Following the decision to close down operations at Fareham after the disastrous fire in 1982, despite my misgivings about site contamination, Donald had struck a deal with a developer whereby his Company and the developer's went into partnership to build several luxury homes. It made a reasonable pot of money for Donald's company, but instead of reinvesting it in setting up a new depot, he squandered it on various dubious commodity schemes a broker friend of his was involved in, and lost the lot, apart from a relatively small investment in some holiday-lets in Spain.

The Waterlooville depot flourished in the years immediately after the departure of Roy Burnside, as it was able to benefit fully from the lucrative contracts it had with the Ministry of Defence, and to take advantage of the eighties' boom. Nevertheless, there were many missed opportunities as Donald in his stubbornness got bogged down in myriad disputes over trivialities. One such related to PAYE arrears owed by the company to H.M. Collector of Taxes. I had explained to him time and again that the money was correctly due on his director's remuneration, but he refused to accept it stupidly on the grounds that he could make better use of it. The amount was not substantial and would not have deprived the company of essential cash flow, not that that was relevant anyway. Finally, the company was taken to court, but because its Registered Office was our premises at Buckingham, the case was heard locally to us. For the first (and only) time ever, he drove up to see me at my Buckingham office for advice on what he should say at the hearing later that day. He moaned incessantly about the length of the journey up, and I reminded him of the times I had made it myself, only to find the appointment at Southsea had been called off once I had arrived.

He phoned me the following morning to say he had lost the case, and to top it all, had not got home until mid-evening. He had come to the conclusion that it was ridiculous having an accountant so far away, and had instructed a local firm in our place. I pointed out that I had always driven down to Portsmouth so as not to inconvenience him, and in any event, I could have transferred his case to our offices in Portsmouth and Southsea if he felt the distance was a problem. However his mind was made up, and he was not going to change it now. This occurred in the mid-eighties

I was not altogether sorry, as it had always been a problem getting him to pay our fees. He was much the same with his suppliers.

~~~~~

Andy and I arrived in Midhurst with time to spare, and wandered around the picturesque streets until 12:30. He explained as we walked, that his firm had been appointed to take on the clients of another company, which had been closed down for fraudulent practice and other irregularities, chiefly blatant evasion of tax on behalf of its client trusts. He freely admitted he was a little out his depth with the complexities of the structure of many of the trusts, particularly groups of inter-connected settlements falling under the jurisdiction of a variety of countries and states.

By 12:30 we were sitting in the bar of The Spread Eagle Hotel, and had ordered soft drinks while we waited for Donald. True to the form of old, he arrived half an hour later with his wife Melanie. She offered an apology, which appeared to irritate Donald sufficiently to discourage her from saying very much more during the time we spent with them.

The head waiter showed us to our reserved table. It was clearly a popular restaurant with business people, as all the tables were occupied, and the noise level making it difficult to hear what our companions were saying.

Donald outlined his problem and how it had arisen. During the height of the 1980s property boom, he had switched his attention to speculating in real estate and allied matters, leaving the depot in the hands of a competent manager. The property transactions were conducted through a Jersey trust, and it very quickly accumulated profits of over five million pounds, all before the onset of the recession of the early 1990s. These profits had been augmented by creaming off part of the gross margin on the supplies to the Waterlooville depot by first channelling them through the trust and passing them on to the depot at an inflated price. The trust's involvement was of course not physical, but simply a paper exercise.

The trust was administered by the Channel Island trust management company which had recently had its licence withdrawn, who had been recommended by the accountants who had replaced us. The management company dealt with all the paperwork including tax returns. Apart from the deeds, etc. setting up the trust, the only documents Donald had been called upon to sign at any time, were the annual accounts. No money had ever been drawn out by Donald or his family. The intention had been to accumulate, in what he had been led to believe was a tax-free environment, the gains and profits for himself and Melanie in retirement, and on his and her demise, their children and grandchildren.

The first inkling Donald had that anything was wrong was when an article appeared in the Financial Times, exposing sharp practice by the management company. It was investigated by the Jersey authorities, resulting in the withdrawal of its licence to operate. Andy's firm was invited to step in, but found it lacked the degree of special expertise of UK trading and property companies, essential to managing some of the trusts it had taken over, Donald's in particular.

Donald informed us that although no enquiry had been ordered by the UK Tax authorities into the trust, they were now raising questions into his personal and the Rhodes companies' tax affairs. He was convinced this was no coincidence. It was Melanie who suggested he contacted me. She had never understood why Donald had left us; she had never felt any confidence in our successors.

As the restaurant customers finished their meals and it began to empty, the noise level subsided, but Donald's voice was not lowered commensurately. I was concerned that our conversation, which was by its nature highly confidential, could be overheard by the remaining diners. I said as much to Donald. I had to be blunt and asked him to lower his voice if we were to continue, either that or we would have to resume our discussions in his car. Andy backed me up, while Melanie nodded in agreement.

It was necessary for me to set out in chapter and verse the terms on which I was prepared to help him. There had to be full cooperation with the Inland Revenue. They would not be satisfied until every stone had been turned over regarding the specific matters they had queried, and there was the likelihood the answers would lead to further lines of questioning. The fines, interest and penalties on unpaid tax because of incomplete disclosure of matters relevant to the calculation of tax were very heavy, but could be mitigated if he were cooperative. Donald resisted my advice, using colourful language to describe what he thought of the tax authorities, but oddly insisted repeatedly that everything must be made clear to them and above board. Andy said nothing. I suspected he had never been involved in tax investigations before.

Donald asked a question, the gist of which had been addressed to me before in other cases. Why should he not hand everything over to the Inland Revenue and let them do all the work of the investigation, rather than him having to pay an accountant to do it? I pointed out that the onus was on him, the tax payer, to provide all the correct and relevant information to them in the tax return and accounts, not for them to determine it. Their job was to seek clarification where the information given did not stack up, or contradicted data they already held, or which subsequently came to light.

Donald looked at his watch, announced that he had a rugby match to go to, and with no further ado, walked out, with Melanie rapidly gathering up her jacket and handbag, and awkwardly following him out of the hotel. Andy and I were flabbergasted. We were left with the bill, which we agreed to share. We accepted that we would probably have picked up the tab anyway, but it would have been courteous of Donald to have offered, rather than rudely walk out on us.

Between us we decided that I would write to Donald summarising what he had told us and what I had said, with a copy going to Andy. We both concluded that it held all the promise of being a wasted day, and an expensive one at that, for both of us.

I used the facilities before returning to the car. Andy had gone ahead to wait by the car and have a smoke. While I was leaving the toilet and making my way through the foyer, I was approached by a lone diner who had been sitting at the table adjacent to ours. He simply offered me his business card, and asked if I would give him a call as soon as possible, and then slunk off without another word.

As I walked towards the car I looked more closely at the card. It bore the name of Denis Smalley, Inland Revenue.

After dropping off Andy at Gatwick, instead of heading north, I drove south for a short distance to Crawley, and found somewhere to park and have a coffee. I found a tea room, and from a relatively secluded corner phoned the number on the card. Denis Smalley was from Enquiry Branch of the Inland Revenue, a section which investigates serious tax fraud, and would like to see me as soon as possible at my office. He did not wish to go into any detail over the phone, but stressed the matter was highly confidential. I was not to say anything to Donald Rhodes in particular, but he agreed I could mention it to a co-partner, or a tax manager in my firm, either or both of whom were welcome to take part in the meeting. Just what I needed in the light of what I had heard on the radio news that morning!

Chapter 36

In Gainsthorpe that evening, we all were on tenterhooks, especially Bernadette and Karen, who had been visited by the police who suspected that the body which had been found was Joe's. This was to be later confirmed by dental records, the body being obviously too badly decomposed for Bernadette to identify. The cause of death was yet to be determined by a pathologist, but initial findings suggested he had been stabbed and died as a result of his injuries.

A thorough examination of the scene where he had been found was being conducted by a team of forensic scientists. Karen and I were asked not to leave the area without informing the police first, in case they 'needed to bring us in for questioning'. They agreed my Buckingham office was not out of bounds.

We were in fact hauled in for questioning late in the following day, and asked in spite of the elapse of eighteen years to recount all we could remember of our movements on the day Joe had vanished. My recollections sounded so far-fetched to the officers questioning us that there seemed to be little point in giving more than a brief summary of my experience at sea. Karen's account of that day and Joe's visit that evening did sound more than a little incriminating in the light of the absence of any explanation as to how Joe had met his death, and of the shouting going on between them when Joe was last seen.

The following morning I contacted Denis Smalley to buy a bit of time for our meeting in view of the police and media activity over Joe. It was preying on our minds to such an extent that for me to concentrate on his matter would be futile. He readily agreed, as he anyway had just received more information concerning the matter he wanted to meet about, and he needed some time to assimilate it. I asked him how he came to be in a Midhurst restaurant at the same time as us. I said I could not believe it was merely coincidence. He confirmed it was not by chance, but refused to elucidate. It was my guess he had been tailing Donald, or more likely Andy Harper, and was probably waiting the previous morning in the Arrivals Hall at Gatwick alongside me.

The latest developments in the Joe case also revived some of the trauma of the trawler and the escape from Poland, which would still come back to me in waves from time to time. Gillian had much the same experiences, although not so for Jack who had been only semi-conscious for most of it, although he occasionally had a nightmare about drowning. He was now in his mid-seventies and since his retirement his health had picked up, and he had grand children to enjoy. As for Gillian, she was based in London living with her partner, also an accountant. She had become a high flyer in one of the major firm of accountants, and specialised in Polish and east European businesses.

Bernadette and Brendan, who had been living with her for the last fifteen ears, invited us over for dinner that evening to go over together all the things we could remember about the time of Joe's murder in case there was some fragment lurking in someone's memory, which might be activated by hearing another's take on the events of those few days. We each agreed that after the elapse of eighteen years, we should be more comfortable with being absolutely candid about the feelings towards one another at that time. We came up with nothing new, but it was a splendid opportunity to extinguish any remaining antipathy between us. The fact that our children had remained friends throughout, and as adults had continued to keep in touch, had put us somewhat to shame, especially over the times we could have benefitted from supporting each other.

The days rolled by with no apparent developments in the solving of Joe's killing. No funeral could be held until there was an inquest, and that would not take place for some time, as time had to be allowed for evidence to come forward.

It was late one evening as Karen and I were contemplating going to bed when the telephone rang. They always seem to sound so much louder at that time of night. It was the local police, who wanted me to come down to the station as soon as I could. There had been a development. Karen came with me as she naturally was as keen as me to discover what had happened.

The forensic people had sifted through every gram of soil around and covering Joe's body, and discovered the remains of a railway ticket. Using some very special equipment they had discerned a date and possible location of where it was issued. The date was Thursday the 27th of May 1982, the day Joe went missing. The location at first was problematical as there were only three letters they were able to identify: ?o??i?_???d. They had sought the help of British Rail, who after a day and a half contemplating the puzzle came up with Bodmin Road, the name of a station which serves Bodmin in Cornwall. This had immediately thrown suspicion on me as I had claimed to have been there at roughly the time in question, but the wealth of evidence produced in the trial of the conspirators in my case ruled that out. However, they had been through all that evidence and the lengthy statements, including those of the conspirators in question, and realised there was one who had not been brought to trial and never traced.

The forensic people had also found traces of vehicle grease and of DNA on the ticket. The grease had helped preserve what was left of the ticket.

The two Britons who had stood trial had now served their sentences and had been tracked down to their current addresses, one in Oxford, the other in Solihull.

They had been approached by the police for the name of the member of the gang who had escaped justice. The Oxford one refused to cooperate, but the one in Solihull considered he had nothing to lose, and scouring the depths of his memory, recollected that he was an apprentice motor engineer by the name of Martin, Martin Homer, the lad I had caught in the woods in Cornwall, and had held his face down in the mud. The partner in crime from Solihull had seen neither hide nor hair of him since that night, but assumed he must have eventually found his way home to Oxford. The police asked me for a description, but after eighteen years there was really nothing I could sensibly say.

That evening, two hours previously, the police had traced Homer's current address and he had been taken into the police station in Oxford and charged with the murder of Joseph Crotty in 1982.

Months later, during Homer's trial, it emerged that further evidence had come to light. Microscopic traces of fibre had been found in the soil closest to where the stab wound in the back of the neck would have been. These had been identified as coming from the carpet of a Ford Escort. DVLA records confirmed that Martin Homer was indeed the owner of an Escort in 1982, which had long since been scrapped. The evidence at best was circumstantial, but it helped paint a picture.

He had a premonition a few weeks before the discovery of Joe's body that his crime was about to be uncovered, and had prepared himself for being arrested and sentenced. He confessed that after the humiliation of allowing me to escape that night in Cornwall he was determined to get his own back. He had found his way back to the road, only to discover that his companions had driven off. He tried to change the wheel of the truck I had 'stolen', but within minutes he saw the blue lights of a police car approaching, and made a run for it.

After several hours of hiking across moorland and along country lanes and quiet side streets, he reached a railway station the other side of Bodmin, and returned to Oxford by train. By then it was well into the evening. From his home he collected a sharp pointed kitchen knife, and set off in his Ford Escort towards Gainsthorpe in the expectation that I, the object of his all-consuming vengeance, would have by then returned from Cornwall.

He parked his car among some trees at the side of a farm track which ran alongside our neighbours' house, and walked back towards our home. A couple were sauntering along the lane in his direction and so he hid behind our neighbours' hedge. It set their dogs barking until someone in the house yelled at them to shut up. As the couple were passing our driveway, Homer saw a man storm out of our house, followed by a woman who was shouting at him. She then turned and went back indoors. Meanwhile the man headed towards Homer, who shuffled in his position to be more securely out of sight. He assumed the man was me. Joe and I were not totally unalike in appearance.

The man passed within feet of Homer muttering and cursing. Homer assumed there had been a row between husband and wife, and he was walking out on her. When Joe reached the farm track, he turned left and headed along it. Once the couple had ambled past his hiding place, Homer, keeping out of sight, followed Joe along the track, past the Escort, and all the while moving closer to Joe who continued to curse, oblivious of being followed. Homer succeeded in drawing within a couple of yards of him, seized his opportunity, pounced and plunge the knife ferociously into the back of Joe's neck. Blood spirted everywhere when Homer withdrew the knife, but the satisfaction of revenge turned to horror when he discovered that his victim was not me. He ran back to his car and brought it up to where Joe's body lay, and hauled it into the boot. He looked at the blood on the track wondering what he could do about it, but by then it had come on to rain, and he concluded it would soon be washed away.

It was an issue raised during the trial as to why the police had not used sniffer dogs in that area in the search for Joe immediately after his disappearance. The police had no answer, as those responsible at the time had since either died or could not remember.

Martin Homer drove to woodland near Buckingham which he had known in his childhood. There were parts of it where the undergrowth was so thick no-one ever ventured into it. He parked as near as he could to the spot, but it was still a good quarter of mile from it. In the darkness and pouring rain he dragged the body until he was satisfied he had reached a place where it was unlikely to be discovered for at least several weeks, not dreaming that it would stretch to eighteen years. He then went back to his car to fetch a spade he kept handy in the boot for clearing snow. The sight of the blood smeared all over the boot and its carpet together with the realisation of what he had just done, made him feel sick. As he buried the body and walked back to the car afterwards, he sobbed bitterly. It put me in mind of Judas Iscariot when I heard Homer giving his testimony in court.

Later he burnt and replaced the carpet from the car boot, and steam cleaned the whole car inside and out, selling it a few weeks later. He tossed the spade into the Thames later on in the night of the murder. The clothing he had worn that day went into an incinerator he discovered in Oxford, not far from Jericho, the part of the city where he lived.

He received a life sentence, despite some suggestion from his defence during the trial that he had suffered severe mental problems. There had been debate about the fact that these had occurred after the crime had been committed, and more an indication of remorse. It could be taken into account during later applications for parole, subject to his behaviour during the serving of his sentence. My chief regret was that Joe's loss of life and the consequent suffering of his family and friends, had been at their expense, rather than mine as intended.

Chapter 37

A month after the discovery of Joe's body, the delayed meeting with Denis Smalley took place at my office in Buckingham. He affirmed that a full scale enquiry would take place into Donald's and his company's and trust's affairs. However, Smalley admitted to me on the quiet after everyone else had left the meeting, that Donald was not their main target. They had bigger fish to fry. I could imagine exactly what he meant. He went on to say that if I were prepared to carry out the detailed work of the investigation and submit it to them together with all the necessary supporting documentation and any other evidence they might request, and there were no obstructions on Donald's part, all fines and penalties could be waived. He tapped the side of his nose with his forefinger. I responded with, "That's always assuming that there are untaxed taxes to be discovered".

"Of course!" he replied.

We shook hands, as I promised to think about taking the work on, but he must not assume it was foregone conclusion.

That night, I lay awake giving it much thought. One does not expect any threat to life and limb in the work we undertake in our profession, but my record to date left me wondering. Besides which, there was a probable mountain to climb in getting Donald to agree to the level of cooperation required, and then there would be the undoubted struggle in having our fees paid at the end of it all. I finally got to sleep when I resolutely concluded I would _not_ take on the assignment.

The following morning, I changed my mind.